There was a thump on the front porch. "Oh, gosh, I thought Daddy was going to keep Grampa away," Amy cried.

"Sounded more like a big newspaper. Is there evening delivery?" Even as I said it, I realized how unlikely it was. The clock over the stove said 8:31; no one brought papers around that late.

Amy ran to the front door. "I don't see Daddy's car," she said, puzzled, peering out the little window. "Just some hot-rodders or something." We could hear the revving engine, the squealing tires.

I pulled open the door. At first I looked down the street, catching a brief glimpse of a big white vehicle careening around the corner. Then Amy gasped, and I looked down at the porch.

A man lay sprawled at the front steps. His head was on the welcome mat. His eyes were open—the two brown ones that I was familiar with from several years of marriage, and a neat black hole like a third eye between them.

Tony had bothered the Sullivans for the last time.

By Lora Roberts
Published by Fawcett Books:

MURDER IN A NICE NEIGHBORHOOD
MURDER IN THE MARKETPLACE
MURDER MILE HIGH

MURDER MILE HIGH

Lora Roberts

FAWCETT GOLD MEDAL • NEW YORK

This is dedicated to the ones I love.

Acknowledgments

I have had a good deal of help with Denver settings from Jean and Rich Mullin, Jackie Edmonds, Judy Gilligan and David Kline, and Detective Metzler of the Denver Police public information office. However, I did make a lot of things up, including everything about the Denver police, who are, in this book, wholly fictional. So if I got something wrong, it's not the fault of any of the above-named people; they did their best, and aren't to blame if the needs of my story got in the way of their carefully-assembled facts.

A Fawcett Gold Medal Book
Published by Ballantine Books
Copyright © 1996 by Lora Roberts Smith

All rights reserved under International and Pan-American Copyright Conventions. Published in the United States by Ballantine Books, a division of Random House, Inc., New York, and simultaneously in Canada by Random House of Canada Limited, Toronto.

Library of Congress Catalog Card Number: 95-90829

ISBN 0-449-14947-1

Manufactured in the United States of America

First Edition: March 1996

10 9 8 7 6 5 4 3 2

1

I got most of the way through the Rockies before Babe checked out on me.

I had turned off I-70 just past the Eisenhower Tunnel to look at the Continental Divide, and to let Barker out. Parking my blue '69 VW microbus (the camper version, without the pop-top) at the scenic vista, I climbed stiffly down from the driver's seat. My niece, Amy, calls the bus Babe. I don't even want to think about what that makes me.

While Barker sniffed the other dogs' deposits and took his time making his own, I watched a pair of hawks hover over bare gray scree patched here and there with fresh mid-September snow. Though the air was thin I didn't feel too dizzy. After spending three days driving through the Sierra and high plains, I'd gotten used to altitude again.

Walking around felt good—I'd been driving uphill since lunch, which I had eaten sitting at my pull-up table, with the side window slats cranked open, overlooking Glenwood Canyon.

Though I was now a relatively plutocratic home owner in Palo Alto, California, the VW bus had once been my only home, the road my only backyard. I liked being on the road again, my universe snug around me like a turtle's shell. It had been easy to fall back into the vagabond rhythm of keeping the sink reservoir filled and heating water for instant soup with an immersion heater plugged into the lighter, or cooking rice and vegetables on the one-burner white-gas stove. In the cold evenings Barker circled his pillow before curling up to sleep, while I pulled out the bed and settled into my sleeping bag, using the battery-powered

1

lamp that had, in that other life, been one of my few luxuries.

Being on the road was fine. What I didn't like was the bad vibes that got stronger with every hour that brought me closer to Denver.

The previous night, we'd camped just outside of Grand Junction beside the Colorado River. The strong rush of the river filled my dreams like the thin, fragrant air filled my lungs. The headache that had dogged me since Lake Tahoe was gone when I woke up, but the sense of foreboding was omnipresent.

Why had I come? I was so happy in Palo Alto, in my small, crumbling house, with Barker growing as if every night the Dog God came in and opened a valve in one paw and blew him up another notch. Although Amy, my niece, had visited for the summer, she'd returned to Denver at the end of August, leaving a bit of blank space that quickly evolved into the peaceful solitude I value.

With some kind of remote sensor, Amy knew I was enjoying the quiet a bit too much, so she contrived to stir me up, long-distance.

It had literally been long distance. I was reading on my front porch, feeling the need of escape after a couple of weeks spent finishing an article on beneficial weeds for *Organic Gardener*. I'd been so deep in *The Woman in White* when Drake had come to tell me about the phone call that I didn't notice him.

"Liz." I looked up. The shadows that had been brief punctuation marks on the edge of the lawn when I'd sat down with my book now reached all the way across. A cool breeze, welcome in the stale September air, stirred the tall spires of the hollyhocks. "Liz. You have a phone call."

"What?" I blinked up at my neighbor. Paul Drake lives in the house in front of mine, the one that faces the street. Both houses became mine after the death of their previous owner, but since I could only afford the upkeep on one, I was selling him the bigger of the two. That monthly payment was the first real financial security I'd known in the fifteen or so years of my adult life.

Drake looked at the spine of my book, then inside.

"You're on page ninety-three," he said, setting Wilkie Collins aside. "Come on."

"Huh?" I looked around for Barker; he was nowhere to be seen.

"You have a phone call." Drake tugged on my hand. "And your dog has made a new hole. Looks like he's trying to dig up the plum tree."

"Where is he?" The plum tree was still standing in the side yard. There was no sign of Barker.

"I shoved him in your back door. He's not black and white any longer. He's brown." Drake gave my hand a squeeze. "Come on, Liz. Get the phone. It's long distance."

"Right." We walked from my front door to his back door. I didn't try to get my hand back. Drake and I are doing that old dance, made fresh and new by our modern fears of commitment, abandonment, and disease. We hadn't gotten to the climactic *pas de deux*, especially with Amy around all summer, but a certain feeling that I both wanted and resisted was building.

"Who's calling, anyway?"

"It's Amy." He glanced at me. "Still part of your life. At least she didn't call collect."

"Would you have accepted?" I don't have a phone. Drake lets me use his, which never used to be a hardship, because I didn't get many calls. It's not just the expense that keeps me from getting my own phone. I don't want to be at the whole universe's beck and call. Salespeople call you, you get a modem, you cruise the Internet, and next thing you know you're just one cell of a vast, uncontrollable organism. I've opted out.

Drake opened his back door and ushered me in. "I might have, but it didn't come up. Anyway, it's long distance on her dime, so you might hustle a little."

Amy was indignant. "Aunt Liz! What took you so long?"

"I was traveling."

"Listen." Amy wasn't in a mood for whimsy, even my extra-special auntly brand. "They don't want me to call you, but I am anyway. Gramma's real sick."

I sat down. My voice sounded calm over the thudding in my ears. "She is?"

"Yeah." Amy gulped a little. "She had the flu when I got back, and she just never got better. She lies in bed all the time. I even made her some of that soup—you know, like I made for you?"

"It's good." It was surprisingly good, considering that the rest of Amy's culinary skills were minimal.

"She had a spoonful, but that was all. She practically doesn't breathe, even." Amy's voice approached a wail. "I don't know what to do. And Aunt Molly and Daddy just stand around and say she should go to the hospital, but they don't make her. Grampa says it must be God's will." Amy dropped her voice. "Here comes Mom. I'll call you again later."

The phone went dead.

"Bad news?" Drake had been leaning against the sink, waiting for the kettle to boil. He's worse than a nanny for thinking hot drinks help settle a person. He was using packaged peppermint tea bags, too, not the homemade ones I had given him.

"My mother's sick." I shivered a little. In the almost sixteen years since I'd left home, she had written once; we hadn't spoken for over a decade. I had been a bad, ungrateful girl, marrying out of the Catholic faith and out of my lower–middle–class station in life. Subsequent events had only reinforced her view that if your daughter offends you, cut her off.

But she was my mother, and it wasn't hard to rewind through the bitterness of my late teens back into my childhood, when we'd had some rapport. I couldn't picture her old and sick. I could see her tying my ponytail ribbon on the first day of kindergarten, holding me off by the shoulders and scrutinizing my green plaid uniform, telling me that I'd do. She was proud of the A's I brought home, supportive of my ambition to attend college, despite my father's opposition. He felt college just made girls unfit for marriage. And when it came to marriage, I'd definitely been unfit.

"I'm sorry to hear that." Drake poured hot water on the tea bags and handed me a cup. "What's the matter?"

"Amy didn't really say. She's had the flu, and she isn't getting over it." I dunked my tea bag up and down. "Didn't I make you some peppermint tea bags? Where are they?"

Drake's gaze slid away. "I used them all up."

"You don't like them." I sniffed the store-bought tea. "They have a lot more flavor than this."

"A lot more," Drake said fervently. "So what does Amy want you to do?"

"I don't know." I sipped the pale tea. "Evidently my brothers and sister don't consider it serious enough to tell me about. And Amy is a little prone to exaggeration."

"Just a little." Drake tried not to smile. "She was dying, I recall, when she had a cold. Convinced she'd never draw breath again."

"A little peppermint tea fixed her right up, though." I studied the pallid fluid in my cup. "She was on her feet in no time."

"You should send your mother some of that tea." Drake refused to be cowed. "Just the threat of having to drink it would cure her."

"I'm drying the coneflowers to make tea with this fall." I grinned at Drake. "Very good for illness, I'm told. Very nasty-tasting, too. The first time you get sick, I'll come over and hold your nose and just pour it down the hatch."

He shuddered. "Please, Liz. Don't get carried away with this picture of yourself as old Mother Herbalist. I'd hate to be called in to investigate a poisoning caused by one of your brews."

I managed a smile, although it wasn't that funny a remark. Drake is a homicide detective with the Palo Alto police department—not that they have many homicides, but when they do, he detects them. And I've had the ill luck to be mixed up in a couple of the investigations. Both of them had involved poison, among other things. I still didn't like remembering them. Drake, however, seemed to have put it all behind him.

The phone rang, and since I was sitting right there, I answered it. Amy's voice came over a clatter and rumble. "Oh, good. It's you, Aunt Liz. I snuck out and I'm calling from a pay phone, so I don't have long."

"I can barely hear you."

"I know." She raised her voice to a shriek. "I can't hear myself either. Aunt Liz, you've got to come! I sat with Gramma for a while this morning and I asked her if she wanted to see you, and she squeezed my hand so hard."

"Amy—"

"She wants you to come, I know she does." Amy gulped, hurrying on before I could get a word in. "Then Grampa came in and I said I was going to call you, and he just had a terrible tantrum and said you'd never set foot in his house again and all kinds of stuff like that, and finally I had to yell at him that he was upsetting Gramma."

"Amy, listen—"

"She was just laying there crying! You have to come right now."

"Amy—" I took a deep breath, unconsciously shaking my head. This time she let me speak. "If Dad doesn't want me there, I won't even get to see her. You should know that."

"You can stay with me. I have twin beds. It'll be fun," Amy said, talking over me as if I weren't saying anything. I guess to her I wasn't. "I'll sneak you in while Grampa is down at the Legion Hall."

"He still goes there?" One thing you could say about my dad, he didn't see any point in changing perfectly good old habits and hatreds for anything newfangled.

"Every Tuesday."

The operator's voice came on, and then bonging noises as Amy fed the phone more money. "Really, Aunt Liz," she cried when she was done. "You have to come. Gramma's counting on it."

"It's at least a three-day drive, maybe more, in my old car. I don't have plane fare." I was pointing out problems, but Amy wouldn't have any of that.

"You can do it in less time. It just took me a couple of days on the Greyhound." She conveniently forgot that someone else had been driving. "You could come that way—it's kind of cheap. But it would be cheapest if you drove. Is there anything wrong with Babe?"

"Babe is as fine as can be expected after two hundred thousand miles—not really up to anything strenuous."

"If you drove, you could bring Barker. How's he doing?"

"He's fine. He misses you, though."

"Bring him." Amy was getting quite good at being the boss. "Aunt Liz, I—I'll be glad to see you. And so will Gramma. I think—I almost think she's afraid of something. She won't talk. But you can find out what it is."

The operator spoke again.

"I'm out of change. Bye." Amy hung up.

I looked at the receiver, as breathless as if I had been the one galloping through sentences, and gently cradled it.

"I gather you're going to Colorado." Drake lifted his cup to me. "Bon voyage."

2 _____

NOW I was standing on top of the world, but I didn't feel like bursting into song. The Continental Divide was a somber place, not a cheerful one. Bard Peak to the north and Grays Peak southward hid their summits in ominous clouds. The sun had gone in while I was driving through the Eisenhower Tunnel, leaving the landscape monochrome; the pines below the timberlines were charcoal accents.

I turned away from the panorama. Barker was finished; he led me back to the bus through the almost empty parking area. The rough gravel under my feet was liberally patched with oil stains; I almost didn't notice the one that spread beneath the bus, until the sun came out and summoned dancing rainbows from its glistening black surface. For one panicky instant of flashback, I thought it might be blood. And it was—car blood, not human. Oil.

Oil dripped onto the gravel with the regularity of a pulse. The dipstick came up nearly clean, showing just a film at the bottom.

Two quarts of 10-30 were jammed into the space beneath the front passenger seat. I poured them in and drove on, barely pushing fifty although it was mostly downhill, watching the oil pressure light flicker on and off. By the time I got to Idaho Springs, it was full on. I knew I wouldn't make Denver before the engine seized up.

I got off the Interstate. The first filling stations I passed didn't have service bays. I was looking for a phone booth, so I could check the listings for a place that knew its way around old VWs. Then I spotted a garage on the corner.

One of the service bays was open, with the familiar shape of a Beetle on the lift. I pulled in.

"We're just closing," the attendant said, greeting me with a small, fast-moving smile. His pocket called him "Hank." A second man was bringing down the lift with the Beetle. "What can I do for you?"

"I'm losing oil."

He cast a professional glance over the bus. "Guess we could take a look. Might be a big problem—blown head gasket, bad cylinder. Have to wait until tomorrow to fix something like that."

I didn't want to spend money on a motel. "But you could fix a little problem tonight?"

"Maybe."

He showed me where to park the bus, beside a small office next to the garage bays. There were vending machines in the office, but no chairs.

I handed Hank my car key. "Where can I wait?"

"Coffee shop across the road." He jerked his head to indicate the direction. I took out my knapsack, put Barker on the leash, and left them to it.

Barker sniffed his way up and down the road before we dashed over to Edna's Coffee Shop. I tied him up at a handy post outside the door. The booth I chose was next to a big window from which I could see both Barker, lying on a patch of grass, and my bus being hoisted slowly up the lift across the way.

I accepted a little metal pot full of lukewarm water and a generic tea bag from the waitress, a young Hispanic woman who also waited on the other four tables of customers. I ordered a chicken salad sandwich and made some notes in my journal.

And I watched my ex-husband drive past in a white panel van.

It wasn't really him, of course. I'd been seeing him everywhere on the road—in pickups, sports cars, sober family sedans. For almost a year, since the dramatic events that left one of my best friends dead and ended in making me a woman of property, I'd put him to rest in my mind. My marriage had been a terrible mistake, and I'd paid in many ways, not the least of which was spending a few years in a correctional facility for trying to keep him from beating me to death. He hadn't been killed by the bullet I'd put into him, which was actually a relief. I don't want to kill anyone, even people who deserve it.

I had welcomed the sentence that accompanied my attempted manslaughter conviction; at least my incarceration had kept him away from me. After parole, I'd gone to ground for years, afraid of being found by him, afraid of re-entering the world.

During the past twelve months I hadn't been afraid anymore. And I wasn't afraid now—at least that's what I told myself while I tried to eat dry chicken and even drier wheat bread. But at some level I must not have believed it. Otherwise I wouldn't keep seeing him, as if he were dogging me, waiting for me to get back into Denver, to invade his territory. That's how I thought of Denver now, as his territory, even though I'd grown up there and my family still lived there.

Over and over I recited my new mantra: Tony had no way of knowing I was on my way; he probably had no interest in my movements since the night I'd faced him and his threats and realized the futility of running. There was no reason for my fear. I held that thought until the panel van was lost to view.

Across the street, Hank and his pal were bringing Babe down off the rack. I paid my tab and took Barker to find out the verdict.

"It was the oil pressure regulator," Hank told me, wiping his hands with a rag. "Lucky I had one. We keep a few in stock. The altitude seems to blow those suckers a lot. Should work okay for you now."

I was astounded. It was just past five. I could make it to Denver that evening, and it hadn't even cost much. My foreboding lessened, I headed back to the Interstate.

The VW bus coasted effortlessly down from the mountains, into the rounded foothills that reminded me of northern California. I seemed poised above the rolling landscape. Patches of green and gold cloaked the hills where aspens were turning. More than anything, the aspens brought my childhood back. We had made a pilgrimage every fall to see the "quakies"; my mother had insisted, over my father's grumbles about wasted time. I wondered if she'd gone for the past fifteen autumns, if she'd be too ill this time.

As I got closer to Denver the traffic thickened. At one point I thought I saw the same panel van pass me. Once more I glimpsed the dark, springy hair and arrogant nose that had reminded me of my ex-husband. The van sped away, and I slowed a bit, content to let it get ahead and carry my ridiculous fears with it.

The closer I got to the city, the more changed everything was. Where I remembered dusty plains and rolling hills, now there were acres of tract houses, their lights twinkling in the dusk, their shopping malls and discount strips blaring from the roadsides. Denver itself appeared as a vast hazy luminosity, blotting out the emerging stars, paling the deep blue of the twilight. Already the crisp mountain air was replaced with the acrid cloud of civilization.

I drove on into it, into my past, my hands in a damp death-grip on the steering wheel.

The street my parents lived on looked narrower than I remembered. I was used to the lush shrubbery and carefully tended gardens of Palo Alto; the bare lawns and shabby housefronts seemed to signal a corresponding bareness of spirit.

My parents' house was no longer white with dark red shutters. The asbestos siding had been painted brown, with black shutters. There was a six- or seven-year-old Chevy in the driveway. The living room curtains were closed, as were those in the front bedroom—the room that had been mine. Paint was peeling off the iron railings that imprisoned the small porch.

I drove on. I had decided to stop at my brother Andy's house first. He and Renee could be said to owe me hospitality, since I'd put Amy up for the summer—and Renee herself had been an uninvited guest.

Andy's house was half a mile from my parents' place. Mom and Dad had moved across town when I was a junior in high school, to be closer to Andy after his hasty marriage. Andy and Renee still lived in the same house, but Andy had tinkered with it over the years. In place of the little tract house I remembered was a big one, with an addition on one side and a big garage growing out of the other side. It crowded the lot. The small trees I'd helped plant years ago were tall and shady, overhanging the little front yard.

Barker jumped down from the front passenger seat and burst out of the door as soon as I opened it. He was wildly curious, sniffing around the yard and whining. He ran up the sidewalk and gave one sharp, peremptory bark at the door.

Amy popped out a moment later. "Barker," she cried. He leaped up at her—which was strictly forbidden—and she knelt on the mat to receive his embraces, glancing guiltily at me.

"I forgot to tell him 'down,' " she said. "Hi, Aunt Liz. I've been waiting and waiting for you."

"Barker's been longing to see you, too." I stopped at the foot of the steps up to the front porch, to give them time for their greeting. "Actually, so have I."

"Well." Renee spoke from the open door, scowling at Barker and giving me a half-hearted smile. "So you did come. Amy was sure you would."

"She said Mom wants to see me."

"She seems to." Renee spoke reluctantly. "I don't know why. It's not like she's at death's door or anything. She just has a bad case of the flu."

"Maybe she doesn't want to wait until she's dying." I decided to leave my valise on the backseat of my bus. I might prefer my own hospitality to Renee's that night.

"You might as well come in." Renee stood aside. "Amy! Stop wrestling with that dog and get in and finish your dinner."

"Am I interrupting you?" I had an impulse to turn around and leave, wondering why I was there and how bad this was going to be.

"Not at all." Barker, never doubting his welcome for a moment, had followed Amy inside, and Renee seemed to remember a "Miss Manners" column she'd once read.

12

"Maybe you'd like to join us. Just roast beef, mashed potatoes, a salad." She glanced at me when I walked past her into the hall. "Or maybe you don't eat meat. I seem to remember a lot of vegetables—"

"I'm only an economic vegetarian." The dinner smelled wonderful. I was, I realized, very hungry after not eating my chicken sandwich. "If I'm not putting you out—"

"No, no." Renee led the way through the kitchen. It glistened with sleek formica cabinets, tiled counters, black glass-fronted appliances. We turned right at the breakfast bar and went into the dining room.

A small chandelier dangled from the low ceiling. The table, chairs, and buffet were a matched set, heavily carved in mock-Spanish style. A tablecloth, candles, nice dishes made a gracious picture, marred by my brother Andy, who occupied what was no doubt the head of the table, since he was there. He had a knife in one hand, a fork in the other, a full plate in front of him. He looked at me suspiciously, as if I might be impersonating myself.

The silence felt awkward. Uneasily, I broke it. "Hey, Andy."

"Liz." His gaze softened. "You look pretty much the same." He would be seeing a short, ordinary-looking woman in her mid-thirties, with badly cut dark hair, wearing jeans, a sweatshirt, and a tentative smile. "Just a little—"

"Older?" I noticed the gray in his hair, the way the lower part of his face had acquired jowls.

"Weathered, I was going to say." He put down his fork and pulled out the chair next to him. "Where'd Amy get to?"

"She's in the backyard with the dog." Renee shot me an accusing look. "I didn't think you'd bring that fool animal. You're not dumping him here, Liz. I'm not having any dogs getting hair all over my rugs."

"Barker's just visiting, like me." I put the linen napkin in my lap—one of my grandmother's, by the monogram. Renee appeared to live with a lot of style. "He'll sleep in the bus at night. He's housebroken."

13

Andy passed me the platter of meat, and Renee offered me mashed potatoes. The aromas were distracting.

"So Amy told you Mom's asking about you." Andy's face tightened again. "We bust our butts trying to help out, take care of her, give her whatever she needs. And our thanks is that she wants you, the one who never gave her anything but trouble."

I held my fork suspended on its way to my mouth. "Andy, I don't intend to impose. I'll see her, I'll set her mind at rest if I can, and then I'll leave."

"You'll have to stay here," Renee said mournfully. "Dad won't let you into the house. He's very bitter against you."

I put down my fork. "Look, we all have reason for bad feelings, don't you think? I've paid for my mistake, and I paid alone. I never got an instant's support or encouragement from any of you the whole time Tony was regularly beating me to a pulp. I might have been able to leave him, if I'd just had someplace to go—"

Aghast, I shut up. After just a few minutes around Andy and Renee, I was whining. I had made my bed. So my mother had said when I first admitted that Tony wasn't the man I'd thought. Marriage was a sacrament, and I had brought it on myself.

Those true words, that certainty, kept me from ever again approaching her. I had been wrong to marry Tony; I was wrong to try to kill him. I had, evidently, been wrong to expect my family to be on my side.

Being wrong was not on my agenda anymore. For the past five years, I had managed to dodge any emotional entanglements. Lately it had been getting harder and harder.

As if my train of thought had conjured it, the telephone rang and Renee said, "Oh, that'll probably be your 'friend' in Palo Alto." Her emphasis put a salacious spin on friendship. "He called earlier to see if you got here okay."

"I'll get it," Amy called in the distance. We sat around the table, all chewing suspended.

"For Aunt Liz," she said when she finally appeared in the doorway. Barker walked beside her, tongue lolling in a pleased doggy smile. "It's Paul Drake."

Self-consciously I went past her down the hall.

"I've got an extension in my room you can use," Amy said, pointing past an open door to a wild tangle of frothy pillows, shaggy stuffed animals, and more sophisticated decor like Roman shades and a poster for Hole showing Courtney Love screaming.

Amy gave me the phone and vanished, taking Barker with her.

"So you finally got there." Drake didn't sound so far away. I could picture him, standing in his kitchen chopping up something exotic for dinner, the phone cradled on his shoulder.

"The bus is a flatlander. It doesn't like mountains." I sat amid the pillows on Amy's bed. "I blew the oil pressure regulator today."

"And did you just pull over and fix it?" He laughed. "It's good to hear your voice, Liz. I was getting kind of worried."

"Why?" The sound of his laugh did strange things to me, and I didn't want that. I didn't want to lie in any more beds of my own making.

"Well, that ex-husband you were so afraid of—doesn't he live in Denver?"

"It's a big city. He'll never know I'm here."

"You sound funny. Are you alone?"

"Probably." There was a phone in the kitchen, and Renee was the world's biggest snoop.

"Oh." Drake was a detective, after all. "Well, listen, if you run into trouble, I know someone on the Denver force. Just try to keep your nose clean this time, okay?"

"I don't run into trouble. It runs into me." I knew I sounded curt, but it was either that or start pouring my insecurities all over him. "Look, Drake, I've got to go."

"Call me if you need to," he said after a pause. "Call collect."

"Yeah, sure. I'll be fine. Bye."

I hung up and wiped my palm on the side of my jeans. I didn't want to be lumping Drake in with Tony or Andy or any of the men who'd let me down. But something about being back in Denver made it seem unavoidable.

15

3 _____

I parked the bus in the shade of a big sycamore,
across the street from my parents' house. It was after eight,
full dark. Even nosy Mrs. Beamish, if she still lived next
door, would have trouble seeing us. Amy sat beside me;
Barker was curled up on the back seat, my personal car
alarm. Andy had driven his own car over to pick up my
dad for his jaunt to the Legion Hall. The front door of
my parents' house opened, and Andy walked out beside my
father.

Dad looked small next to his son. He was bent—the leg-
acy of so many construction jobs—and his hair had pro-
gressed from iron-gray to white, combed back carefully as
always.

I felt shocked. I remembered him as he had looked the
day I brought Tony home after our hasty marriage. He had
risen out of his big chair when my mother starting crying
at my announcement. Leaving the Sunday afternoon game
blaring on the TV, he had escorted us to the door. Standing
there, tall and broad and forbidding, he'd told me I was
never to come back, since I'd hurt my mother so much.
That wouldn't have kept me away, if it hadn't been for the
grim satisfaction behind his words. He'd always said that
letting me go to college would end in disaster; once again,
he was proved right.

Now I looked at his shrunken form, the thinning hair, and
wondered why we were tiptoeing around this man, what fire
he could possibly still possess that made Andy reluctantly
agree to get him out of the house for me, as if the old man
could physically bar the door to his errant daughter.

Andy scowled over at us after shutting the passenger door, before he climbed into his side of the car and drove away.

"That's Daddy," Amy said blithely. "He doesn't want us to think he likes doing us a favor. But he's not so bad, really."

"That's not what you said last summer."

Her brow wrinkled. "Well, he was different when I got home. Like—I don't know, like he almost respected me or something." She giggled. "Fat chance, huh. Well, they're gone. Let's go in."

She led the way across the street and used her key to open the door. "Hi, Gramma, it's me!"

I stopped in the doorway, overcome by the familiar smells of lemon oil and my dad's pipe tobacco and the faint, musty scent of old house. The couch was the same, its striped upholstery faded now into a soft haze of blue and gray, its cushions saggier. My dad's armchair still stood in front of the TV, but the TV was bigger, dominating the room. Through the archway I could see the chrome dinette set in the dining nook. The curtains looked new—not the faded draperies of nubby polyester I remembered, but some cheerful, homemade ones with sunflowers. The rooms seemed much smaller, cramped and crammed with doilies and plastic flowers and my mother's collections of silver state teaspoons and china leprechauns.

"Come on," Amy hissed from the hallway. "I've told her you're here. She wants to see you."

I followed her into the short hall. On the left was my parents' bedroom, on the right my old room; the one bathroom was at the end of the hall.

"Amy?" It was my mother's voice. "Lizzie?"

"She's right here, Gramma." Amy pushed me through the doorway. "I'll make us some tea."

I hesitated, feeling awkward, just inside the room. The woman in the bed had changed. She had always been short, like me, but she was no longer pleasingly plump, as she had called herself; now her face looked thin, and the hand she held out to me trembled.

"Well, come here then." Her voice was the same, unexpectedly steely. "You've come all this way. Sit down here." She patted the bed, beside her.

"You don't look good, Mom. Shouldn't you be in the hospital?"

"No." Her hand closed around mine, hot and dry but still with enough strength to pull me down beside her. "I'm getting over it now. There were a couple of days when I thought I would die, and that's when I knew we'd have to talk."

I looked at her carefully, while she fumbled on the bedside table for her glasses. Her hair had gone from the gray I remembered to snowy white. My dad would be in his eighties, my mother pushing seventy-five, and neither had led the easy lives that keep a person young-looking. My mother's hands were lumpy with arthritis, and I wondered if she could still hold a crochet hook or embroidery needle. Her blue eyes were filmed, her eyebrows sparser. Beneath the covers, her outline was insubstantial.

"Well, you've changed a great deal," she announced after examining me. Her hand moved restlessly, picking at the chenille bedspread, and I took it before I realized I was going to. After a moment, she squeezed my hand gently. "I'm sorry, Lizzie. I was sorry right after I wrote you last summer, but I didn't know how to make things better. He wouldn't let me."

"Dad? Is he still so bitter?"

She shook her head slowly, side to side. "You know your father." Her eyelids drifted closed, and she spoke with a kind of detachment. "Although he probably doesn't really care. He just goes through the motions these days, you know. I can tell. He acts the same and says the same old things, but he's not really here." She opened her eyes and fixed a painful gaze on me. "It's not your father that's worrying me so much. It's Tony."

I couldn't speak; my throat was closed with fear.

"Tony," she said again, helpfully. "You know. Your husband."

"Ex-husband," I managed to whisper.

"Divorce is not sanctioned by the Church." For a moment the stern disciplinarian of my youth was there before me. I almost expected her to ask me to say the Act of Contrition. Then she closed her eyes again and let her head sink back into the pillow. "You should never have married him. He's a very bad man."

"How—how do you . . ."

"He came here a few weeks ago." Her eyes were still closed, and her voice was becoming thready. "His car had broken down nearby, and he wanted to use the phone— that's what he said. After he made a phone call, we talked. At first I had sympathy for him. He said he'd never gotten over you, that he'd spent a lot of money to try and find you and was broke." Her eyes flicked open. "I gave him some money."

I tightened my grip on her hand. "Mom—"

"Let me finish. I felt sorry for him, like I said. It stirred up all that upset, all the disappointment I felt in you." She was watching me now. "He was back in a couple of weeks. I told him I didn't have any more money, and he suggested that I get some. He said—he said you'd told him that—" She drew in a deep breath. "That your father had—that there had been—episodes—when you were little."

I couldn't be silent any longer. "He lied, Mom. I wouldn't have told him anything like that, because it wasn't true."

Something in her face relaxed. She was quiet for a moment. "I wondered," she said at last. "You think you know a man, but you never do, really." She pressed my hand again. "Thank you."

"So Tony was trying to blackmail you." I started to get angry. "All you had to do was tell me. You could have written again, asked me about it. You could have gotten Drake's phone number from Amy."

"I—couldn't." She turned her head away, nestling it into the pillow as if seeking refuge. "I didn't want to think about it or deal with it. I got some money and gave it to him, and he said he wouldn't be back."

"But of course he didn't mean it." I felt hot rage. "He didn't hurt you, did he?"

She didn't answer, her head turned away. Then she said, "No. Not really." She must have felt my anger. She put her other hand over our joined ones. "He was sorry, right away. He said he wouldn't be back." She fought for a deep breath, and I held my own, sensing she wasn't ready to yield the floor.

"Your dad came in then, with Byron." She looked at me. "Your nephew—Molly's youngest boy."

"I know." I didn't know, really. All I remembered about my sister Molly's kids was that they were all boys—maybe two, maybe three of them. "What did Dad do?"

She sighed. "He went into a rage, of course. If it hadn't been for young Byron, it could have been bad. Byron—Biff, they call him—is a good-sized boy. He was ready to fight. Then your dad got his gun out, and Tony left."

"Dad has a gun?" That sounded like a recipe for disaster. "So did Tony come back?"

She moved her head weakly from side to side on the pillow. "No. But there've been phone calls—breathing, and muttering. When I got sick, I worried about it a lot—that he would come back when Byron wasn't here, get hold of your father, and there'd be a fight or worse, and your father would be killed—"

"Relax, Mom." I pushed her back on the pillow. Her breathing was light and fast, and two red spots burned on her cheeks. "There's nothing to worry about. The threat he made is untrue, and he won't be back if there's no profit. I'll take care of it for you. I'll take care of him."

She took a deep, shuddering breath. "I knew you would. After all, you brought him into the family. You have to settle this, Lizzie."

I swallowed the retort that rose to my lips. She was right, as far as she saw it.

We sat for a moment, holding hands. She was almost smiling, and then I realized she'd fallen asleep. I disengaged my hand gently and went to find Amy.

"So how did it go?" Amy sat at the dinette, sipping tea, eating a large peanut butter sandwich, and reading from a big textbook. "I was dying to come in, but I thought you needed some privacy."

"You're perceptive." I found another cup and poured from the old blue and white teapot. "She's sleeping."

"You set her mind at rest?" Amy spoke around a mouthful of peanut butter. "Something was really eating at her."

"I'll take care of it." I stared into my cup, wondering just how I was going to do that. I didn't want to see or confront Tony in any way. And yet somehow I was going to have to make him quit threatening my family.

There was a thump on the front porch. "Oh, gosh, I thought Daddy was going to keep Grampa away," Amy cried.

"Sounded more like a big newspaper. Is there evening delivery?" Even as I said it, I realized how unlikely it was. The clock over the stove said 8:31; no one brought papers around that late.

Amy ran to the front door. "I don't see Daddy's car," she said, puzzled, peering out the little window. "Just some hot-rodders or something." We could hear the revving engine, the squealing tires.

I pulled open the door. At first I looked toward the street, catching a brief glimpse of a big white vehicle careening around the corner. Then Amy gasped, and I looked down.

A man lay sprawled on the front steps. His head was on the welcome mat. His eyes were open—the two brown ones that I was familiar with from several years of marriage, and a neat black hole like a third eye between them.

Tony had bothered the Sullivans for the last time.

4

TONY was dead.

For one instant my own heart stopped. A tidal wave of emotion rushed through me, leaving my knees weak. I clutched the doorknob, staring at that round third eye. It was as if I had time-traveled back ten years, with Tony's gun smoking in my hand after my feeble attempt to kill him, as if everything between that moment and the present had been wiped out, and I was that terrified young woman again.

Then it washed away, and I recognized the emotion that flooded me. Relief.

Amy screamed. The present snapped back around me like a rubber band.

I put an arm around Amy, turning her horrified gaze away from Tony's body. Cold night air poured through the open door; across the street, Barker hurled himself against the car window, yelping furiously. My mother cried out from the bedroom.

"Don't let Mom get up. Don't let her come out here." I squeezed Amy's shoulders and nudged her toward the hallway. "You'll have to get a grip on yourself."

Amy drew a deep, shuddering breath. "I—I—was it a dead man, Aunt Liz?" She sagged against me.

"Yes, he's dead. You can't help him. Help your gramma." The next nudge was not so gentle.

"Right. Right." Noises came from my mother's room, and Amy ran down the hall. "Gramma—no. It's okay." I heard her close the bedroom door behind her.

Without Amy to bolster, I felt shaky again. Light streamed out of the house onto the porch, casting golden bars onto Tony's face and open eyes, giving him a lively air. For a moment I wondered if he really was dead. The hole in his forehead seemed pretty conclusive.

It was important to call the police. I knew that. But I was rooted to the floor, while all kinds of mad ideas rushed through my head—getting rid of the body, wafting myself away from Denver, turning the clock back so I could decide not to visit my family in the first place. Such thoughts were futile. That blessed moment of intense relief would have to be balanced by hours, maybe days, of close encounters with the police.

A light flashed on the porch of the house next door, and a little figure scuttled out. Mrs. Beamish, like my father, seemed much smaller than my memory of her, but her voice was the same commanding boom.

"What's going on there? Mary, is that you?"

"It's Liz, Mrs. Beamish."

"Liz?" She came to the edge of her porch, peering over the railing. "Liz who? What's that there?"

"Liz Sullivan. Could you call nine-one-one, Mrs. Beamish?"

"Nine-one-one? Is your mother taken bad?"

"Not my mother." I tried to sound calm. "There's been an accident, though. Please call for me."

"You haven't been around in a long time." She sounded accusing.

"Yes, I've just come for a visit. Mrs. Beamish—"

"Fine, I'll call for you. I don't understand why you don't do it, though. What's the matter? Has someone passed out or something?" Mrs. Beamish lingered another moment before going back into her house.

I could have made the call, but I couldn't shake the feeling that if I turned my back, Tony's body would vanish. That would be fine, actually, but Paul Drake's voice in the back of my head was telling me not to leave the scene, not to touch anything.

To hell with Drake. I took a deep breath and knelt beside the body of my ex-husband.

He was wearing jeans, a flannel shirt with the sleeves rolled up, and scuffed hiking boots. I put my fingers on his neck. No pulse. No gun concealed under his arms, in his front pockets. I fished a tissue from my own pocket and, wrapping it around my fingers, angled behind him for his wallet. His body shifted, the dead weight pinning my hand. With something like panic, I pulled out my hand, his wallet in it.

His face stared back at me from the driver's license. I repeated the address given there a couple of times, hoping I'd remember it. There was money in the wallet—I saw a couple of hundred-dollar bills, and didn't count any further. He had a Visa card that bore a woman's name: Maud Riegert. I stared at it for a moment, wondering why the name was familiar. Then I heard a noise from next door and quickly stuffed the card back into the wallet, the wallet into Tony's pocket.

"So what's the matter with him?" Mrs. Beamish, booming her questions, scuttled down her front walk and up my parents' walk. "Drunk, is he?"

I got to my feet, fighting off the urge to stand between her and Tony. "Actually, he's dead."

"Dead?" She stopped, halfway up the walk, and stared up at me. Her thick glasses caught the light from the open front door. I hoped her eyesight was bad enough that she hadn't seen me rifling Tony's wallet.

"Yes. Are they coming?"

"Who? I told the girl there was a drunk passed out, not a dead man. Maybe you'd better call again."

She came a step farther, peering avidly up at the sprawled form that decorated my mother's front porch. "Poor Mary," she added in passing. "Certainly not good for her in her condition."

"I'll call," I said, driven to desperation. "Please don't let anyone else up here, Mrs. Beamish. The police will likely consider it a crime scene."

Her mouth opened a little farther at that, dentures gleaming in anticipation.

My parents' phone didn't have a long cord. I was trapped inside the little kitchen, not knowing what Mrs. Beamish was up to. The brisk voice at the other end of the phone didn't hesitate when I gave her the address and said the drunk that had been reported was actually dead.

"No hurry for the ambulance, then."

"I beg your pardon?"

"Any evidence of foul play?"

"There's a bullet hole in his forehead."

The brisk voice paused briefly. "Any firearms around?"

"No. He was dead when he got here."

Another pause. "The officers will be right over. Please stay on the line."

"That's not such a good idea."

"Wait! I didn't get your name—"

I hung up the phone and rushed back to the porch. Mrs. Beamish had come as far as the foot of the steps. She transferred her glittering gaze to me.

"So, Lizzie. When did you get back into town?" As loudly as she said it, I was sure the whole neighborhood would be out soon.

"Just tonight, actually. Thanks for your help, Mrs. Beamish. The police will be here soon."

She backed up a couple of feet. "The police, is it? Does your father know you're here?"

"He will." There was no possibility, now, of keeping my presence away from my father. And after my earlier glimpse of him, I didn't care anymore. The stern disciplinarian of my youth, the fearsome authority figure, had no more power to cow me. I was only amazed that my brother still found it necessary to placate our father.

A police cruiser rounded the corner, lights flashing but no siren. Perhaps the dispatcher had conveyed that there was no emergency. Mrs. Beamish edged off the walk and into the shadows of the big catalpa tree that grew between her yard and my folks'.

"I'll just be getting on home," she said more softly than usual. "Let me know if your mother needs any help, Lizzie."

"Thanks. I will." I watched the police car pull up to the curb, facing the wrong way. Barker had quieted down, but he was still watching me, his wet nose pressed against the window glass to make slimy smudges I'd have to clean off later. If I were free to wield my window cleaner.

Amy came out of my mother's room and joined me at the door. She shivered in the cold. "Gramma's resting. I told her everything was all right." She glanced at me anxiously. "Did I lie?"

"Probably."

The cruiser's doors popped open and the officers made an appearance. "Do you have any weapons?" The driver of the cruiser was a tall, beefy-looking silhouette, just out of range of the porch light.

"Weapons?" Amy squeaked. "Jesus God, Aunt Liz. Do they think we killed this guy?"

"Probably." I raised my empty hands, fingers spread. "Show them, Amy. They do have weapons, you see."

The other officer approached us slowly, watchfully. As the figure came into view, I saw it was a woman, looking bulky in her thick waist-length jacket, her peaked hat casting a shadow over her face. She had one hand on the gun at her side; her other hand held a cell phone close to her mouth.

"Come down here, please," she said. Her voice was neither demanding nor harsh, carrying the lilt of Hispanic pronunciation. Something in it compelled, besides the hand on the gun. We went down the steps, me first, Amy shrinking away from Tony's body as she negotiated the steps.

The woman cop waited until we were level with her, then pocketed her cell phone and patted me down. Amy's skimpy leggings and hooded T-shirt took even less of her attention. "No weapons," she tossed over her shoulder to the guy, who still waited, using the cruiser as a shield against our potential violence.

The woman flashed her badge at us. "Officer Gutierrez," she said. "Hear you've got a dead body you want to get rid of."

5

"JEEZ, Gutierrez." The big cop came out from behind the patrol car, finally. "They might be kin to the stiff—the dead guy."

"As a matter of fact," I said, clearing my throat, "he's my ex-husband."

Amy gasped. "Why didn't you tell me? Aunt Liz—"

"Listen." I turned to the woman cop, thinking she could more easily understand. "My mother is sick in bed in there, and my niece should be taking care of her instead of standing out here shivering. Can you let her go back in while I give you the story? You can talk to her later."

Officer Gutierrez thought about it for a minute. "Guess so," she said finally. "He wasn't killed here?"

"No, he was just dumped out. It was around eight-thirty."

Amy started shivering again. "Go on in," I told her. "Make some more tea or something—make some for Gramma, too. Tell her I'll be in later if she wants to talk about it."

Amy nodded and sidestepped Tony's body on her way up the stairs. Her back was stiff with holding in her usually volatile emotions. I had to give her credit for keeping her cool.

The male cop stopped at the front of the steps. "You been through here, right? Anyone else?"

"Just my niece."

He went up a couple of steps, examining Tony's body critically, as if we were holding a body-dumping contest and he was the judge. "You move him at all?"

"No." I saw no reason to mention my snooping, and hoped Mrs. Beamish wouldn't either.

Officer Gutierrez took out a notebook. "Let's have the story."

I told her as briefly as I could how I'd just gotten into town, stopped at my brother's, come over to my mother's sickbed. There was a small-to-nonexistent chance they would finish grilling me and cart Tony's body away before my dad came back. I made my story as quick as possible.

"My dad's down at the VFW," I finished up. "He's old and frail. Any chance we can clean this up before he gets back?"

Officer Gutierrez tilted her head, examining me under the porch light. "You're pretty cool about your ex-husband's murder," she said slowly.

"Yeah, well, he was ex for a reason." I sighed. "Look, you're going to find all kinds of great stuff when you start up your computer on this one. He beat me, I shot him—ten years ago." She had stiffened, her hand going to her gun. "I did time for it, then I left for California. I haven't been back until now—tonight. Just my luck that someone offs him the instant I get back. If you want to arrest me, get it over with and let's get out of here before my dad comes back and has a heart attack."

Gutierrez stepped away from me and spoke into her cell phone. I watched the male cop put on plastic gloves and begin going over Tony, his pudgy fingers moving with surprising delicacy. Shooting off my big mouth wouldn't get me anywhere—I knew that already, but I'm still apt to do it in moments of stress.

"The Homicide guys are coming," Gutierrez announced, flipping her phone shut. There was a hint of hostility in her voice when she spoke of Homicide. "I'm just going to keep the scene intact and take statements from your niece and any neighbors who might know something." She looked narrowly at me. "Are you planning to leave town?"

"Not anymore, I guess."

"After we secure the scene, you'll be coming with us for further questioning. The Homicide guys will decide whether to detain you or not."

That was that. A few minutes later, a van full of equipment and people pulled up, and they took pictures, fingerprints, scrapings, and sweepings, of this and that. The lights they rigged made the whole front yard glow like a scene from a science fiction movie. Neighbors started to gather just outside the circle of light. I could hear Mrs. Beamish's foghorn voice broadcasting everything she knew.

After a few minutes of that, I asked to sit with my mother, and received an absent-minded permission from Gutierrez. Just before I shut the front door, an ambulance pulled up to take away Tony's mortal remains.

There were people inside, too, doing a rough but efficient job of tossing my mother's living room. It gave me a horrible feeling to see her antimaccassars and embroidered cushions strewn every which way. They barely looked at me when I walked toward the hall.

Amy was curled up on the bed beside my mother. She lifted a scared face to me. I could see a million questions trembling on the tip of her tongue, but mercifully she suppressed them. I didn't notice the stolid policewoman in the corner until I shut the door. My mother lay back on her pillows, her face white and exhausted. Her eyes, worried, flicked open when I came over to the bed.

"Amy said your husband is dead, that that's what this is all about."

"Yes, he's dead."

"Did—did you—"

"Gramma!" Amy let the word explode. "I keep telling you, Aunt Liz has been with us—with me—since nearly seven this evening. She couldn't possibly—"

"I didn't shoot him this time." I leaned against the wall, fatigue washing over me, as tired as if I'd walked all the miles between Grand Junction and Denver that day instead of driving them. "I'm sorry, Mom. Whoever dumped him on your doorstep must have been hoping I'd take the fall. I just don't understand how that person knew I'd be here."

"It's punishment for our sins," my mother said gloomily. "I doubted your father, so I'm being punished."

"Bullshit." She winced, and I tried to moderate my voice. "It's sheer bad luck, is all it is. And anyway, like Amy says, I have an alibi for most of the evening, so probably everything will be okay." I studied her face. "This isn't doing you any good. You need your sleep."

"I'll sleep later." She reached out, grasping my hand, her fingers surprisingly strong. "Will they arrest you?"

"They'll take me to the station for questioning, and then I'm sure they'll let me go. The investigation will take some time, and while it's going on I'll be around. Then, hopefully, they'll find out who killed Tony, and it'll all be finished." I squeezed her hand, and her grip slackened. "You'll be over the flu by then, back on your feet."

"I hope so." Her voice was feathery, her eyelids drooping. "Your father—he's going to be—"

"Upset, I'm sure." From the corner of my eye, I could see the policewoman taking notes. "He'll deal with it." I stood up. "Amy, let's get out of here and let Mom sleep."

The policewoman waited for us at the bedroom door. I turned the bedside lamp low and pulled the covers up around my mother's shoulders. She smiled a little and nestled her head into the pillow.

In the living room, Amy looked around at the mess. "My God, what did they do here? What were they looking for?"

The uniform who accompanied us shuffled her feet sheepishly. "Anything—blood, bullet casings—that ties this place to the crime."

"Well, are they done?" I glanced into the kitchen, where the same chaos reigned. "Can we put things back?"

She went to the door and had a low-voiced conversation with someone there. "Yeah," she said, coming back. "They're finished in here. Be all done in ten, twenty minutes."

It was nine-thirty. My dad would be home pretty soon. Amy and I fell in to the living room, tidying the magazines, putting cushions back on furniture and books in the bookcase. After a few minutes the uniform started helping, so I went into the kitchen and cleaned up spilled flour and sugar, put staples back in the cabinets. It burned me to have my parents go through this, but it wasn't exactly new to me. I've been involved in crime scenes before.

Amy came in as I finished sweeping. "It looks better now." She wrapped her arms around herself. "What happens next?"

"Next, I let you drive Babe."

"Wow." Her smile was a pale imitation of the usual beam. "I'm overcome."

"Take it back to your house, and take Barker for a walk if you would. He's going to be antsy." I put the broom back in the closet. "Go now, before your grampa gets back. It'll save trouble."

"What about you?"

"I'll call Andy if I need anything, but probably I'll just creep in quietly when the police are done with me and sleep in the bus. You can put Barker in there after his walk if you want—that way your mom won't have a conniption."

Amy's smile was less forced. "What is a conniption, anyway? Gramma's always talking about them."

"You'll find out if you're not out of here before your grampa comes home." I found my knapsack where the police had dumped it beside the refrigerator, and dug out my keys. "Drive carefully, now. Just park on the street in front of your house."

"Okay." Amy took the keys, said a polite good-bye to the policewoman, and headed out the door.

I followed her. The front porch was empty of everything, even the welcome mat. Outside, the ambulance and the evidence van were both gone, along with the glaring lights. Except for the police cars and a few neighbors still hanging around, it looked normal again.

"That didn't take long." I said it to the other policewoman, but Officer Gutierrez answered.

"He probably wasn't killed here, as you said. There wasn't much to find." She nodded to the policewoman, who clumped down to a second cruiser and got in. "Are you ready to go?"

"Yeah." Gutierrez and the beefy guy cop were the last ones there. "Is anyone going to hang around to tell my dad about it?"

"Nope." She looked at the neighbors. "He'll probably get the unofficial word, or you can tell him later."

"That will be fun." I got into the back seat of the patrol car. A murmur went up from the small group of people clustered on the sidewalk in front of Mrs. Beamish's house, centered by her foghorn bray. I waved cheerfully as we pulled away.

6

OFFICER Gutierrez ushered me through the institutional halls of police headquarters and into a drafty office where two bleary-eyed, middle-aged men sat at desks covered by mountains of paperwork.

"It'll be a minute." The man at the nearest desk didn't even raise his head.

The second man smiled at Officer Gutierrez. "Hey, we can always make some time for Ms. Gutierrez, can't we, O'Malley?"

O'Malley looked up at that. "Oh, it's you, Eva honey. Look, I'll clean out my desk for you tomorrow, okay? I got work to do right now."

Officer Gutierrez reddened perceptibly, but managed a smile. "I'm not after your job tonight, O'Malley. Just bringing you a customer."

"I got enough customers." O'Malley looked at me without the teasing smile he kept for his female cohort. "What's it about?"

"Homicide," Officer Gutierrez said. She gestured me into the chair in front of O'Malley's desk and leaned against the doorframe just behind my shoulder. "Body dumped on the front porch of this woman's family. Her ex-husband, she says."

"Did you do a make?"

"Asked for it on the way in. They'll bring it along as soon as the printer is free."

O'Malley nodded, his attention still fixed on me. "Why don't you tell me about it, missus? Or ex-missus, whatever."

I told him about it, as succinctly as I could. My head was

pounding, and for some reason all I could think about was Barker—if he was behaving, if he'd get too cold in the bus without me there to curl up with. At least, that's what occupied the front of my mind. The back of it was wondering how long it would be before Paul Drake's name came into the conversation. It was humiliating to think I might need his help, as if he were an all-powerful Lord Peter Wimsey to my Harriet Vane. Finally I understood what she was so upset about in those books.

"So either him showing up like that on the doorstep was one hell of a coincidence," O'Malley said slowly, after I quit talking, "or else someone really has it in for you big-time, missus. Is that your story?"

"I don't have a story." Other people I knew didn't spend significant portions of their time being questioned by police. I allowed myself a bit of self-pity, since I was no less well-behaved than anyone else. "I'm just telling you what happened. My mother isn't well; I came back here for the first time in over ten years to see her. I've been driving since Saturday, and didn't pass the city limits of Denver until after six tonight. I went right to my brother's house. I don't know when Tony was killed, but I've been with my brother and his family and my mom since seven."

"That's nice," O'Malley said. His tone of voice was bored. Behind me, Officer Gutierrez shifted from one foot to another, her belt clanking slightly, the fabric of her uniform brushing sibilantly against itself. O'Malley let the silence lengthen.

"Hey!" I had a happy thought. "I was at a garage in Idaho Springs just before five. My bus sprang an oil leak, and they were able to fix it. They'll tell you I wasn't in Denver earlier. If you've ever driven an old VW bus, you'd know how long it took me to get from there to my brother's in rush-hour traffic."

"Yeah, yeah." O'Malley checked the shelf behind him. "Phil, you have the phone book I need." The other man, talking into his telephone with the receiver cradled between his ear and shoulder while he typed on a computer keyboard, just shrugged. "What was the name of the garage?"

I reached for my knapsack, which had already been

searched once, and fished out the receipt I'd gotten from Hank. For the first time in a while, fortune smiled on me. Hank's garage had the kind of cash register that printed date and time on the receipt. Both were there to confirm what I'd said: I'd paid cash for the repair at 5:15 that very afternoon.

O'Malley dialed the number on the receipt, but nobody answered at the garage. He hung up the phone just as a uniformed officer came in with some papers and dumped them on his desk.

"Is that the make on the victim?" Officer Gutierrez stretched out her hand toward the papers, but O'Malley, elaborately casual, moved them out of her reach.

"Nothing out of the ordinary," he said, looking up at us, but it seemed to me the papers had contained information he'd rather not have had. He stared at the wall for a moment. Officer Gutierrez looked confused.

O'Malley seemed to see me again; there was more curiosity in his gaze than before. "Get the usual stuff and let her go. We'll keep this for a while," he said fluttering the paper from Hank's garage. "Eva will give you a receipt for your receipt." The ghost of a smile visited his dour mouth. "Hope you enjoy your family reunion, because you're going to be around for a while. We'll be in very close touch with you until we get a handle on this investigation."

Following Officer Gutierrez down the hall, I started breathing again, thanking the Goddess of Travelers for that blown oil pressure regulator. Hank would surely remember me, the last customer of the day. I wasn't home free, but at least I had an alibi of sorts. And Paul Drake hadn't come into it at all.

"Sit here," Eva Gutierrez said, pulling out a chair in front of a desk on one side of the busy charge room. She sat at the desk and began pulling out forms. The noise and bustle going on all around helped mask our voices, making us almost cozily private.

"Paperwork," she explained, rolling a form into the typewriter and beginning to type, her fingers flying across the keyboard. "I thought I'd get away from clerical stuff in law enforcement, but there's forms to fill out before you can blow your nose, almost."

I smiled perfunctorily, and she concentrated on her typing, passing things over to me as she finished them. I read every word of the evidence receipt, the interview report, the preliminary statement, and all the rest of them. After they were signed she stuffed them into a folder.

"Could you copy all those for me?" It was an impulsive question, born of my experience with correctional bureaucracy.

She hesitated. "Well, okay. No rule against it for this stuff."

"I'll copy it if you don't have time."

"It won't take long. We'll do it on the way out."

It didn't take long. I pushed the door and turned to her. "Thanks. It was as painless as possible, I suppose."

"Good." She raised her eyebrows at me. "I'm driving you home."

"Oh." Of course, there was no Babe waiting for me outside. I felt cast adrift. "Thanks."

"Just checking out that you're going where you said you were, and that your brother's recollection of events matches yours."

I didn't enjoy the thought of facing Andy's anger, and later my dad's inevitable hostility. "Well, I'm sure he'll tell the truth, anyway," I said, trying to convince myself.

We drove in silence for a while. The inside of the cruiser was warm and crowded, with all kinds of lethal-looking stuff bristling out of it here and there.

"So why'd you shoot him the first time?" Her question came out of the warm darkness. I could see her profile etched against the window—a straight, rather long nose and a firm chin. She was still pretty young—late twenties, at a guess. Efficient, ambitious. Maybe even honest.

"It was him or me, or at least that's what I thought at the time." I shrugged. "Didn't really solve anything, though. If he'd killed me, I would no longer have to worry about having a police record every time there's a bad deed done nearby. If I'd killed him, I'd still be in jail, probably."

"At least you're alive."

"For what it's worth." I pointed out Andy's street, and she turned the cruiser. Babe was parked in the driveway, with no new dings or scratches that I could see, so Amy had made it home all right.

Officer Gutierrez walked me up to the door. Andy opened it before we got there and stood waiting, fists on hips. His dark silhouette loomed in the lighted doorway, reminding me of my father years ago, when I'd come home past my curfew.

"Andy, Officer Gutierrez." I introduced them on the step, hoping he'd be polite enough to invite her in, if not me. "She wants to talk to you."

"Now you're dragging me into it—and my daughter!" Andy thrust his face forward, into the light. There was an ugly look in his eyes. "You actually contaminated my daughter with your convict behavior!" Renee peeked out from behind him, her mouth making a tight upside-down smile, as if she were confronted with something nasty.

"Perhaps you wouldn't mind talking to him out here." I turned politely to Officer Gutierrez.

"Certainly." She took out her notebook. "Mr. Sullivan—"

"Come on in." He had the grace to look slightly ashamed. "But if you're arresting her, I can't afford any bail."

Officer Gutierrez raised her eyebrows. "Ms. Sullivan is not under arrest, sir, anymore than you are. I merely wish to verify some points in her statement."

"In here." Renee led the way into the sleek kitchen. She carried a coffee mug, and she did mumble an invitation to Officer Gutierrez, which was declined.

"Ms. Sullivan states she got here about seven. Can either of you confirm that?"

Renee turned to Andy. "It was just about then. I'd just put dinner on the table."

"Yeah, why we can't eat at a decent hour," Andy began, and then stopped. "Anyway, that's about right. Sometime around seven."

"And she was here until you left to pick up your father, is that right?"

"Yeah."

Renee chipped in. "She and Amy left about ten minutes later, to give Andy time to get Dad out of the way. He would have had a fit—"

"That's enough." Andy glowered, and Renee shut up.

Eva Gutierrez stood up. "That's all I need for now, Mr. Sullivan, Mrs. Sullivan. Thanks for your cooperation. You'll be hearing from us if you can help us further."

I walked her out, and after she drove away, I didn't go back in. Barker jumped up on the passenger seat when he saw me headed toward him. I let him out and put on the leash, and we walked briskly around several blocks until the tension started to leave the back of my neck.

When I opened the side door on the bus, Andy came out of the house as if he'd been waiting for that noise.

"Where are you going?"

I ushered Barker into the bus and turned to face my brother. "The police think I'm staying here, so I planned to stay here. Right here in the driveway. But I can park in the street if you'd rather."

He blinked. "You'll sleep out here?"

"I prefer it that way."

"Well—" It took him a moment to deal with this. "I just came out to say—you'd have to stay here, because I won't be a party to you skipping out."

It had really been a long day. That's my excuse for losing my temper. "I never have skipped out. Any debt I owed to society has been paid—many times. Can you say as much?" I climbed in the side door. "Good night, Andy."

He didn't say anything, so I shut the door, and just after it closed he yelled, "And stay away from Amy!"

It was a little easier to take his hostility when I realized that a lot of it was prompted by concern about Amy. I slid the window open to talk about it, but he was already stalking back inside.

The little battery-powered lamp shed a soft glow over my chilly abode. I used the immersion heater to make myself a cup of tea—my own mixture, homegrown chamomile and mint. Amy had called it Peter Rabbit tea after I'd dosed her with it. A little honey made it perfect.

Barker jumped up beside me on the back bench seat. He

looked very comfortable sitting there, his tongue lolling out, his head on a level with mine—maybe topping me a little, if truth be known. I am not a tall woman, and he sits very tall, especially when he gets to sit on the furniture. "Down," I said, but without my usual emphasis. Practically everything in the bus counts as furniture of one kind or another.

After the tea was gone, I brushed my teeth in the little sink, pulled out the Z-bed and fluffed up my sleeping bag. I opened the side window and shook Barker's rug out. I turned out the lamp and used the bucket I'd kept for traveling, wishing I had taken a stand on my principles after visiting Andy's bathroom instead of before. Nestled in my sleeping bag, I thought about using my newest toy, a pencil-thin but bright halogen flashlight that, worn on a headband, made reading in a sleeping bag easier than ever. Before I could complete the thought, I was asleep.

7

BARKER woke me early. I was stiff from the chill that seeped into my sleeping bag. There was no morning sun, just a lowering gray sky only a little lighter than night.

I pulled on clothes and took Barker for his walk, hoping Andy would go to work before I got back so I could use one of his bathrooms without enduring a rant from him. Of course, Renee would still be around, dealing out her slings and arrows.

While we walked, I tried to figure out what I was going to do. First and foremost in my concerns was my mother and her fragile health. Tony's murder might have made her really ill—I would have to brave my father's doddering fury to find out. And maybe she didn't want to see me any more than he did.

My own situation also required a good deal of thought. Tony's death had turned my already problematic reunion with my folks into something that threatened my personal freedom. It was almost enough to make me sorry he was dead.

For a little while I imagined heading west, driving back through the Rockies and the Sierra, back to my ancient computer and the queries I was compiling for the more lucrative magazines that had bought stuff from me in the past. Trying to make a living as a freelance writer is like being on a furiously moving treadmill—tumble off for any length of time and you have to scramble to get back on.

But instead of heading back to my home and livelihood, I had to stick around Denver. And a lot of issues that had been swept under the rug in my family years ago might get shaken out. I had always nursed a grievance over the way my parents had severed me from their life. Lately I'd been telling myself that even though they were wrong to act so, they were still my parents and we should communicate with each other. It came from living several years in California, I suppose, where everybody talks like a therapist because everybody's seeing one—except me, probably the last holdout from counseling in the entire Bay Area. I had seen enough psychologists during my incarceration.

My parents could have used some counseling back then, too. It might not even be possible to communicate after all this time, so encrusted was our relationship with past issues. But they were old, and I felt on some basic level that they deserved a daughter's duty from me. If they hadn't been there for me over the past years, the obverse was true.

The streets Barker and I walked down were lined with small, older ranch-style houses interspersed with big, brassy new remodels like Andy's. I thought about Palo Alto, about my own small house and the sunshine that bathed it this time of year, about my garden, my veggies and flowers, and about Drake.

Once I allowed Drake into my thoughts, he took up way too much space. It wouldn't be long before he found out about my reunion from hell, given that police departments have fax machines and computer linkups and are prone to checking up on people who get involved in murders. Then he wouldn't just be in my thoughts anymore. He'd be in my ear, yelling at me on the phone. I could hardly wait.

The trees were starting to turn already; every so often dead leaves floated down to litter the sidewalk. Barker hadn't experienced fall before; he took personal exception to all the leaves, shying away from them when they drifted near him, then attacking the helpless ones at his feet. I pulled my sweatshirt hood up against the uncompromising nip in the air, so different from the moist coolness of Bay Area September mornings.

Renee's kitchen light was on when I got back. I slipped the plastic bag holding Barker's morning deposit into Andy's garbage can and ushered the dog into Babe's front passenger door, closing the door behind us with as little noise as possible.

I was turning the Z-bed back into a seat when the side door squealed open. "Hi," Amy said lugubriously. "Are you okay?"

"I'm fine." I pulled up the table and got my cup out of its place in the cupboard. "Just trying to be real quiet and not bother anyone. How are you? Okay after all you went through last night?"

"I had dreams." Amy shivered and let it go at that. "You went through more than me. Did the police give you the third degree?"

"I don't think they do that anymore. They were quite polite, actually. Do you want some tea?"

"No, thanks." I winced when the cupboard door banged, and Amy said, "Daddy's already gone, and you'd have to be invisible not to bother Mom." The kitchen curtain twitched. "She'll be out here pretty soon, waking up the whole neighborhood."

"She's just protecting her family." Barker gazed blissfully at Amy while she combed her fingers through the silky fur of his ruff. "Maybe you should go back in."

"It's not fair," Amy burst out. "You're part of the family. And they won't even let you sleep in the house—"

"It was my idea to stay out here. I enjoy living in the bus again." All except the lack of a bathroom.

The front door opened, and Renee motioned to Amy. I stayed where I was, planning to drive around and find a filling station or a construction site with portable toilets.

Amy pulled on my arm. "You come, too," she hissed. "I'll make you some breakfast."

By my calculations, it was Wednesday—a school day. "Don't you have school?"

Renee stomped toward us. Amy turned her back on her mother. "I'm thinking of cutting."

"You will not!" Renee glared at me. "This is all your fault, Liz."

"Tell the world, why don't you?" Amy returned her mother's glare.

I dropped a meek sentence into their verbal battle. "Do you mind if I use the bathroom?"

Renee was taken aback. "Well, I guess it's okay. I mean, I guess you'll have to."

Amy pulled me toward the house, and Barker bounded joyfully in our wake. "Come on, Aunt Liz. You can use my bathroom."

"Don't let that dog in the house!"

"He'll stay in my room." Amy still wouldn't look at her mom. Renee trailed us through the front door, arguing.

She was still arguing when Amy and I left, half an hour later. I'd had a very quick shower, and a cup of tea made by Amy, and had offered her a ride to school, which went a short way toward placating Renee. But she still had to wring her hands and wail whenever she thought of the disgrace of having the police come around, and her last words to Amy were not to talk to reporters.

"Will there be any?" Amy bounced on the passenger seat. "Like, TV guys? There's one on channel four—he's killer, for an old guy."

I judged from this that the reporter in question was probably several years younger than me. "I doubt they'll seek you out, but your mom is right—the less you say, the better you come off on TV."

"Like, woman of mystery, hmm?" Amy shook back her hair, which was now totally orange, instead of the multicolored hanks it had been a month ago. "I can do that. What will you be doing today, Aunt Liz?"

A sideways glance showed her looking concerned. "I don't know. Surviving, I guess."

"I'm worried," Amy burst out. "I mean—what if someone tries to kill you, or the police arrest you—"

"I'll be fine." I projected as much calm certainty as I could. "Even if I'm arrested, which I don't expect, they'll have to turn me loose again—lack of evidence. Besides, jail is a pretty safe place." This was a lie, but Amy accepted it.

She rooted in her backpack and came up with a small tape recorder. "Here," she said, shoving it into the open top of my knapsack as we pulled up in front of the high school. "It's voice-activated. I got it for school, but I won't need it today. You keep it with you, and then if someone tries something, you have a record."

It didn't sound that useful to me, but I didn't mind toting it around if it made her feel better.

Knots of young people in various outlandish outfits stood around in front of the school building; an immense parking lot nearby showed how things had changed. In my day, very few kids drove themselves to school. Now the lot was full of low-rider trucks and rusty-looking sedans and a sprinkling of newer cars.

"Good," Amy said in relief. "The bell hasn't rung." She zipped up her heavy book bag and gave Barker's head a final pat. "Thanks for the ride, Aunt Liz."

"Amy!" A loud female shriek sounded nearby. "Is this Babe? Killer!"

"Kimberly!" Amy shrieked back. She jumped down, turning to me. "This is my friend Kimberly. I told her all about you."

"Hi!" Kimberly peered out from between long strands of improbably pink hair with dark roots. Underneath the Morticia-inspired makeup was a round, cheerful face. "Nice to meet you!"

A sleek white pickup truck screeched to the curb just in front of my bus. Brawny young men swarmed out of its cab. The driver caught sight of Amy and Kimberly and came sauntering over, followed by his passengers.

"Why, it's my little cousin Amy," he said in a high, fake-sounding falsetto. "You hanging with the hippie chicks, honey?" His insolent grin flicked over me and the bus. Barker started a low, rumbling growl.

Amy barely glanced at him. "Chill, Biff." She started to shut the door, but the young man grabbed it.

"No, no. Let's see who your friend is." He peered through the door. "Kind of old for you, isn't she? Or do you little dykettes like older women?"

"This is our aunt, Byron," Amy said, emphasizing the name. "Aunt Liz, this is one of your nephews, Byron Fahey."

My sister Molly's boy—the youngest one, who'd helped my dad chuck Tony out a few weeks ago. I looked at him with interest. He didn't much resemble my memories of Bill Fahey, the up-and-coming accountant my sister had married when I was thirteen. But I could see the Sullivan in him. In fact, he was like a **young** version of the father I'd grown up with—big, and simmering with resentments.

His lowered eyebrows made him look as if a two-year-old had taken possession of his burly body. "No way. I don't have no Deadhead aunt."

"Not everyone who drives a VW bus is a Deadhead," I said, trying to be polite. "Nice meeting you, Byron."

"The name is Biff." His lip stuck out now. "Oh, yeah. You're the man-killer aunt, right?"

I didn't like his tone of voice, nor the way his eyes had lingered on Amy's all-too-visible cleavage when he'd called her his little cousin. I'm not too fond of macho men at the best of times.

"I did once try to eliminate an obnoxious testosterone-based life form." I kept my smile pleasant. "So long, Amy. Perhaps we'll meet again, Byron."

He slammed the door shut, the noise it made swallowing the uncomplimentary word I saw on his pouting lips. Amy and Kimberly, laughing, were halfway up the steps. Biff started after them, but one of his friends, grabbing his arm, pointed at a man in a suit, obviously some school official, who watched them from the top of the stairs. Somewhere a bell rang, and I drove away.

I would have spent more time worrying about Amy's situation with her hostile cousin, but instead I chose to worry about my upcoming interview with my father. I just hoped I could get through the encounter without shouting at him.

I parked on the street, behind a nondescript sedan. Barker sat up expectantly in the passenger seat, but I told him to stay.

After knocking, I turned the knob and went right in, without waiting to be invited. My dad sat in his chair in the living room. The man I'd seen the night before at the police station, O'Malley, sat across from him on the couch.

O'Malley raised an eyebrow at my entrance. "Missus Sullivan? Or is it Naylor?"

"Sullivan." I looked at my dad. His face was slowly turning red—a familiar sign from my childhood. He was much more lined than I remembered; his scalp, also flushing with anger, showed clearly through thinning white hair. His eyes were filmy behind thick-lensed glasses with heavy, dark frames.

"So. Your mother said you were back." His voice was the same—gravelly, with an incipient snarl that went with the angry red tide washing over his face. "Who invited you? Look at the trouble you bring." He turned to O'Malley, who wore an expression of courteous boredom. "Always too smart for her own good, that one."

O'Malley's glance flicked to me. "Do you think your daughter arranged this crime—had her ex-husband killed and dumped on your doorstep?"

My dad drew back in his chair. "I didn't say that. She wouldn't do that anyway. Girl has nothing—that's what my daughter-in-law said. Lives in a little tumbledown place somewhere in San Francisco with all those hippies and all." He shook a knobby forefinger at O'Malley. "How could she afford to hire anybody killed? Tell me that! She's poor as a church mouse!"

"Is that true, Missus Sullivan?" O'Malley's bright, observant eyes gave nothing away. "You too poor to hire a hit?"

"I'm poor, and I don't kill people, in person or by proxy." I gave both the men a disgusted look. "I'm here to see my mom."

"You're not welcome in this house. That hasn't changed." My dad clutched the arms of his chair, ready to rise to his unsteady feet and throw me out.

"Right. When I've seen Mom, I'll leave."

He sank back in his chair again, looking exhausted and old even beyond his eighty-three years. Suppressing a qualm, I left them in the living room.

Mom was propped up on her pillows, her mouth slightly open, the *Catholic Register* lying on her lap between limp hands. A breathy snore rent the air, relieving my alarm at seeing her looking so unconscious. I moved slowly around the room, tidying up some of my dad's clothes on the floor.

Renee had mentioned, sniffing, that she had cleaned the old people's house a couple of days before; that she and my sister Molly took turns doing this, although Molly occasionally sent her housekeeper over instead of doing the work herself. I didn't want to like Renee, but I had to admit she did her part looking after her in-laws. Again I felt guilt for being such a bad daughter.

When I came in from straightening the towels in the bathroom, my mother was looking at me. "Lizzie." She sounded better. "Did you—did your father—"

"I'm here to check on you, then I'll go."

"You don't need to check on me." She coughed a little into her fist. "Molly and Renee and Andy help me all I need. Dan and his wife would, too, but they're in Montana right now."

"So you don't want me to come again."

"I didn't say that." She coughed once more.

"Look, Mom." I sat in the chair that I'd cleared of dirty clothes. "I came all the way out here because I thought we might be able to forgive each other and keep the lines open in the future. So if you still feel I'm unworthy or whatever, just say so now, and I'll save myself the trouble of trying to talk to you."

She looked at me for a moment, and then tears began to leak out of her eyes. "You never used to want the trouble of talking to me—to your father either."

"You didn't want to hear what I had to say." I handed her the box of tissues, but she ignored it.

"I had such hopes for you—you were such a bright little thing." Washed by tears, she looked at me sadly. "And look at you—no family, messing around with that writing stuff— and Renee told us about how you live in some little old chicken coop. Your brothers and sister have all done better for themselves—why, Molly's house is like a palace, almost. Even Andy's done fine, in spite of—"

"In spite of knocking up his girlfriend and having to get married?" It was spiteful, but I said it anyway. Perhaps my siblings had surpassed me in material goods, but if Biff was a symbol of how much better Molly had done than I, I was glad to have been spared the pleasures of motherhood.

46

My mother gave me a look I recognized although I hadn't seen it in years. "You should talk, Lizzie. I just want you to know that we can't afford to support you if you move back here."

Patience is not my long suit. "I like my life fine, and I wouldn't dream of moving back and burdening you." The words came out loud, defiant; those old patterns of behavior were powerful. I tried to sound like a rational adult. "Sorry, Mom. I'm just upsetting you, not helping at all. I'll probably be around for a few more days until Tony's death is settled. If you want to see me, let Amy or Renee know. Otherwise, I won't come back."

I had my hand on the doorknob when she spoke. "What do you want me to say, that I'm sorry, that we treated you badly?" Her voice had a little more strength in it. "Well, maybe we did. But you were so headstrong. You wouldn't listen—just like your father, both of you going to extremes. I couldn't go against him, and I was angry with you, too—oh, so angry, the way you threw my hopes away."

"I'm sorry I didn't live my life to please you," I said tightly, not turning. "It's all over with now."

"But it's not, is it?" Her voice gentled a little. "See, here you are in trouble again just because of that foolish marriage." I bit my lip to keep from replying, and her voice went on, tempered with that know-it-all motherly condescension that so sets our teeth on edge. "And I never asked you to live your life to please me. Has it pleased you, Lizzie? Have you done so well by ignoring your parents' advice?"

"Good or bad, my life is of my fashioning, and as you pointed out before, none of your concern." I glanced over my shoulder for one last look at her face, set inflexibly in righteousness. "Good-bye."

At least I didn't slam the door.

8

O'MALLEY was still talking to my dad. I hurried through the living room with only a nod to them, trying to avoid negative comments about my horrible personality.

At least Barker was thrilled to see me. Isn't that why people have pets? Uncritical acceptance is so rare among humans. I didn't have long to bask in it. Before I even had my seat belt untangled, O'Malley was standing by the driver's window.

At his motion, I rolled the window down. Barker growled from the passenger seat, his hackles rising. I put a hand on his ruff. "Yes, Officer? Lieutenant? Detective? How do I address you?"

"You call me O'Malley, I'll call you Lizzie."

"Liz." I pulled Barker back. "Put your fur down."

"I don't keep it up," O'Malley said with a grin.

I gazed at him stonily. "My dog doesn't like men much. What do you want?"

"I want to tell you I'm sorry about the way your parents feel." O'Malley shook his head. "Boy, the last time you tried to kill your husband they sure got upset, huh?"

"Yes." I put the key in the ignition. "I gather you don't accept my alibi, O'Malley?"

"Your alibi's fine." He smiled amiably. "That fellow at the garage ID'd you right away. Even saw you sitting across the street in the cafe while he had your car on the rack. Looks like you didn't pull the trigger."

"I didn't have anything at all to do with it." I took a deep breath, trying to calm the panic that threatened me. The justice system isn't really about justice. It's about expediency, in a bungling sort of way. People who've already been

48

through it can be processed quite easily. As far as the system was concerned, I was being served up on a silver platter.

"So you say." O'Malley was still smiling. "You know, things are different now than they were last time you tried to kill your husband. Battered wives get off light these days. Sometimes they just get probation. A good lawyer, now, and you might not do any time at all."

"Are you arresting me?" My hand tightened in Barker's fur.

"No, no. Don't go getting ideas into your head." He regarded me brightly. "Just telling you some facts, Liz. We aren't ready to arrest anyone yet—still investigating." He rubbed the sparse, graying bristles on his chin. The hair on his head, what there was of it, wasn't much longer. "For instance," he said in a conversational tone, "the neighbor next door mentioned that a man who looked a lot like your ex has been visiting here a few times lately. Last time, your dad and some young guy helped him out the door. She thought she saw a gun involved." O'Malley smiled at me. "Of course, you weren't around then, so you wouldn't know anything about it. But maybe killing this guy is a hobby of your family."

I felt a chill, but tried to keep my expression bland. "Boy, you people will settle for anyone as a perp—me, who wasn't here, my dad, who's no threat to anyone anymore—"

"Even an old guy can off someone if he has a gun," O'Malley pointed out. "Course, it could have been the young guy. You know him?"

"I wasn't here, as you said yourself. I was home, peacefully trying to make an honest buck. And if you want confirmation—"

"We got that already." He gave me a sly smile. "Friends on the force, that's what you have. Too bad your cop buddy didn't come along to Denver with you. What an alibi that would be!"

I was about to make a heated reply, when it occurred to me that what was missing in this conversation was any sense from O'Malley that it mattered. He didn't have the air of a man intent on doing his job. These offhand, lei-sured remarks were his way of going through the motions.

"If you really believe my dad would kill Tony, when I was the one he was mad at, then you're obviously hard up for valid suspects. Why don't you go find some, and stop bothering us?"

Even that didn't get him riled. He stepped back from the bus, smiling a little. "We're looking. Everywhere. Depend on it, Missus. And we'll be having some more chats with you sometime soon. Eva will keep in touch with you on that."

He waved, climbed into the nondescript car, and drove off. I watched him go, feeling hollow.

Then, before my dad could come out and harangue me, I drove off, too. I didn't have a destination in mind. No point in going back to Andy's house so Renee could give me the cold shoulder. No point in hanging around my mother, either. I was surprised at how much her rigid dis-approval hurt. I thought I'd cured myself of ever need-ing my parents' approval years ago, but deep down, that "I'll show them" attitude still lingered. And I hadn't man-aged to show them. Though just getting through each day without a financial crisis was a triumph for me, they natu-rally didn't see it that way.

Aimlessly, I drove through the streets of little houses, finding myself finally at a small park I remembered from high school, where the disaffected youth used to hang out evenings and weekends until the police would come and make them move. This time of day it was deserted except for a couple of moms at the tiny playground, pushing their toddlers in swings. I clipped the leash on Barker and walked slowly through the park, scuffling in the leaves, ad-miring the bed of dahlias that rose stiff and triumphant from their knobby bark mulch.

It sounded as if O'Malley would settle for me, or, if he couldn't figure out some way to blame me for master-minding the killing, my dad and Biff. Much as I thought Biff deserved the chastising of Fate, a murder charge was probably overdoing it. And yet, did I want to take the rap myself? Was there any way out of that? I couldn't marshal any coherent thoughts about my situation; instead I was awash in stoic helplessness.

Rabbits caught in headlights must have something of that heavy passivity, that acceptance of a danger so overwhelming that the only thing to do is hunker down and hope it goes over you without hurting too much.

Usually, it kills you.

What I needed was a plan. What I had was a primal need to call Drake and blubber in panic.

Barker strained at the leash after a squirrel. I didn't know if Denver had a leash law, and under the circumstances I didn't care about the wrath of the animal control department. I took off his leash and let him run.

Watching him dash from tree to tree, I tried to control my fragmented thoughts. I didn't want to be the premier suspect, and I didn't want my family suspected either. I certainly didn't want the murderer out free under the blue sky while I was locked up for killing my ex-husband.

Given O'Malley's snide remarks about Drake, the Denver police must already have contacted him to see if I'd actually been hanging around the Rockies longer than I'd said. Maybe Drake was already calling Renee's, looking for me. Anxious for me. I allowed myself the comforting warmth of that thought. Drake, I was pretty sure, was genuinely interested in my welfare—at the least, as a friend. Perhaps even as more.

But that was too scary to think about—even scarier than O'Malley's friendly concern. I couldn't—didn't want to—confront the possibility of a close, loving bond with a man. The very idea had been anathema to me for too long, because of Tony. And now Tony was dead.

That was the most disorienting thing that had happened in the past twenty-four hours. Tony was truly dead, gone out of my life, unable to personally threaten me again. I kept feeling that he was about to sit down beside me on the park bench any moment, grabbing my arm in that affectionate-looking squeeze that left bruises behind.

Barker panted up to flop in front of me, tongue hanging out. I put the leash back on him and sat awhile longer, staring at the path, waiting for Tony to feel dead to me.

He had been so exciting when I was nineteen, so different from the rest of the college boys. I had felt sophisticated and glamorous with him—and grateful, because no one had ever before treated me as if I were a beautiful woman. Later, I knew he treated any woman that way when he wanted something from her—sex or power or just an afternoon's amusement. His insistence had led to our marriage—I was too infatuated, too envied by other girls, to care whether we married or not.

And afterward it didn't take long before I became clumsy, awkward, dowdy, too shy—or so he told the friends he'd made at the brokerage house—to mingle socially in the evenings. I believed all that, even when I defied him, left him. I still believed it, on some level.

So I pushed the thought of Drake away. I wasn't ready to give him the right to be concerned about me, involved in my actions. I would stand on my own two feet, and I would take care of my own problems. If I had to do it alone, without friends, I would do it, and not just be the blind, panic-stricken rabbit, paralyzed by its own fear and relentlessly squashed.

I got up, leading Barker toward the street and trying to kick-start my brain. I knew nothing about Tony's friends and associates these days. But I had known some of them years ago, and they might know what he was up to that had gotten him killed.

Just as I opened the side door for Barker, a name slipped into my mind. Maud Riegert. Tony had been carrying her credit card, and now I remembered her—a thin, chain-smoking junior commodities broker at the same firm where Tony worked. I had met her a couple of times at office parties Tony couldn't get out of taking me to, and the reactions of his coworkers at the second party had made it clear to me that Tony and Maud were linked in office gossip. That night I had offered him a divorce—a mistake I paid for with a black eye and a chipped tooth. When Maud called a month or so later to ask why I wouldn't let Tony go where his heart was, I was so overcome with hysterical laughter I couldn't speak.

The branch library was still in the same place, though I

got lost on some one-way streets trying to get to it. I started with the Denver telephone directory and hit pay dirt right away. She was listed, though her address was not.

I used the pay phone next to the library, without much hope that she would be home this late on a Wednesday morning. But a sleepy female voice answered on the third ring.

"Maud?"

"Yes, who is it?"

"This is Liz Sullivan." I cleared my throat. "Tony Naylor's ex-wife."

There was a moment of silence. "Who?"

"Tony Naylor. He's dead, you know. He was killed last night."

More silence. Then she whispered, "Who told you to call me? Was it Kyle?"

"Er—no one told me. I just remembered that you and Tony—I wondered if you knew—"

"Look," she interrupted. "I don't know you or what you're talking about. The police already asked me about this Tony person. Evidently he'd stolen my credit card somehow. I don't know anything more about it, okay? Just leave me alone!"

The phone banged in my ear, and the dial tone buzzed gently. I set the receiver back in its cradle.

Ten years is a long time to remember anyone's voice, but I thought she'd recognized mine. No matter what she said, Maud Riegert knew something about Tony. And she'd told me something, too.

Kyle. Kyle had been Tony's buddy, and I'd met him many times—mostly when they were both drunk, but sometimes on ordinary occasions, when he'd been kind to me. A couple of times, when Tony had taken a swing at me, Kyle had stopped him. Once, shortly before the end of my life in Denver, he'd come over when Tony wasn't home, and I'd received the distinct impression that he would be glad to comfort me, especially in the bedroom. By then sex was not my idea of a treat, and fear of Tony's retaliation would have kept me from enjoying it anyway, but I had appreciated the offer, which briefly made me feel like a woman again instead of a cowed, beaten thing.

I tried to remember Kyle's last name, standing there with my hand on the receiver, but it eluded me. Instead, I went back into the library and consulted the phone book again. Among a list of brokerage houses I found the one Tony had worked for.

Digging out all my change, I lined it up on the little shelf by the phone where a phone book was supposed to be but wasn't. I summoned my best office-temp voice, and when the receptionist at Baker Mulshine Hollenbeck answered, I asked dulcetly for personnel.

"I'm verifying a reference," I cooed when personnel answered. "This is for a job that requires a great deal of background checking."

"Oh, at Rocky Flats?" The woman on the other end sounded inclined to be chatty.

"I'm not allowed to say," I said primly. "But you're close."

"How can I help you?"

"The applicant wrote down your firm on his employment history—although his handwriting is difficult to read." That much was true, anyway—Tony always had a horrible scrawl. "One of his references also works for you, but I can't make out more than Kyle Something."

"Can you tell me the applicant's name? We have two Kyles here."

"It's Anthony Naylor." I held my breath hopefully.

"Naylor, Naylor," she muttered. "Was he recently employed here?"

"The date he left is smudged, but the start date was several years ago."

"Oh, Tony. Tony Naylor. He was—terminated—over a year ago." Her voice was a blend of curiosity and formality. "It must be Kyle Baldridge he put down as a reference. They were always close."

"Was Mr. Baldridge his supervisor?"

"No, that was Mr. Tobin—Leonard Tobin. He recently retired. And Kyle's been on leave for the past month—he won't be back until the beginning of October. Just a minute." She put me on hold, long enough to make me wonder if she had some way of tracing my call. I fed the phone when the digitized voice told me to, and hoped it wouldn't ask for more.

"Sorry about that." She was back. "When did you get an application from Tony?"

Someone had obviously just filled her in. Suppressed excitement simmered in her voice.

"It was a couple of weeks ago." I made my voice sound apologetic. "I've been on vacation, too, and it came in while I was gone. I can't get hold of Mr. Naylor to verify these names."

"That's because he's dead," the woman in personnel said triumphantly. "Gladys just told me that the police were here this morning, trying to find out where he's been working since he left."

"Goodness, I'd better get in touch with them. And I guess I won't need to check references after all. The police have probably already talked to this Kyle person."

"I don't know if they have." She sounded thoughtful now. "He's volunteering on a dig in the Four Corners area—he likes that archaeology stuff."

"Thanks for your help." I hung up quickly, before she could demand information from me. At least I had gotten Kyle's last name—and I remembered Leonard Tobin, too. I'd met him at one of those functions, and then Tony had railed loudly about him more than once, about Leonard taking his credit and obstructing his advancement. I hadn't paid much attention—Tony suspected most people of those crimes. I didn't think Tobin was that much older—certainly not retirement age. But perhaps, as senior broker, he'd made his pile and was ready to spend it.

Back to the phone book again. This time I was lucky. Both Kyle and Leonard were listed, Kyle in the chic old section near downtown that Amy had referred to as LoDo, for Lower Denver, and Leonard in the Cherry Creek area. I wrote down their addresses and phone numbers and went back to the bus, where Barker munched dog food while I munched peanut butter and jelly, trying to figure out how I would talk to these people, and hoping that somehow what I heard could help me.

9

SINCE Kyle Baldridge was out of town, I decided to head for Cherry Creek to see if Leonard Tobin was at home. After my experience with Maud, I didn't phone first. It's too easy to hang up on someone.

Leonard Tobin lived in one of those subdivisions with roads winding through landscaping that captures the dichotomy of Colorado—one house sprawls in a Southwestern jumble of cactus, sand, boulders; the next one is a mock Tudor enveloped in a lush cottage garden. Tobin's was discreetly middle-of-the-road ranch style, with foundation shrubs and a brick path to the door. A FOR SALE sign swung in the front yard.

I parked on the street. My bus was an anomaly among all the gleaming Cadillacs and sport utility vehicles that ornamented the driveways. There was no car in Tobin's driveway; the garage was shut.

The doorbell made a hollow sound inside the house. I was about to turn away when the door opened.

"Yes?"

I suddenly felt jittery—I hadn't really thought he'd be home, framed the right approach.

"Uh—Mr. Tobin?"

"Yes?" He peered at me suspiciously. I recognized him when he moved into the sunlight: the thin face, the high-bridged nose. His hair was much sparser. "What do you want?"

"I'm Liz Sullivan. Tony Naylor's ex-wife."

His face changed; for one instant, fear lanced out. Then he looked down. "Sorry. I don't know you."

The door began to close. "Wait. Mr. Tobin—I just want to ask you some questions. Tony's dead. Did you know?"

He froze, one hand on the doorknob. "Dead?" His other hand passed, trembling, over his mouth. "I—didn't know." He looked up again. "What do you want? Why have you come here?"

"Some answers." I could see I was losing him. "The police suspect me."

"And you want to throw suspicion on me?" His face tightened. I could see that the past decade had left a heavy mark on him. "Look, if I'd killed Tony, I would have done it awhile ago, when it would still have benefited me. But now—" he pointed at the sign on his front lawn—"now there's no reason. I've already lost it all. My job. My wife. My home's next to go." He leaned toward me, his mouth twisted, and I smelled the whiskey on his breath. "He won, you see. He won over a year ago. Why would I wait so long to kill the bastard?"

"I'm sorry." I didn't know what else to say. "But weren't you his boss? How could he get that much power over you?"

"You're his wife. Didn't you know?" For the first time he seemed to see me. "Oh, you might as well come in. I've got to leave in a little while—the realtor is showing the house. But you might as well have a drink."

I followed him down the hall; he staggered a little. The living room contained a couple of plastic lawn chairs with a brass-and-glass coffee table between them, and some nicely framed and matted photographs on the wall. "My wife took most of the furniture—my ex-wife," he said, settling into one of the lawn chairs. "Yeah, now I remember. You shot Tony—tried to kill him a few years ago, right? He was on sick leave for a couple of months. So were you more successful this time?"

"I wasn't even in Denver, but the police think I was behind it somehow." I sat in the other chair, uninvited. A huge bottle of Jack Daniels stood on the coffee table, next to a glass.

Tobin poured himself a drink. He didn't offer me one.

"That Naylor. What a bastard." He raised his glass in a salute, then drank half the whiskey.

"I wondered where Tony had been working recently. Can you tell me? I gather he was fired from the brokerage."

"He was blackmailing me, you know." Tobin looked at me earnestly, clutching his glass. "Just a little mistake—little bad margin call on my part. Had to cover myself. Dipped into a trust fund I was managing." He took a morose sip. "Tony found out somehow. I was a VP by then. Couldn't let them know."

"So what did he want?"

"Money." Tobin gave me a sharp look, the muzziness momentarily gone. "And immunity from his own depredations. I told him I couldn't protect him forever, but he pushed. Got found out, and took me down with him, the bastard." His hand clenched on the glass. "God, I hate him." Then he focused on me again. "But I didn't kill him. Didn't know where he was or what he was doing. I had enough trouble on my own account." He sloshed a little more whiskey into his glass.

"Do you think Maud Riegert might know more? Were they still—friends?"

He shrugged and tossed off his drink. "Good old Maudie. She moved on a few years ago. Dunno if she still saw Tony. Got a job in another firm." He giggled a little. "She had a black eye once, you know. Said she got it in the shower. Then she left. Nice little ass that girl had." He made a vague gesture in the air and reached for the bottle, but his hand groped without finding it. Then slowly, peacefully, his eyes closed. A breathy snore bubbled out of his mouth, followed, in a moment, by another.

I pitied the real estate agent who was bringing a client over. And though I had gotten some information, it wasn't the information I wanted.

Tobin slumped farther in his chair. His sport coat fell open, revealing a small notebook in the inside pocket. As I looked at it, he snored again.

He didn't move when I stood beside him for a while. So I fished the notebook out. It was one of those little pocket daily calendars with an address section in the back. Maud

58

Riegert's address and phone number were written down under *R*. The phone number was the same one I had reached her at earlier. I copied the address, and then leafed through the book again. Kyle's name was there, but I already had his location.

Tony was in there, too—with several scratched-out addresses under his name. The last one, with a big angry X drawn through it, was the same as Kyle Baldridge's. So Tony had moved in with Kyle at some point. Perhaps he had still lived there at the time of his death. I had looked at his driver's license but I couldn't remember now what had been written there, and I knew from my own experience that licenses weren't always accurate.

I needed to talk to Kyle, even if I had to drive to the Four Corners to do it.

Leonard Tobin snored again. I tucked the notebook back into his pocket and tiptoed out of the house.

10 _____

MAUD Riegert was a lot closer than the Four Corners. I drove back across town to her apartment, which was near the Capitol Hill area of older mansions and elegant apartments.

I found a place to park on the street. Barker let me know in no uncertain terms that he was growing tired of staying alone in the bus. I promised him a nice walk later, and went into the lobby of the building. The marble floor shone, and so did the plate glass of the locked door between me and the elevators. I wondered if Maud would let me in.

The elevator on the other side of the glass door opened and a rottweiler charged out, towing a woman in jogging clothes. She pushed the inner door open, and as the dog pulled her inexorably toward the sidewalk, I caught it before it could close.

Maud was on the sixth floor. I rang the doorbell, waited, rang again. The door had a peephole, but she probably wouldn't recognize me—it had been a long time, and we hadn't seen that much of each other. I might not recognize her, if given the chance.

The door opened to the length of the chain lock; a narrow sliver of suspicious face appeared in the opening. "Who are you?"

"Ms. Riegert?"

"What do you want?"

I cleared my throat. "The county has some questions. About the death of Tony Naylor."

She sighed. "I've already talked to the police. Can't you get your information from them?"

"It's better if I talk to you."

The one visible eye looked me up and down and found me nonthreatening. My anonymous outfit—khaki pants and windbreaker jacket from the Junior League Thrift Shop—makes me look like thousands of other nondescript women in their mid-thirties who can't be bothered to fix up. She shut the door briefly and then opened it without the chain.

"Come in." She hustled me into the living room. "Make it snappy, can't you? I'm busy."

She certainly was. Through an open door I could see her bedroom; the bed was piled high with clothes and suitcases. A big cardboard packing crate took up center stage in the living room.

"Are you moving?"

She gave me a sharp look. "I'm going on sabbatical for a little while, and I don't want the sublet to ruin my things."

"That's sensible."

"You don't mind if I work while we talk, do you? I don't have long before the truck comes."

"It's fine." I fidgeted with the notebook I had taken out of my knapsack in the interests of verisimilitude. "Actually, I'm not from the county, although I imagine they do have questions about Tony's death."

She froze in the act of wrapping a towel around a watercolor depicting the quaint Main Street of an old mining town. "Who—what—"

"I'm Liz Sullivan. I called you earlier, but you wouldn't talk to me. I really need to know some things, Maud."

"Liz?" She put the watercolor down and peered at me. "You don't look at all the same. Your hair's short, for one thing."

I could see by her expression that she had no great opinion of my hairstyle. "It's low-maintenance. Do you know where Tony's been working lately?"

She sat down on the love seat opposite the one I occupied. "You don't beat around the bush. Why do you care? You've been out of the picture for a while." Her eyes narrowed. "Say, how long have you been back in Denver, anyway? Do the police know you're here?"

"Yes. They think I had something to do with Tony's death."

"Did you?" Her gaze turned speculative. "You tried something like that before, I recall."

"I had nothing to do with it." I cleared my throat. "Can't even quite take it in that he's really dead."

She shook her head. "I know. It—it's been a shock."

"Is that why you're going away? Because of grief over Tony?"

"Grief?" She laughed, a harsh sound. "It'll be a warm day on Pikes Peak before I spend any tears on that two-timing, lying bastard."

"Then why are you going away?"

She laughed again. "Boy, you don't give up." Her voice held a contemptuous tolerance. "Honey, you never did have a clue. The times Tony and I had sex in your bed while you were out at your dreary job! I had him in his car, in my car, at my place—even at the office, one night, on the vice president's desk." She shivered, wrapping her arms around herself and smiling. "He was quite a guy, Tony. You didn't have a prayer of handling a man like that. He liked it rough and wild, and so did I."

"Did you like the black eye, too?" I studied her thin, well-toned body, picturing her with my husband in all those places she'd mentioned. It stirred nothing but a faint wish for a nice hot shower.

"Who told you about that?" She jumped up. "The bastard. He was writing you about me or something, wasn't he?"

"I know a bit about it." I fiddled with my notebook. "You left the brokerage firm after that."

"I told him off, and I got a new job." Her gaze slid away. "Oh, hell. You might as well know. He was scaring me a little—really acting out of control, and talking wild about how he could make people do anything he wanted them to. I heard later that he was caught cooking an account, and he implicated poor old Leonard. That was mean."

"So when he blackmailed you, it wasn't a total surprise."

She collapsed back into the love seat, her eyes blank. "How did you know that?"

"I heard he had your credit card, that you gave it to him."

"He stole it." She recovered a little. "I reported it stolen."

"When was this?"

"Look, what makes you think you can ask me these questions? You're not the police." Her lips pressed together in a firm line.

"The police think I had something to do with it, and I didn't. I'm trying to find out what Tony's been doing since he left the brokerage house. I thought you might know. Did you start seeing him again?"

Her gaze slid away. "It was stupid, wasn't it? I knew what he was like. But he came around—so charming. He brought me that picture." She nodded toward the watercolor. "We had spent such wonderful weekends there—our private place. I—let him take me out to dinner and everything."

"Was this recently?"

She twisted away. "Oh, well, I already told the cops, so I guess I can tell you. We went around for a little while. Other people will tell them that, I'm sure—my so-called friends. Then he got offensive again, and I told him to get out. That's when he said—that's when he stole my credit card. I realized it the next day and reported it missing, and they closed the account. That was a couple of weeks ago. I hadn't heard anything from him since."

"He took you out." I spoke slowly. "So he had money. Where was he getting it?"

"He had money then." She shrugged elaborately. "I didn't know where it came from, and I didn't ask."

"He ran out of money." I leaned forward, but she wouldn't meet my eyes. "Is that when he blackmailed you?"

She scooted farther away on the sofa. "I don't—look, this is none of your business. Tony was a bastard, only interested in himself."

"He seemed to be hitting a lot of folks up for money about then."

She gave another bark of that humorless laughter. "I'm not surprised. He was really sweating for some cash—" She stopped.

"Why?"

"How should I know?" She wrapped the towel tighter around the picture. "Probably cooked the books again and needed to cover. That was his style." Her lips snapped together tightly.

"You know where he was working."

"No." She shook her head. "I don't know." Leaning forward, she looked deliberately into my eyes. "I don't know anything. And you can tell anyone who asks you that I said so."

"Okay. I'll tell them that. But why don't you tell me what you're so afraid of? Maybe I know something that will help."

"You are so naive!" She jumped up and shoved the painting into a crate. "I'm giving myself a nice vacation in a mountain cabin until this all blows over. So if anybody's looking for me, they won't find me."

"Tony was doing something illegal, is that it? Drugs?"

"I suggest you leave now." Maud came over to stand beside me. "I can't help you anymore."

"Maud, you don't have to tell me. But you should tell the police. Maybe they can protect you, if you need it. And they need the information to conduct an investigation."

"Look, as far as I'm concerned, whoever killed Tony was just cleaning up one of Mother Nature's mistakes." Her gaze slid away from mine. "I mean, it was only a question of time before he took someone out, if you ask me. The way he was acting—" She stopped again, then took my arm and jerked me toward the door. "You should feel the same way." She stood there, her hand on the doorknob. "You tried to kill him, too, after all. The police can find out stuff on their own, if they're inclined." For a moment she looked almost sympathetic. "I'll tell you this much. It wasn't the police Tony was afraid of, probably because he had something on someone there. He had something on a lot of people. He would have been rich if he'd had any idea how to manage money." She opened the door.

"Wait, Maud. Did he tell you what he had on them?"

She pushed me out the door, firmly. "Good-bye, Liz. Hope you manage to avoid the rap this time."

The door closed behind me, and a moment later I heard the rattle of the chain lock.

11 _____

I still didn't know what Tony had done for the past year, but it seemed likely to have been shady. And the harder it was to find out, the more it looked like a clue to his murder. Obviously, he'd had enemies. In fact, some members of my family could look suspicious, as O'Malley had pointed out.

But I preferred to scrutinize other potential murderers. Both Leonard and Maud looked good for this purpose. Of the two, I would pick Maud as cold-blooded enough to kill someone who got in her way or threatened her. Had Tony threatened her? And why the panic-stricken flight?

With Barker on the leash, I roamed through Cheesman Park and the botanical garden. I couldn't keep my mind on the flowers or the distant view of Pikes Peak to the south. I kept thinking about Maud's description of Tony as a lover. It was hard to deal with having Tony on my mind, after years of carefully screening myself against a single thought of him. He had been a totally different person to her than to me, and yet I knew he could woo and seduce. He had always said his violence toward me was my own fault; perhaps I had brought it on by my lukewarm response to him.

Collapsing onto a bench, I stared at a bed of late roses. There it was, the victim mind-set I'd inhabited far too long. In the past couple of years, I'd started to come out of that, to take my place among ordinary people who don't automatically cringe when a man raises his voice. The only blame I accepted was for not leaving town before I tried to shoot my husband, instead of after the jail term I served for doing so. I wouldn't be responsible for Tony's actions anymore.

"He's dead." I said it out loud, trying to convince myself. "He's dead."

"Just tired, I think." The elderly man walking by looked at me reproachfully. "He could use a drink of water."

"Huh?" I gaped at him a moment before I realized he was talking about Barker, who sprawled at my feet, tongue lolling out. The man went on by, shaking his head over my obtuseness, and I led Barker to the water fountain, where he politely accepted some water from my cupped hand.

Then I really looked at the roses for a little while. The bushes were small; I had forgotten, after years in California where a grandiflora like Queen Elizabeth could reach to the eaves, that in the Mile High City, roses must be covered every year against frost, and are extensively cut back for that purpose. Many old favorite hybrid teas were blooming, as well as some newer ones I didn't recognize.

Back at the bus, I got Barker a bowl of water and looked at Kyle Baldridge's address in my notebook. He didn't live that far away, and perhaps one of his neighbors would know how I could get in touch with him.

"Can you believe it?" I spoke to Barker while I maneuvered through traffic. He was in his favorite spot in the front passenger seat, sitting up tall to observe the action. "I forgot to ask Maud where Tony was living!"

For a moment I debated going back to her house. But she might already be gone, and I might not be so lucky next time at getting through that lobby door.

Instead I stopped at the next pay phone. Maud's answering machine answered after the third ring. I debated leaving a message. When it beeped I said, "Maud, this is Liz Sullivan. There's one more thing I'd like to ask if you're still there. Would you pick up the phone, please? It won't take—"

She picked up, cutting into my flow of words. "What is it? I told you, I know nothing."

"But you know where Tony was living, right?"

She was silent a moment. "Not really," she said, grudgingly. "Around, is my best guess. Here when I let him, with Kyle sometimes, with other people probably—women, no doubt."

So my ex-husband had also become a kind of vaga-bond—the moocher kind. "How do you know?"

"He gave me his pager number, not a real phone number. Then he'd call back. And when he stole my credit card I called Kyle's to tell him to give it back, and Kyle said he hadn't seen Tony for quite a while. So he didn't always live there. Look, I've got to go. The movers are here."

She slammed down the phone. I got back in the bus and headed on to Kyle's. I had to find some way to get in touch with him. He might know something, even if Tony hadn't been living there recently.

It was after four. Traffic was thick on Eighth Avenue. I turned off on Pennsylvania, partly to escape the traffic, and also to look at the last place Tony and I had lived together, an old brick apartment building with ten small units. I drove slowly down the block, searching for it, but there was no trace. The building had vanished, along with several of its equally rickety neighbors. Southwestern-style condos with tiny patios covered the area.

I drove on to Kyle's, feeling disoriented. Denver had changed more than I had. I kept trying to turn onto streets that were now one-way in the other direction. I kept look-ing for familiar landmarks and not finding them, or finding them metamorphosed. An old house whose mini-turrets and battlements I had always admired had been modern-ized with a huge, featureless addition across its backside. The strip mall I had patronized now housed offices—chiropractor, orthodontist, and optometrist—instead of dry cleaners, bakery, and convenience store.

Larimer Square and all of what Amy called LoDo was also changed. The area had been undergoing a renaissance ever since I could remember, but it was still a pretty funky place when I'd left Denver. Now it resonated with expen-sive, urban-rustic chic. Kyle's apartment was in an old warehouse converted into living units. Mailboxes and door-ways crowded the front hall; years of use had polished the wooden handrail along the curving stairs.

The mailbox with Baldridge on it was for apartment 2D. I started up the stairs just as Officer Eva Gutierrez turned the corner down them.

She looked at me, unsmiling, and I looked back. Finally she spoke. "So what brings you here?"

"I could be looking to rent an apartment."

"There's no vacancy here." She nodded toward the front door, where a plaque announced that we had entered the Glenarvon Apartments. Beneath the plaque were two empty hooks, obviously meant to hold a VACANCY sign.

"Well, I'm looking up an old friend, actually. Kyle Baldridge. He was a friend of Tony's, too, so that's probably why you're here." I'm not too good at being ingratiating, but I gave it a try. "If I'm in the way, I'll come back later."

Officer Gutierrez stood there for a moment, planted squarely on the landing above me. She appeared to come to a decision. "Come up here for a minute. We'll have a chat."

At the end of the upstairs hallway, a bench beneath a window gave a view of the street. Officer Gutierrez settled herself on it, gun and baton clanking, as if she had the rest of the afternoon. "Now," she said. "What have you been up to?"

"Why should I have been up to anything?" I leaned against the wall and glanced out the window. My bus was parked a little way down the street. I could see Barker doing sentinel duty in the driver's seat. He likes climbing up there when I'm not in the car.

She studied me for a moment. "I spoke with Leonard Tobin this afternoon."

"Oh."

"He said you were asking him questions. That's our job, Ms. Sullivan. All we want from you is to stay put while we investigate."

"That's not what I heard this morning." I studied her in turn. She looked brisk and competent, but I wondered how much clout she had in the department.

"What do you mean?"

"Your Detective O'Malley was at my mom and dad's this morning, and he pretty much told me he'd decided I fit the bill perfectly as a suspect. I expect he'll arrest me

69

soon." Either me or my poor old dad. Or my obnoxious nephew Biff.

She frowned. "O'Malley said that?"

"He said women rarely do jail time anymore for killing their abusive husbands, and that I'd probably get off lightly."

"Hmm." She looked troubled. "Well, whatever he may think, he's assigned me to follow up some leads, and I assure you I'll do a thorough job."

I wondered if Leonard had told her as much as he had me. "So who's your favorite suspect?"

"I don't have favorites." She glanced at her watch. "I'm just gathering facts."

"Kyle's out of town, someone said," I volunteered.

"So why did you come here?"

"I was going to ask around and see if a neighbor knew how to get in touch with him."

"We've gotten in touch." She smiled triumphantly. "He's supposed to show up soon to talk to me."

"Can I sit in?"

"Ms. Sullivan. This is not *Murder, She Wrote*. Amateurs are not invited into our investigation. I assure you, I'll get all the information you need."

"Did you get it all from Leonard?" I knew it was dumb to argue with a cop. But once in a while my mouth gets ahead of my brain. "Did you find out everything from Maud?" I fished in my knapsack, which was slung over one shoulder, and pulled out the little voice-activated tape recorder Amy had given me that morning. "Did Leonard tell you how Tony got him fired? Did Maud mention that she's so scared of whoever he's been hanging out with that she's leaving town? Did you find out yet where Tony was working, how he was getting money, who else he was blackmailing?"

Her jaw was tight. "We will find that out, given time," she said, reaching for the tape recorder. "You taped their conversations? Without their knowledge?"

"Is that against the law?" I held the tape recorder out of her reach. I could feel it faintly vibrating, taking down every word we said.

"You know it is, Ms. Sullivan."

"Then I didn't do it." I put the tape recorder back into my pack and sat on the bench.

"I have reason to think otherwise."

"Get a search warrant and find out." I folded my arms and glared stubbornly at her. "Anyone can carry a tape recorder around, as far as I know. I mean, we are still in the United States here, aren't we? And I'm free to sit on this bench and wait for my friend if I want to. And unless you're arresting me, I'm going to."

For a minute I thought she was going to arm wrestle me for the knapsack. Then her lips twitched and she burst out laughing.

"Okay. You win. Do me a favor and don't get killed for that tape."

"What tape?" I felt kind of foolish, glaring, when she was having a nice laugh on me.

She shook her head. "This is the weirdest case I ever worked on," she said. "Usually I go look for the junkie who knocked over the liquor store, or the hood who shook down the wrong person."

"Do you do much homicide work?"

"I've helped out a little." She glanced at me curiously.

"I have a friend in Homicide in Palo Alto," I said lamely. "I thought maybe from what O'Malley said last night that you were hoping to get a desk next to theirs."

She shrugged. "Lots of uniformed cops want to move into Homicide. Better pay, more interesting work."

"Longer hours, I bet. Especially in a city this size. Drake doesn't get many murder cases in Palo Alto, so he does lots of low-level investigation and gets home for dinner most nights."

"Drake is your buddy's name?" She whipped out her notebook. "Maybe I'll be in touch with him."

"Great." It wasn't great. He'd be burning up the telephone wires to yell at me as soon as he heard from the Denver police that I was a murder suspect, an activity of mine he deplores. I've thought before that it's something in my karma. I used to be a suspect because anyone who lives in their car is considered abnormal by the police. But now

I live in a house most of the time, and have been published in a couple of good rags and have even held down jobs—a series of temp jobs, it's true, but I do have an income of sorts. And still the bad vibes were landing on me regularly. It's enough to make a person seriously consider the cloister.

A man ran up the steps and paused before the door to apartment 2D. He was in his mid-thirties, tall, sunburned, and wiry in worn Levis, a chambray work shirt, and scuffed cowboy boots. His light brown hair was longish, straight, and glossy. He folded away a pair of sunglasses and put on some horn-rims, looking at Officer Gutierrez. "Are you here to see me? I'm Kyle Baldridge." His glance slid over me, then returned. The blue eyes widened. "Liz? Is that you? My God, how did you know?"

I started to smile, but his face changed. "Don't tell me you—that you finally—My God!"

Shaking his head, he backed away. The smile froze on my face. Officer Gutierrez looked at me curiously before she spoke.

"Mr. Baldridge." She spoke firmly. "I'm here to ask you some questions about Tony Naylor's death. And Ms. Sullivan isn't under arrest." She gave me a dissatisfied look. "She shouldn't be here at all, actually."

"Liz." Kyle came forward again, his expression shamefaced. "Forgive me. I'm sorry—I should have known—well, I'm not too clear on the circumstances of Tony's death. All I heard was he'd been shot."

I let him take my hand. He squeezed it gently. "I was actually trying to think how I could get in touch with you, and here you are."

Officer Gutierrez cleared her throat.

"I would like to talk to you, Mr. Baldridge." She glanced meaningfully at me.

"Can Liz come in, too?" Kyle smiled at me, and I remembered how his smile always seemed to light up his rather sober face. "We have to talk about stuff." He guided me over to the door of his apartment, which he unlocked one-handed. "Was it a terrible shock for you? It was for me. Tony wasn't always the best person but—he was my best friend for too long. I always made an excuse for him."

He ducked his head and looked at me sidewise. "Not for what he did to you," he said awkwardly. "I couldn't understand that. Every time he'd say he wasn't going to anymore. You know."

"I know." I moved away from him when we were in the apartment, looking around at the comfortable leather furniture, the polished wood floor and Navaho rugs, the old trade blankets draped over sofa and chair. Baskets and pots lined a shelf under the window. It didn't look like Tony's kind of pad.

"So what about the memorial service?" Kyle put one hand on my shoulder, looking at me earnestly. "I was just going to get something together. Is there—do you want—am I horning in?"

"Not at all." I looked at Kyle, and remembered the times he'd helped me. I hadn't asked often, because if Tony had known he would have assumed a sexual relationship between us, which was the only kind he knew about between men and women. But Kyle and I had been friends, and more important even than the times he'd helped me hide from Tony were the conversations we'd had about artifacts and the Anasazi, his true passion in life. "Kyle, I have to say I don't care about Tony's memorial service. Did you get hold of his mother?"

"She died a couple of years ago." Kyle looked grieved. "Tony would never talk about it, but he brooded. Then he got a lead on where you were in California and went out to see you. Did he touch base?"

"You could say so." Officer Gutierrez looked at me again. I could see her making a mental note to have yet more conversation with me. "Anyway, the memorial service is all yours. I wouldn't dream of interfering."

"I guess it's dumb to have a service for a man with as many enemies as Tony had," Kyle said, sighing. He moved over to Officer Gutierrez, who was examining a small black and white pot. "That's Chaco work," he said, taking the pot from her to trace the design. "You can see the characteristic—" he broke off and laughed. "Sorry. I don't mean to jump on my hobbyhorse." Somehow he ended up with the figurine in his hand. He set the pot back carefully on its stand and offered Eva Gutierrez a seat. "Would either of you like a drink? Coffee? Mineral water?"

Officer Gutierrez glanced at the pots and then at Kyle, vanishing into the kitchen. "Just some conversation," she called after him as he disappeared into the kitchen. She frowned at me. "You can make yourself scarce, Ms. Sullivan. I'm not going to smash up your friend's artifacts or anything."

"No, let Liz stay." Kyle reappeared, drinking a mineral water and carrying two more bottles. I accepted the one he offered me, more as an excuse to stay than because I was thirsty. Office Gutierrez didn't take one.

"You say Mr. Naylor had enemies." She had her notebook open now. I wished I had mine out, but I was counting on the tape recorder. "Can you tell me who they were?"

"Afraid not." Kyle smiled at her, but his eyes looked worried. "Tony didn't really tell me, and after a couple of incidents year before last, I didn't ask. I let him stay here when he needed a place, but to tell the truth I was always glad when he moved on." He sat on the sofa, staring at his clasped hands. "I loved him like a brother," he said quietly. "And he was always a brother to me. Both of us grew up without dads, you know. My mom is dead, too, and Tony's was a hopeless alcoholic. He sent her money, but he couldn't stand to visit her very often, because she was just going downhill. I think in the end she was homeless or something." He looked up briefly, and I saw the moisture in his eyes. "I always thought he'd straighten out. He was a lot of fun. He just—never grew up. Now he doesn't have a chance to anymore."

"So you don't know who his enemies were?"

Kyle looked at her carefully. "I kind of thought," he said, choosing his words, "that it was someone local. In the police department, actually."

12

OFFICER Gutierrez froze. She sent a glance toward my knapsack, probably wondering if my tape recorder was on. "What do you mean by that?"

Kyle shrugged. "Something Tony said awhile ago. He'd been working for some big trucking place, getting accounts from shippers and stuff. And then all of a sudden he was looking for a place to stay and didn't want anyone to know—would never answer the phone or go to the store or anything. This went on for a while, and finally I told him it wasn't going to work for me much longer." He looked at me a little apologetically. "Sometimes he could just get on your nerves."

"Look, you don't have to spare my tender feelings about Tony." I was tired of being treated as the grieving widow. "I'm surprised you could even stay friends with him."

"I didn't really," Kyle mumbled, tearing at the label on his mineral water bottle. "I kinda lost patience then. He said he couldn't leave because someone would kill him. And I told him to go to the police for protection, because I sure couldn't provide it, and frankly didn't want to be involved." Kyle got fired up a little, recounting this. "Then he said that's who was trying to kill him."

"Who?" Officer Gutierrez looked up from her notebook.

"The police." Kyle set the bottle down on the coffee table. "He said they were after him."

"Did he say why?" Officer Gutierrez looked skeptical.

"No. Next day, I come home from work, he's gone. All his stuff moved out, not a sign of him. At first I thought maybe whoever they were had got to him, but then I noticed a lot of groceries were gone, too. That didn't seem to indicate a hit." Kyle smiled faintly. "I didn't hear from him until his mother's death. We got tight again for a while after that, but he never stayed long."

"Was he still working at the shipping place?" This had become a burning question for me; I was determined to get an answer. Officer Gutierrez frowned, but Kyle answered.

"I don't know. He said he was working contract stuff, and by that point I didn't want to know what he was up to." Kyle picked up his bottle again and finished the drink. "Every so often he'd call, we'd go out and have a meal, go to a concert or have a few beers. He always looked fine—I mean, not like he didn't know where his next bath was coming from, or anything. Just ordinary." He pushed his glasses up on his nose and smiled hopefully at me. "Liz, can you have dinner with me tonight? I mean—excuse me, ma'am." He turned politely to Officer Gutierrez. "Is that all you wanted to ask?"

"For now, anyway." She stood up and turned to me. "I do, however, have further questions for Ms. Sullivan. If you would accompany me?"

"Just a minute." Kyle got up, too. "Liz, would that be okay? Dinner? I feel awful that I suspected you, even for a second. I want to make it up to you."

I glanced at Officer Gutierrez, who was visibly fuming. "That's nice, Kyle, but probably not. I'm staying with my brother, and he'll want some time to yell at me. Thanks anyway."

Kyle stood in the apartment door, gazing wistfully after us. After me, it seemed. I was immensely flattered at his wish to spend time with me. Despite the horn-rims and the shaggy hair, Kyle was good-looking, and all that weekend trenching hadn't done his shoulders any harm. I remembered him as impressive in his power suit and usual haircut, a kind of financial Clark Kent.

But attention from men still made me uneasy. After nearly a year of being neighbors with Drake and seeing each other often, I was just getting comfortable with him. It was infuriating to feel that I owed him any kind of sexual loyalty, seeing that neither of us had made that kind of claim on the other. But that's how I felt.

I followed Officer Gutierrez down the stairs. Outside the door she turned to me. I noticed that she had a few inches on me, and she was mad.

"We'll talk in your car."

"Fine." I led the way and unlocked the side door. "Watch out for Barker. He isn't getting as much exercise as he likes these days."

Barker was giving contradictory messages—his neck fur was up but his tail wagged furiously. He sniffed Officer Gutierrez's outstretched hand, then stuck his nose in her crotch.

"Barker!" I yanked on the choke chain and he sat apologetically. "Sorry. He's a rude teenager of a dog."

"That's okay." Officer Gutierrez scratched him behind the ears and ducked to enter the bus. She slid behind the fold-up table, and I took the backward-facing seat across from her.

"What did you want to talk about?"

"I want you to give me that tape." She stared straight at me and put her hand on the table, palm up.

"No." I met her gaze. "You don't have a search warrant. The only way you can get it is to beat me up."

"That's right." Her gaze didn't waver.

"My dog will bite you."

Her shoulders lost their tense look. "Sure he will." Barker was sitting right beside her—probably on her feet. He gazed adoringly at her, and her free hand fondled his ears.

"Look, Officer Gutierrez."

She took her hand off the table and rubbed her eyes. "Oh, just call me Eva."

"I was stupid to even indicate I might have a tape. Let's just forget about it, okay?"

"No, let's not." She folded her arms across her chest. Deprived of caresses, Barker urged himself closer. "How long did you talk to Leonard Tobin?"

"Maybe half an hour."

"How long to Maud Riegert?"

"About the same."

"So your crummy little tape probably ran out before

77

Baldridge's left-field remark about Tony getting on the wrong side of cops." She shrugged. "And if it is on the tape, such allegations should be investigated. I want to hear what else is on there, too. O'Malley wants the whole picture, and I think you have some pieces of the puzzle we haven't seen."

"What you say has merit." I knew I'd only gotten this far with my ridiculous defiance because Eva was a straight shooter. Any other cop would simply have taken the tape recorder from me already. Probably deep-sixed the tape, too. I remembered O'Malley's response to the printout on Tony he'd gotten. Certainly someone in the police knew more about Tony than they were letting on.

"Let me think about it, okay?"

She shook her head. "And while you're thinking about it, someone comes along and takes the evidence. How will you feel then?"

"Really stupid." I had to smile. "But I still know what was said."

"Right. You, too, could be a danger to anyone interested in the tape." She spoke slowly, carefully. "Duh."

I squirmed a little. "Well, you're the only one I told about the tape recorder. And there might have been a malfunction. The batteries might have died. This is all conjectural."

"Your niece knows you carried the tape recorder. Anyone that she blabbed to knows—and believe me, that age can blab." She leaned closer. "Play it now."

I glanced around at people walking along the street, at the big bulk of Kyle's apartment building. "Look, Kyle can probably see us from his windows. Anyone could hear. And I might get towed if I stay in this parking spot much longer."

"You won't get towed." She, too, glanced at the apartment building. "But you're right. We'll go to headquarters."

"I don't like the sound of that."

She gazed at me stonily. "You're not in much position to choose, are you? I'll follow your car. You remember how to get there?"

"Yeah, sure." My voice sounded hollow, even to me.

Once at the police station, I was definitely at risk for continued detention. O'Malley could probably come up with three or four things to hold me on, pending a murder charge. Perhaps taping people without their permission would be one of them.

Eva got out and shut the side door, and I got into the driver's seat, wondering if I should just make a bolt for it. The police are notoriously overworked, and she might not have the time free to pursue me, figuring I'd just turn up at my brother's eventually. But it seemed so counterproductive. I pulled into traffic, and she followed me. At least she spared me the blinking lights.

We drove sedately along, past strip malls and discount houses and tacky little stores side by side. At one light I noticed adult bookstores on all four corners, along with support industries like a lingerie store, a massage parlor, and a video transfer studio. Staring at this last, I accelerated away from the stoplight and into a curbside parking spot one lane of traffic away, narrowly missing a collision with an old Ford pickup.

The video transfer shop was just a countertop, with a lot of samples of racy-looking video stills hanging around. The woman behind the counter was too bored even to look at me when I ran in.

"Do you do audiotape transfer as well?"

Slowly she turned her head, making me aware that I had interrupted her contemplation. She sighed. "Yes," she said.

"Can you do these little tapes?" I opened the tape recorder gingerly, copying the way Amy had done it. I had seen Drake do the same thing with his, but even so it eluded me for precious seconds. Then the back popped open and the tiny tape glinted up at me.

The clerk barely glanced at it. "Yes."

"Well, can you do it now, or can someone, while I wait? On a regular cassette?"

She looked into the distance over my head. "Yes."

I pried the tape out while she languidly assembled a printed envelope and a pen and put them on the counter in front of me. Hastily I scrawled my name and Andy's phone number, and stuck the tape in. It was taking Officer Eva a long time to disentangle herself from the traffic. That was good.

The clerk disappeared into the back room with my tape just as Eva burst through the front door.

"What do you think you're doing?" She had one hand on her nightstick, as if she thought she would need to club some sense into me.

"I'm getting the tape duplicated. Then you can have it if you want it, and we can part company here." I tried a polite smile. "You'll understand if I have a fear of police stations."

Some of the anger died out of her face. "Liz—" She stared at me, shaking her head. "You should be under lock and key now, if you ask me. This is no way to behave with the law."

"I did everything right the last time." I shoved my hands into my pockets and returned her glare. "I called the cops, I cooperated—I ended up in jail. This time I figure I've got nothing to lose. I'm looking out for myself, and not depending on the poor understaffed police to do it for me."

"You're endangering yourself every minute," she sputtered. "Any one of these people you're getting so cozy with could be planning how to get you in deeper right now. Just lay low, why don't you, and let us do our job?"

"Because your job is looking for evidence against me, and my job is looking for the truth. Truth gets swallowed by expediency nine times out of ten."

The clerk came back in. "That's right," she said in a monotone. "Ten minutes." She looked at Officer Eva.

Officer Eva looked back. "We'll wait."

For the first time a trace of animation appeared on the clerk's face. "Here? You're going to wait here?" She turned to me. "We don't do police work."

"I'm not the police."

"You're not?"

"No."

"But she is!"

"Yes."

Sullenly the clerk retired to the far end of the counter.

There were no chairs. Eva and I leaned against the counter and looked at each other for a moment.

"Oh, what the hell," she said finally. "Come on. There's a burger joint down the street. I'll buy you something greasy."

"Okay." I was hungry, I realized. Very hungry. But not anxious to eat Andy's food. "Back soon for the tapes," I told the clerk.

"Pay in advance, please." She punched a button or two on the cash register and showed me the amount. "And we close at five-thirty. Sharp."

"Sharp, it is." I pocketed my change and followed Eva out the door.

13 _____

IT was only five. We had the fast-food place mostly to ourselves. My chicken sandwich was actually not bad. Eva had some coffee and a little bag of french fries that she appeared to enjoy.

"So what did the others say on this tape of yours?" She wiped her fingers on a napkin, then looked at me over the rim of her coffee cup. "See if you can give me the gist of it."

I thought about it while I contained an eruption of sauce from the side of my sandwich. "Leonard's hitting bottom and blames Tony for it because Tony was blackmailing him and finked to the bosses."

She blinked. "Well, that about covers it. And you saw Maud Riegert, too? What did she say?"

This was harder. "You'll get the tape. Then you'll know."

"I want to know now." She pointed a french fry at me. "I think you owe it to me, Liz."

"Maud," I said reluctantly, "has been involved with Tony since before I—"

"Before you tried to kill him."

"The first time, as your O'Malley kept saying this morning."

She waved that away. "He's not my O'Malley, thank heavens. So they were carrying on behind your back. Or did you know?"

"Yeah. It went on for quite a while." I looked down at the molded plastic tabletop, tracing a coffee ring with my finger. "Several times I told him he could have a divorce, but he would laugh or say something mean, or—hit me. The last time, he said that 'till death do us part' wasn't just rhetoric to him. I said that divorce was preferable to death from my perspective, and he went berserk. That's when I shot him."

She whistled softly. "I hadn't realized you were discussing her when that happened. It must have been pretty uncomfortable to confront her today."

"She didn't know why I shot him." I glanced up at Eva. "It never came out then. My court-appointed attorney said it would make me look like a jealous cat, so it kind of got lost."

"What did she say today?"

"Lots of stuff. But she didn't know where Tony was living lately or what he was doing. Last she heard was a few weeks ago when they got together, and it ended with him stealing her credit card."

Eva was silent for a moment. "She didn't report it stolen."

"Huh? She said she did."

Eva shook her head. "Nope."

I pushed away the last bit of sandwich. "That's interesting."

"Is it?"

I ignored her bland question. "She must have let him have it. So he *was* blackmailing her. What would he have on her?"

"Something she didn't want her current employer to hear about, maybe." Officer Eva got to her feet, stretching a little. She was a strapping woman, not one of your anorectic types, with sturdy legs and big, capable hands. She wore no rings. "Well, let's go pick up the tape, and hope it sheds some light."

"It's not admissible for evidence, right?"

She shot me a look. "O'Malley and I will listen to it. And then we'll reconfirm what we hear in follow-up interviews, which will be admissible as evidence."

"Uh, Maud said she was planning to leave right away. She was spooked by Tony's death. Packing up stuff and everything."

"What?" Eva stopped short, then strode faster down the

street to the tape transfer shop. "Thanks for keeping that till last."

"I told you she was leaving." I hurried to keep up with her—she had five or six inches on me, and just then it all seemed to be in her legs. "And she might still be around. When I called her just before I got to Kyle's, the movers were there."

"Movers." She was almost running now.

The clerk had my tape and the copy on the counter, along with the paid invoice. She pretended she hadn't seen us, so I snatched the tapes and gave Eva the copy.

"Keep your nose clean," she said from the sidewalk. "I'll probably be checking up on you tonight, so if you get together with your friend back there, make it short. I want to be able to talk to you whenever I feel the need."

She had the police cruiser in traffic, screeching into a U-turn at the next traffic signal and roaring back the way we'd come, before I even opened my door. Barker regarded me expectantly from the passenger seat.

"Okay," I told him. "We'll go see Amy."

That met with his approval. I drove back to Andy's house, my head whirling with information overload. Also, I puzzled over Officer Eva's perplexing friendliness. I'd thought she was just stringing me along so I'd spill my guts to her. But then she'd given me that little nugget about Maud's credit card to chew over—why? I couldn't help her with inside knowledge about people I hadn't seen for close to ten years.

And that made me wonder about Kyle. His insistence about dinner was surely not just for the pleasure of my company. Despite his earnest science-fair approach, Kyle had always been popular with women. Perhaps because of it.

At any rate, I hadn't accepted his invitation, and the reason, I felt sure, was because of Drake. That rankled a bit. Why should I feel any sense of commitment to Drake, who was the lack-of-commitment poster boy? I decided that if Kyle made any more overtures, I would be more responsive in the future.

Barker came to attention when I turned onto Andy's

street. I parked in front of the house, but I told the dog to stay. He slumped with disappointment.

"Amy will come out if she's here," I promised. "But better not let Renee see you."

Amy was there. She bounced out of the house before I got to the door.

"Aunt Liz! I've been worried about you all day. What's happened? Mom says Grampa called up in a terrible rage this morning. Was Barker a good boy today?" She opened the passenger door and he sprang down. There was a storm of licking and mutual hugging, and then they looked at me, both of them evidently much refreshed.

I saw Renee's sour face in the kitchen window. "Let's talk out here for a minute, Amy." Opening the side door, I reached into the refrigerator and got out a bottle of mineral water for her and one for me.

Amy's eyes grew round. "Aunt Liz! You bought bottled water? I can't believe it."

"I don't want to impose. I had dinner already, so let your mother know when you go back in, okay?"

"Aren't you coming in?" Her face clouded. "Don't you need the bathroom or anything?"

As a matter of fact I did; Amy saw my hesitation. "You can hang out with me in my room," she urged. "You could sleep there, too; I've got twin beds."

"I might take you up on the bathroom part."

"I wanted to show you something anyway." Amy bounced on the backseat of the bus. "I did an InfoTrac search at school today and turned up some information about the brokerage firm your hus—your ex-husband worked for."

"What's InfoTrac?"

"It's an on-line database search thing you do." Amy waved that away impatiently. "Anyway, a little over a year ago there was a big investigation of local brokerage houses, and Baker Mulshine Hollenbeck was really shaken up by it. Several senior guys left, and there was talk around that that was just the tip of the iceberg." She looked thoughtful. "But I didn't find any later information. Does that help you?"

It was nothing I hadn't heard already, but she looked so eager. "It's great to know. Actually, someone who works there and knew Tony turned up today, so we found out about that stuff."

"We?"

"Officer Eva and me." I grinned a little at Amy. "She's evidently letting me check into things if I don't get in her way."

"Excellent." Amy took a swig of her mineral water. "Did you find out anything vital?"

"Not really. Just bits and pieces." I pulled the tape recorder out of my bag. "Thanks for letting me use this. I'll get you a new tape tomorrow—I filled this one up."

"Can I listen?" She fished in the pocket of her baggy overalls and pulled out a pair of headphones.

I shook my head. "I'm just going to file it away in case I need it. Officer Eva already has a copy of it."

Renee opened the front door and thundered down the path. "What are you doing here?" Her eyes went suspiciously from me to Amy, lingering on the bottle of water. "What's that?"

"Calistoga." Amy showed her mother the label, with a roll of the eyes in my direction.

"Isn't that the little tape recorder you got for Christmas, to help you with schoolwork? What's it doing out here?"

"I wanted Aunt Liz to hear a tape from English class," Amy said hurriedly, pushing the headphones toward me. "I'll finish my homework, and then we can do that Internet crawl we were talking about, Aunt Liz."

She slid out of the bus and into the house, taking Barker with her. Renee didn't seem to notice. She was too busy tearing into me.

"You should leave her alone," she snarled. "Do you want to ruin her life, too?"

"Not really. That's your job." I pulled my typewriter case out of the narrow cupboard next to the sliding door. "By the way, Renee, I had dinner already. Don't worry that you have to feed me—I can take care of myself."

Patchy color washed her cheeks. "I suppose this is a slam at me for taking advantage of your hospitality last summer?" Her intonation made "hospitality" a dirty word. "Well, suit yourself, Ms. High and Mighty Sullivan. If you want to act like a poor-relation martyr, go right ahead! Just don't think you can go over to Mom and Dad Sullivan's for your comforts. They don't want you there." She tossed her head triumphantly. "I thought Dad was going to have a stroke when he called this morning. Said the police as good as told him you'd killed your ex, even if Amy says you couldn't have pulled the trigger." She drew back from the sliding door and delivered her final admonition. "Just keep Amy out of it from now on, or you'll really be sorry!"

She stormed back into the house. I rolled a piece of paper into my old Royal, plugged the headphones into the tape recorder, and started typing up a transcript. It reminded me of a summer job I'd had right after high school, working for Reliance Insurance to transcribe adjusters' field tapes.

But summer was over, and now I wasn't even getting paid.

14

I worked for nearly an hour, laboriously stopping and starting the tape recorder to get every word, no matter how muffled or obscure, and hoping that the batteries wouldn't conk out until I was done. While I worked Andy drove up in his big Ford pickup. After one glance my way he stomped on into the house, ignoring my wave. Shortly thereafter the kitchen curtain lifted so they could peek out at me.

Other than that, they left me alone. The sky lost color, paling to translucence and then, as the light failed, to gray. I was typing more by touch than by sight—the batteries in my halogen head-flashlight were also growing weak, and I didn't want to kill it before I could get new ones. The vagabond life was much more demanding of batteries than the last time I lived it.

The tape didn't run out until most of the way through our encounter with Kyle, right up to his dinner invitation to me. Including, of course, Maud's remark that Tony had some dirt on someone in the police hierarchy, and Kyle's comment about Tony having police as enemies, all of which would doubtless make Officer Eva unhappy. In fact, when O'Malley and his buddy listened to the tape, I might be in real trouble. I hadn't managed to figure out yet whether O'Malley belonged with the police-for-hire group or not, though Eva appeared to be on the straight and narrow. With law enforcement people you couldn't always tell. They have so many opportunities to be on the take, in ways that can seem pretty innocent.

I finished the transcript and took the headphones out of my ears. A goodish pile of paper sat next to the Royal. I stretched my hands, then stepped out of the bus to unkink my back. In the backyard, Amy called to Barker. Picking up the transcript, tape recorder, and earphones, I headed for the sound.

"No, no, you silly dog." Amy was grabbing for the ragbone, which dangled from Barker's smiling jaws. Each time she grabbed, he whisked the bone away. "How can I throw it if you won't let me have it?"

"He's still not too strong on the fetch aspect." I handed Amy the tape recorder and earphones. "Thanks for lending this. I'll get you some new batteries tomorrow—think I must have worn them down."

"Thank you, Aunt Liz." She grinned at me. "Mom and Dad hate for me to ask for batteries, and I'm stony this week."

"Broke?" I looked at Andy's house. "You made money this summer."

"Yeah, but I put it all in the market." She snatched the bone away from Barker and tossed it to the other end of the long, narrow yard. Barker tore after it. "We have this investment group which is really getting, like, max return. But I don't want to pull my money out, and Dad's, like, sitting on my allowance because I blew my curfew last weekend." She shrugged. "It doesn't matter that much—my allowance is such a tiny, minuscule thing that I hardly miss it."

I held up the tape and the transcript. "I want to mail these. Do you have a couple of envelopes I can use? I'll pay you back for those as well."

"Aunt Liz, chill." Amy stuffed the tape recorder into the front of her overalls and hung the earphones around her neck. "You don't have to, like, pay me back for every last little thing. I mean, I'll cut you some slack. You're my favorite aunt, for God's sake."

"You're my favorite niece, too."

Amy hooted. "I'm your only niece, fool!"

We smiled at each other. Then I remembered the reason why I'd come to Denver in the first place.

"Would you call your grandma for me? I guess I'm in

the doghouse there again, but I want to know how she's doing."

"Sure." Amy snapped her fingers for Barker. "You missed a good dinner, Aunt Liz. Maybe Mom has some leftovers—should we check?"

"I'm not really hungry." The fast food in my stomach was making a leaden statement about heartburn.

The darkness was nearly complete. Amy's white T-shirt glimmered, and Barker was a collection of light and dark blobs. I shivered; though not as cold as the night before, it was too brisk for the sweatshirt I wore.

"Time to go in," Amy told Barker. He picked up the ragbone and flourished it one more time, but she refused to be drawn. "Come on."

"I could put him in the bus if your mom minds him inside."

"I want him inside." Amy stuck out her lower lip, making one of those lightning changes from mature young person to spoiled child that teenagers can accomplish at will. Then she smiled. "I'll shut the door to my room and then all the dog hair will stay in one place."

I felt a sneaking sympathy for Renee, despite her hostility and lethal mouth; she and Amy didn't show each other their good sides very often.

She was waiting inside the back door; had been watching us, evidently. "Have you finished your homework?"

Amy rolled her eyes. "Yes, Mother."

"That dog shouldn't be in here."

"I'll vacuum up each and every hair he loses, Mother."

Renee flicked a disparaging eye at the baggy overalls and turned to me. "Did you plan to leave that car of yours in front of our house forever?"

"Where did you want me to park it?"

"Down the block a little ways or something. It makes us look like white trash."

"Maybe we are white trash, Mother. Did you ever think of that?"

I threw myself into the breach. "Could I use the bathroom, please?"

"Yeah, sure." Renee gestured down the hall. "And you

didn't wipe off the counter after you filled the dishwasher, Amy. Do it now, please."

Grumbling, Amy followed her mother. Barker followed Amy. I seized a few moments of noncombative peace in the bathroom.

When I came out, I could hear the muted mutter of the TV from the room Andy called his den. Barker sat outside the kitchen, gazing expectantly at the door. After a moment Amy came out and gave him the extravagant petting he thought he deserved.

I was still holding my transcript and the little tape that had the information on it. Amy led me to her room and dug out a couple of Priority Mail envelopes. "Some prospectuses came in them," she explained. "It should hold your stuff."

"Thanks." I addressed the transcript to my post office box in Palo Alto and the tape to Drake's address. Not a very clever dodge, perhaps, but if it worked in all those mystery stories, probably it would work for me. While I was sealing the envelopes, the phone rang.

"Sure," Amy said blithely into the receiver, which she had sprung for after a warning bellow. "She's right here." She handed me the receiver, mouthing "Drake," and then slipped tactfully from the room.

"Hi." I figured I might as well get a word or two in before he started scolding me. "Wish you were here."

"I'll bet you do." The sound of his voice caused a sudden stricture in my diaphragm that interfered with my breathing. "Can't you be out of my sight for a week without getting into trouble?"

"It hasn't been that long." I forced my vocal cords to operate, despite their momentary paralysis.

"Are you okay?" Drake dropped the scolding tone. His voice deepened. "You sound funny."

"I'm fine."

"I heard from some of your new friends out there." He was making tea; I could hear his teakettle singing in the background. "First an e-mail message from the Homicide department, wanting a background check on you, and then a personal phone call just before I left from an Officer Gutierrez."

"You shouldn't work so late." I made myself sound casual. "What did you tell her?"

"The truth, of course—that you don't have the sense to keep your nose out of other people's business, but you're not violent, just weak in the head." He waited a moment. "You're supposed to laugh."

"Maybe later." I didn't like the way his voice was making me feel—soft and dependent, in need of his help. I told myself to get a grip. Instead I said, "O'Malley, one of the Homicide guys, already has me pegged for it."

"Has you pegged for—don't be ridiculous. It's an obvious hit. They're probably looking into underworld or gang connections right now. The stooges are singing even as we speak."

His robust common sense was comforting. "O'Malley mentioned this morning that women who kill their abusive husbands get off light these days. He referred to my former attempt as the first time I tried to kill my husband."

Drake was silent for a moment. "He thinks you know something, and he's trying to rattle it out of you."

I took a deep breath. "I'm rattled."

Another pause. "I never expected to hear you admit that." He sounded worried. "This Gutierrez I talked to—she seemed okay. Just wanted the usual about any past interactions with our department."

"So what did you say?"

"I told the truth, of course."

"Truth is so subjective, Drake."

I could hear his sigh. "Do we have to have this argument again? Truth is what's written down in our files, Liz. That's what I told your officer friend about."

I let it drop. "How are the roses?"

He told me how my garden grew—although his descriptions didn't make a whole lot of sense. We spoke of our friend Bridget, of his partner Bruno. I built a picture in my mind while we talked: my little cottage tucked behind the bigger house Drake was buying from me, the tall redwoods at the back, the orderly beds of vegetables and flowers I tended there.

"I'm cutting the salad stuff like you showed me." He smacked his lips. "Good, too. You're really missing out."

"Thanks, Drake. I had fast food tonight."

"Was it your first time?" He laughed. "Can't picture you in the plastic seats, Liz."

"I ate it before, on the way out here."

He was quiet for a moment. "Listen up, woman. I can't do anything illegal for you, but I might happen to find something about your ex-husband in the databases. If I think you should know it, I'll get it to you somehow."

"Don't go Federal Expressing things." Amy opened the door and peeked in. "That would just mean I'd have to pay you back, and I can't afford it. Regular mail is fine."

Amy bounded into the room and pointed at her computer. Puzzled, I shook my head. She scrawled something on a piece of paper and handed it to me. Drake was offering overnight mail, but I interrupted him.

"Amy has an e-mail address." I read it to him over the phone. "She'll pass along anything you send."

He understood the subtext there. "Anything confidential I'll get to you some other way. And you won't pay me back. I'm eating your designer lettuce, remember?"

I hung up the phone after a rather lingering good-bye. Amy dove for the receiver practically before it left my hand, so I assumed that's what she'd come back for. I headed for the bathroom with my bag of washing stuff. I needed a little time alone to sort through my reactions to that phone call.

15 _____

"GRAMMA is still feeling poorly," Amy announced. She was just hanging up the phone when I came back into her room. "Aunt Molly is there. She says Gramma did eat some dinner, though. And Grampa won't talk at all, Aunt Molly says. He just grunts when she speaks to him." Amy faltered. "She—said some stuff about you, too, but, I—I don't remember it."

"I can fill it in, thanks."

"Aunt Liz, why are they all so mad at you? Seems to me that you're the one who should be mad."

I didn't know how to answer that, because I agreed with Amy. Maybe that's why they were mad. If I'd come and penitently admitted my mistakes, accepted their pronouncements on my poor judgment, perhaps I could have been forgiven. But for years I had felt that I would apologize when they did. I could perfectly understand their resentment—I shared it.

"So is Drake going to send us e-mail?" Amy put one hand lovingly on her computer. "I love to get e-mail."

"Any kind of mail is fine with me, but the kind with a check is the best."

Her face clouded. "You're not getting to pick up your checks while you're here, are you?"

I shrugged. Picking up checks wasn't a regular occurrence in my life. Vacation pay, insurance, sick leave—not the perks of my line of work, as Drake pointed out with irritating frequency. I'm used to working without the safety net; personal responsibility is an archaic concept in our culture, but I embrace it anyway.

I didn't dwell on thoughts of my disappearing savings. I

would manage, as long as Drake didn't let the snails get to my seedlings, which I depended on for next spring's veggies.

"Aunt Molly said you'll probably be arrested again and drag the family through the mud even worse, because now you're back to calling yourself Sullivan." Amy was still worrying over her aunt's conversation. "But there's almost as many Sullivans as Smiths or Browns, so I don't know what she's kicking about. And you're not going to be arrested, are you?"

"Since I didn't do the murder, they won't be arresting me." I tried to speak with a calm certainty. "The police will find the real killer."

Amy looked pensive for a moment, stroking Barker's ear and reducing him to slit-eyed ecstasy. "So is Drake missing you?" She glanced slyly at me.

"Why should he? He's getting all my baby lettuces to himself. And there'll be raspberries, too."

"Come on, Aunt Liz." Amy made an impatient face. "You know he wants to jump your bones."

My face grew hot, despite a need to remain cool. I was at a loss for a reply. I could return a gentle reminder about making personal remarks, which would have a dampening effect on future communications. I could take some moral stance about how men and women could be friends without sex, but were Drake and I friends? Though we didn't act on it, sexual attraction was an undercurrent in all our dealings.

I elected a change-the-subject approach. "If we're going to talk love lives, how about yours? Who are you dating?"

"Dating?" Amy tasted the word, as if it were a foreign concept. "We don't 'date,' Aunt Liz. We just sort of—" she gestured helplessly "—are. I mean, you know, we have coffee, we talk, maybe go to a show—"

"You and your boyfriend?"

"My friends and me." She shook her head, and the long, shiny hair slid over her face. "You know—a bunch of us." She shuddered. "I haven't met a guy I want to date. I mean, that's for the prom-queen crowd. Everyone would assume you were sleeping together, and it's just too gross."

A few months ago I would have agreed. But now Drake

was messing with my head. I made a determined effort to stop thinking about him.

"I don't know how to do Mom any good at all," I said, finding something fresh to feel inadequate about. "Not without giving Dad a stroke, or Molly a conniption fit."

"I shouldn't have made you come out here." Amy sat up straight on the bed, gazing down at her knees through holes in the overalls. "I thought—" she looked at me, and tears glittered in her eyes. Barker scooted closer to her, his head on her knee. "I thought if you came out, if they saw what a great person you are, everything would be better."

"It's not your fault, Amy." I sat on the bed beside her and gave her a cautious hug. Despite living in California now, hugging is still not an everyday thing with me. "I was ready to approach them, and you gave me the reason I needed. Now it's up to them. If it doesn't work out, it doesn't. Anyway, I'm glad for the opportunity to see Gramma and Grampa again. And you."

"Well, you'll see me lots if you want to." Amy dried her eyes and smiled. "I like the Bay Area. I'm thinking of applying to Stanford and Santa Clara University and UC Santa Cruz." She glanced at me. "That's a couple of years away, of course."

"I'll look forward to it." I stood up. "But for now I'm tired. Think I'll get to bed."

"You're sleeping outside again?" Amy's face was wistful. "I have this other bed." She pointed to it.

"I like the bus." I snapped my fingers, and Barker jumped up. "And Barker likes it, too."

Amy pulled me into the kitchen on my way out to offer me a snack, but I declined on the grounds of just having brushed my teeth. I smiled at Renee, who sat at the table with a mug of coffee and a catalogue, and received a grudging nod in return.

It was cold outside. I pulled the Z-bed out, fluffed my sleeping bag, got my sweats out of the cupboard, and put them by my pillow. Barker curled up under the bed, waiting until I was trapped in the sleeping bag before making his move to sleep next to me. My book and headlamp waited on the other side of the pillow.

I was ready to shut myself in for the night when Officer Eva drove up in her patrol car.

She came over to the bus. I climbed back out again, standing by the open side door. "So," she said. "Going nighty-night?"

"You got it."

She glanced over her shoulder at Andy's house. Renee was at the curtain again. "They won't let you inside?"

"I prefer my own space."

She looked at me. In the weak dome light, her face was impassive, her dark eyes unreadable. "You still have that tape?"

"No." I had left it in Amy's bedroom. "My niece needed it back."

"You just gave it to her?"

I shrugged. "It doesn't take long to erase, you know. Didn't your copy work out?"

"It worked." She took a breath. "I gave it to O'Malley."

"Thanks for putting me on the spot."

"You put yourself there." Her glance slid away from me. "It's evidence in a major case, even if improperly obtained."

"How did he like what Kyle said?"

"He laughed." She gave me the ghost of a grin. "Your friend Kyle is going to receive a visit first thing in the morning. Good thing you're not keeping him up late."

"Everybody seems so interested in my social life all of a sudden." I gestured to the dog, the sleeping bag. "You can see it's a real lively one."

"Your friend Drake asked me about it, too." She smiled more openly. "Man almost leaped down the phone line when I said you were mixed up in a murder case."

"Yeah, and then he leaped down my throat. You're really making my life easy, aren't you? I guess O'Malley will be here right after he gets Kyle out of bed, hmm? My brother will love that." I nodded at the patrol car. "You're bringing down the tone of the neighborhood, you know?"

She lifted her eyebrows. "So are you."

"That's already been pointed out to me." I glanced at the

kitchen window again. The curtain was back down. "But I'm not parking down the block tonight. Maybe tomorrow."

Her face changed. "They don't want you to park in front of their house? Your family really knows from hospitality, Liz."

"Families can be strange. Say, did you get hold of Maud?"

Her face sobered. "She was already gone, everything locked up. We'll have to find that mountain cabin. I'm searching the property records tomorrow."

I shivered. "Is that all you wanted to talk about? It's cold out here."

She studied me for a moment. "That's all for now. I'll be in touch."

Sitting on the Z-bed, I shut the door and the dome light went off. All the curtains were closed, so I couldn't see Officer Eva leaving. But I heard her car drive away as I scrambled into my sweats and parked my old Birkenstocks by the door.

I didn't use the headlamp to read. While I was lying awake in the dark, a truck roared by, and I saw Tony's body again, sprawled on the steps, his head dark against the welcome mat. And then the scene changed to Tony falling backward, staring in surprise, while I felt the heavy weight of the gun in my hand. Only this time, instead of a bright triangle of blood on his shirt, there was a neat hole in his forehead, and his eyes were fixed accusingly on me.

I woke up, realizing it was a nightmare, but despite Barker's reassuring warmth by my leg, I didn't feel safe and invisible, like I used to when the bus was my only refuge.

16_____

IT was another gray morning. At the neighborhood park, Barker strained to go after some squirrels. I let him off the leash and leaned against the slide, watching him flash across the damp grass, scattering the squirrels and birds as if life could hold no greater pleasure. And probably, for a dog who'd been neutered a few short weeks ago, that was true.

I tried to think what in my life gave me that rush. Getting an acceptance from a magazine was up there, especially if a check was enclosed—usually by the time I was paid for my work, months, if not years, had passed from the time it was accepted. Another small but richly enjoyable experience was diving into the pool for my swim, cleaving the water, switching elements in an instant. And seeing a whole row of carrots pop up in the seedling bed was also something to savor. I resolved to notice such things more often. Without that kind of sweetening, the dull fiber of life gets mighty hard to swallow.

Homesickness washed over me. Three years ago I would have scoffed at the notion that I could feel so grounded in one particular place. But now I wanted my house, my own bed, my kitchen full of rickety, last-legs appliances, my garden and flowers and redwood trees. I even wanted my neighbor—and maybe on more than a purely platonic basis, if my dreams were anything to go by. Besides, having Drake live in the house in front of me was like having a shield against the outside world. Not that I would tell him so, of course. It was too shaming to admit that after years of solitary vigilance, I liked having a man to guard my portal.

Barker finished with the squirrels, driving the final tree-rat into the branches. He found a stick and brought it to me; I threw it several times before he decided not to play anymore and refused to drop it. I snapped the leash on. We walked back with him carrying the stick proudly, ears up, tail wagging.

I took a circuitous route back to Andy's, trying to decide what to do with my day. Since I had come to Denver in the first place to help with my mother, I thought I would give it another chance. If Dad wasn't speaking to Molly, it shouldn't bother me that he wouldn't speak to me, either. At least I could wash dishes and do some laundry, maybe cook them a meal. My dad should enjoy seeing me do women's work.

Turning the corner onto Andy's street, I saw a car pulled up in front of mine—the car Detective O'Malley had been driving the day before. He was sitting in the open side door of the bus.

Barker didn't like that much. As we approached, the fur on his neck got tall, and he started growling deep in his throat, around the stick he still clutched.

O'Malley put out a cigarette and glanced up placidly when I stopped in front of him, holding Barker by the collar. "You shouldn't leave your door unlocked." He shut the book he'd been reading and put it down beside him.

I recognized the book. "Did you lose my place?"

He shrugged. "Might have. Didn't know you had a place." Negligently he held a hand down toward Barker. After a suspicious sniff, Barker dropped the stick and backed away. His fur was still up, but he wasn't growling anymore. "Didn't have you pegged for the kind of person who reads Juvenal," he went on. "He's big among police officers, you know."

I didn't tell him that the Juvenal, a translation borrowed from Drake, was my current sleeping-pill book. It's my habit to read myself to sleep, and an exciting mystery or my favorite Victorian authors don't work too well for that. "Did you want to talk to me, Detective? Kind of early for that, isn't it?"

"I was driving by," he said, shifting over to make more

room in the doorway. "Saw that your door was open, and was afraid something awful had happened to you—like your relatives tossing you in the Platte. Thought I'd wait a while."

I handed him Barker's leash. "Well, I don't have many comforts, but I can do better than sitting in the doorway. Hold this for a minute."

He stood beside the bus, watching Barker with a wary expression that mirrored the dog's. I folded the bed back, tossed my sleeping bag into the cargo area, pulled up the table, and got a couple of oranges out of the cupboard. I noticed while I was in there that some papers in my file box were rearranged. I always stack them neatly, because the box is just barely big enough to hold my file folders. O'Malley had made himself at home, it seemed. I began to wonder if he'd watched for me to leave so he could search my space.

I put the oranges on the table. *"Voilá."*

"Nice little place you got here." He climbed in and handed me the leash. Barker's fur was still up, so I made him sit by me after I took the leash off. He sat on the bench seat, staring fixedly at O'Malley, who took the seat that faced backward behind the driver's seat.

"It's good for traveling." I rolled an orange toward him. "I can heat some water if you'd like tea."

He looked a little uncomfortable. "No thanks."

I peeled my orange. I was hungry. "Officer Gutierrez seemed to think you'd be badgering Kyle this morning, not me."

"I wondered if I could kill two birds with one stone, so to speak." He glanced around.

"You think I would have brought him here?" I began to laugh. "My brother would really hit the ceiling then. Might be amusing at that."

"You didn't go to his place."

"No, of course not. We're just sort of friends—at least we were ten years ago. He's a nice guy."

"What did he say when you told him you were coming back for a visit?"

I put the orange down. "Maybe you'd better spell out

what you're after here, O'Malley. I didn't tell him or anyone I was coming back. My niece told me my mother was ill, and I decided on the spur of the minute. I would never have told Kyle even if I'd known how to reach him."

"Why's that?" He leaned forward, his voice soft and persuasive. "Because you knew he would want to protect you against your ex-husband? Because you knew he would kill Naylor and dump the body where you'd find it?" He sat back a little. "Just like this old cat I had once," he added. "Used to bring ground squirrels she'd killed and lay 'em right on the doormat."

I shook my head, trying not to dwell on the monstrous picture he'd conjured. "You're really reaching here, O'Malley. Kyle's probably got a girlfriend—it's a sure bet he hasn't been pining for me the past ten years. And nobody knew—I didn't know myself—when I'd get here. I'm sure when you talk to Kyle he'll be able to set your mind at rest. He was Tony's friend more than mine. The only person I know who'd kill someone because of me is—was—Tony. And the person he'd kill wasn't Kyle."

O'Malley frowned. "What do you mean? Do you have other old boyfriends around?"

I shook my head. I had gotten into the habit of talking to Drake, forgetting that other policemen aren't always willing to listen with an open mind. "The person Tony would have killed is me, Detective. He came close a couple of times. Not over other men, because there weren't any." It was too much. All the feelings I had been trying to revise for the past year came boiling to the surface—the anger, the fear, the disgust. "Do you suppose I could have trusted any man that way—after Tony?"

He studied me a moment, curiously. "So you like women, is that it?"

Barker's cold nose shoved in my arm a couple of times helped me control myself. "You really need to know about my sex life? I'll tell you. There is none. It's that simple."

For the first time, his gaze fell, and a slight blush appeared. "Okay, already."

Heady with the power of discomfiting him, I pushed.

"So you'll have to drop me and my family from your list of potential bad guys, right?"

He shook his head. "You wish. Think about it, Missus. Your ex-husband didn't end up on your parents' doorstep by accident. Someone put him there for a reason."

"Someone who heard that he was bothering my mom, that my dad threatened him—"

O'Malley cocked an eyebrow at me. "Your dad doesn't admit that, of course. And your nephew, young Byron—" He pursed his lips. "That boy's inches away from trouble."

"Look, O'Malley. You're wasting your time trying to find a culprit among the Sullivans. Do us both a favor here." I realized I was leaning forward, jabbing my finger toward his bemused face. I tried to relax in my seat. "Stop concentrating on me and my family. We didn't do anything. Find out who did, and give them the third degree. And do it soon. I want to go home."

O'Malley shook his head. "You got a lot of gall, talking to me like that." He didn't sound angry, just surprised. "I could haul your ass in, you know."

"On what grounds? Your case is so flimsy you couldn't even hold me." I had learned a few things from listening to Drake talk, and one was that arrests were expensive, prisoners were expensive, and the DA didn't like having to let people go again because there was no evidence. "And if you think you can railroad me, or use me to obscure any funny business that's going on among your fellow cops, think again. I'm a writer, you know. In my experience, local papers always like to run exposés of police misbehavior."

"Are you threatening me?" His face turned dull purple, all traces of amusement gone. I had gone too far; it was a bad habit of mine.

"No more than you were threatening me yesterday, when you pointed out how well I'd come out of a trial. I'm keeping a journal, O'Malley. I'll have lots of material for a series of articles—'Justice in Denver' sounds like a good title." I tried to sound calm. "Up to you whether it has a period or a question mark behind it."

O'Malley stared at me for a moment longer and then

turned on his heel. I watched through the windshield as he slammed his car door and drove away. Now he was my enemy, and I had only my own big mouth to blame for it.

Andy opened the front door, staring after the departing O'Malley, then at me. "Come in for breakfast." It was not a question.

I was still fired up to slash and burn, but Barker had no ambiguities. He jumped down and pranced up the sidewalk, ready to see his idol, Amy.

I followed, trying to conceal my surliness beneath a thin veneer of decent civility. It was hard.

In the kitchen, Renee was dishing up plates of ham and eggs, with hot biscuits and red-eye gravy. It was an instant flashback to my growing up. Every morning my dad would sit with arms guarding his heaped-up plate, waiting for us to get to the table—absence wasn't tolerated. The theory was that he burned it all off, and certainly my mother filled his lunch box to the brim as well. He never seemed to get fat, but I noticed that Andy was no longer very trim around the waist. My brothers had joined my dad in the laborer's breakfast when they started working construction, but Andy was a foreman now, though he still ate like a laborer.

I accepted my plate and sat down beside Amy, who managed to smile at me, chew an enormous bite, and highlight something in a big textbook at the same time. The food was good, although I noticed the spiral cardboard of a refrigerator-biscuit carton in the trash and immediately felt less inadequate. Renee served me with a parody of hospitality, which seemed to be saying, "Remember how badly you fed me when I was your guest?" True, I'd never fixed her ham and eggs—or anyone, for that matter. The rich food tasted good going down, but sat in my stomach like a lump. I should have eaten granola in my bus.

"Fooling around with that computer instead of getting your homework done," Andy growled between bites. Renee refilled his coffee cup and her own, and silently offered me a cup with a tea bag string sticking out of it. Lipton. And lukewarm water, too. It was thoughtful of her not to offer coffee, though. I thanked her and wondered how soon I could escape.

"I'm getting it done, okay? Get off my back," Amy said in that prefight tone of voice that I recognized from my own adolescence. "What are you doing today, Aunt Liz?"

I cleared my throat and took a sip of the lukewarm tea. "Well, I'm going to see if I can do laundry or marketing or cleaning for your gramma."

"Don't upset the old man," Renee said sharply. "You've done enough, I'd say."

I shook my head. "I came to help, and I'm stuck for now, so I'll help. What especially needs doing? Clean the bathroom?"

She said grudgingly, "Well, if you want something to do, that would save me from the job. And you can clean the kitchen cabinets if you like."

Andy started to protest, and Renee rounded on him. "Well, why shouldn't she?" Her voice was shrill with passion. "God knows I slave over there on top of my own work to keep that place going, now that your mom is laid up and your dad just sits there, expecting to be waited on like always. Let Liz get her hands dirty with it. She's never helped before!"

Andy turned to me, a little shamefaced. "I've been thinking. About what you said last night." He glanced around, as if dissatisfied with his audience, but went on resolutely. "You have a point. We could of at least beat the shit out of Tony when we knew he was hitting you, but we kind of thought it was between the two of you." He stared at Renee. "God knows women can drive you crazy."

"Marriage is hazardous." I stood up. "I'd better get going. I have some errands to do. Can I pick anything up for you, Renee? Groceries or such?"

She shook her head. "Thanks." It was reluctantly said, but at least it happened.

"You're welcome."

"Don't you want a shower, Aunt Liz?" Amy pushed her wet hair out of her eyes.

"If it wouldn't be a bother."

"Go ahead." Renee shrugged, picking up plates.

"Can I help with the dishes?"

"I just load the dishwasher," she said, flouncing off.

Amy slapped her book shut and came out to the bus with me while I collected my washing stuff. "You can give me a ride again if you're fast enough," she suggested.

I agreed to this. It doesn't take me long to clean up, and I wanted desperately to get out of my brother's house. Despite his (for him) handsome apology, I felt smothered there.

Amy and I were climbing into the bus when a white pickup roared up and dived for the curb right in front of Babe. Biff leaped out of the driver's seat and came striding over to us. This time he didn't have his chorus of muscle-bound friends along. The scowling eyebrows gave his face a Neanderthal air.

"Look," he said without preamble. "I don't like cop-loving snitches." He came to a halt in front of me, his big fists clenching and unclenching.

"Get out of here, Byron." Amy jumped between us, and he pushed her out of the way.

"You get out, freak." He didn't take his angry gaze from me. "Stay out of my space, Auntie." He gave the word a mean emphasis. "We don't want nosy bitches like you around. The sooner you get out of here, the safer you'll be."

I felt paralyzed by the raw anger that poured from him. He got back in his truck and roared away just as Andy came out.

"What did Biff want?" He looked from Amy to me.

"The usual," Amy answered, sounding a little dazed. "Total world domination."

Andy laughed indulgently. "That Biff."

Neither of us joined in.

17

MY mom was leaning against the kitchen counter while she filled the glass pot of the coffeemaker with water. The only sign of my dad was the faint sound of water running from the bathroom.

"Should you be out of bed?" I took the carafe from her trembling hands and poured the water into the coffeemaker.

"Lizzie." She sank into a chair and rested her arms on the table. "Thought you weren't coming back. Your father isn't going to like you being here."

"Tough." I studied the coffeemaker and flipped it on; it was a relatively simple machine, not like Drake's Italian monster. "I came to help out, and I can't help if I'm not here. What does Dad get for breakfast these days?"

"The doctor told him, no more bacon." She smiled a little. "He doesn't like that, but he wouldn't cook it for himself, so it works out okay. I make him an egg, over easy, and some toast."

"I can handle that." I found the little cast-iron skillet, then exchanged it for a bigger one. "You'd like an egg, too, right?"

She sighed. "I just don't feel hungry at all."

"You can eat one egg, though." The butter was in the same white melamine butter dish embossed with butterflies that had once been gold but were now pale and streaky. The eggs occupied their usual spot in a bin inside the avocado-green refrigerator. I remembered when that refrigerator was new, when I was in high school. The whole kitchen was in a time warp.

"So, you must be feeling better if you're up." I mixed

some frozen orange juice while the butter melted. "What did you eat yesterday?"

She told me about the soup Molly had brought. Encounters with Biff fresh in my mind, I asked about Molly's kids.

"Those boys are so spirited." Mom beamed when she talked about them. They sounded like out-of-control, hormone-driven wild men to me, but I'm admittedly a maiden aunt where rowdy nephews are concerned. I remembered the oldest, Brendan, as a malevolent six-year-old, tormenting his younger brother and the new baby.

"So Amy and Byron go to the same school?"

"He likes to be called Biff, for some reason." Mom shook her head, smiling fondly. "We saw two of the boys on Labor Day. Brewster and Biff are so tall. Had to bend way down to kiss their gramma."

"You haven't seen them since then?"

Her face clouded. "Biff was here the other day—you know. I told you about it. When him and your dad found Tony here. It certainly made me feel better to have a strong young man like Biff around then."

"Right." As long as he's on your side.

"He came by once more for just a minute, but he didn't have time to sit with his gramma. The boys are so busy, and so is Molly, just running around everywhere, never a moment to sit and talk." She sighed. "I've been such a burden on them with this illness."

Guilt struck like a well-thrown dart. I had been no help at all for the past sixteen years. Long-buried experience told me I would never be able to expiate my overdue account. I stifled an urge to burst into self-justification. My mother stated nothing more than the truth. If anyone should be doing more to care for her, it would be my dad. She had cared for him so long.

I turned back to the eggs, using the familiar old pancake turner, its wooden handle worn smooth. The faint sound of water stopped. I put toast in the toaster and poured another glass of juice. My mother sat up a little straighter when I put the juice and some silverware at the head of the table, facing into the living room, the place Dad sat in my memories.

The toast popped up, and I arranged it in buttered triangles on the faded blue forget-me-nots of the melamine plates. The eggs were done, too. Footsteps shuffled down the hall—not the ponderous strides I remembered.

"Smells good." My dad appeared in the archway, sniffing. With his bent back and sunken chin, he was much smaller than the imposing, intimidating figure of my youth. He saw me and grabbed at the back of a chair.

"Hi, Dad." I dished up the eggs, two on his plate, one on Mom's. "I'm cooking this morning."

Those bushy eyebrows came down; his mouth worked. His freshly shaven skin looked pink, but papery; the big nose was seamed with veins. His hands, the knuckles swollen and red, clutched the chair back for a moment before he drew himself up.

"We don't need your help." His voice was thick. He cleared his throat impatiently. "You're not welcome here."

My mother made a faint sound of protest. He shot her a fierce look.

Somehow, though, the melodramatic words tickled my funny bone. That big, stern lay-down-the-law man from my childhood was much more frightening than this old fellow.

"Welcome or not, I've made your breakfast." I put the plate down at his place, and set one in front of my mother. I brought them each a cup of coffee, though I wasn't sure my mother should have any, and a cup of tea I'd brewed for myself. "Sit down, Dad. Eat it while it's hot."

He moved around the table until he was staring down at the food. For a moment I thought he would throw the plate on the floor, like the ungovernable child he'd sometimes seemed. I pulled out the chair across from my mother and sat down with my tea. She was paler than ever, her eyes fixed on him in mute appeal.

He didn't even notice. He sat down, pulled the salt over, and started eating.

My mother sighed, picked up her own fork, and cut into her egg, looking critically at the flood of yolk she'd released before using her toast to dam the flow. How many times had I seen her do that? When my dad looked around, I knew he wanted the apple jelly he liked on his toast. Silently I fetched it, and he accepted it. I sipped my tea and watched them. My mother, though downcast, finished most of her egg and a piece of toast. My father methodically worked his way through everything on his plate, ending with a final swipe of the toast across the forget-me-nots.

He pushed his plate away, took a noisy swallow of coffee, and fixed me with one cloudy eye. I reminded myself that he was eighty-three, past changing any of his prejudices.

"So, girl." He sounded fierce. "Have you been to confession lately?"

"Not lately." I shrugged. "Nothing to confess. I live a very quiet life."

"In a shack, Renee said." He looked at my mother, who nodded.

I was prepared for this. "It's little and old—but I own it free and clear." I pulled a picture out of my pocket. Drake had taken it just before Amy had left the previous month. The two of us were standing at the walk that led to my front door. Behind us was my house, softened out of focus into something quaint and English-looking, with Shasta daisies and scabiosa in full bloom on either side of the walk, and the glossy foliage of a Lady Banks rose climbing over the porch. "I think it's nice, actually. Maybe not all modern like Andy's place, but I get along fine there."

Mom looked solemnly at the picture and handed it to Dad. "It's not so bad." She sounded tolerant. "Renee is spoiled by that nice kitchen." She shook her head. "Those fancy black appliances show every finger mark, if you ask me."

My dad looked at the picture and tossed it down. "Foundation's going."

I tucked the picture away and cleared the plates. "Well, anyway, I came here to help Mom through her illness, and I'm going to help today."

"Molly was going to come, and bring her housekeeper." Mom sounded hesitant.

"Housekeeper," Dad grunted. "Fancy word for a wetback hired girl."

110

Mom sat up straighter. "You know she doesn't like you talking that way, Fergus."

"She can come," I said, interrupting before it could get out of hand. I filled Dad's coffee cup; he looked up in surprised approval. "The work will be done before she gets here. Do your sheets need changing?"

I cleaned the kitchen quickly, while Dad finished his coffee, and then changed the sheets on their bed. Mom was glad to get back into it.

"My legs are so wobbly," she complained. "I don't know what I'll do."

"You're much better, anyway." I picked up the bundle of used sheets. "Get a nap, now. I'll wake you before I leave."

She pulled the afghan up around her shoulders, but she still looked worried. "Your dad—"

"He'll be okay." I wasn't so sure of that, but I had lost my fear of the old man. "I won't pay any attention to him."

"You should go to confession." Her voice trailed. "He's right about that, you know."

"Uh-huh." I slipped out of the room as her eyes closed.

The sheets and towels made as much of a load as I ventured to put in the washer. I wondered how she'd kept all these ancient appliances going. The stairs out of the narrow cellar were steep; I couldn't see my frail mother carrying laundry up and down.

My dad was still waiting in the kitchen when I went in to look under the sink for cleaning supplies. "What do you think you're doing here?" His bark sounded much like it used to.

"I'm helping." I sat down across from him. "Let's make peace, Dad. I'll forgive you for casting me out when you should have helped me, if you'll forgive me for ignoring your advice about my marriage."

"You forgive!" He looked genuinely astonished. "You, a jailbird, a divorced woman who tried to kill her own husband! What could you possibly have to forgive?"

"The Bible," I reminded him, "sets a precedent for the way to treat sinners and prodigals."

"The devil quotes scripture for his own ends." Dad

crossed himself. "You were an undutiful daughter. I should have taken my belt to you."

"You did." I sat rigid, keeping my temper. "Many's the time you lambasted me. It only made me hate and resent you, so as a treatment for undutifulness, it failed. Let's try talking to each other, Dad. I'm willing to listen. Get it out of your system."

He wouldn't say another word, just buttoned his lips together and glowered from under his bushy brows. After a moment I shrugged and gathered the cleaning stuff together. In the intervals of running water in the bathroom, I could hear him moving around.

I put fresh towels out and left the bathroom sparkling. My mom was snoring gently, flat on her back with the afghan tucked under her chin.

Dad was in his chair in the living room, the TV turned on to some news babble. He watched me through the room, but didn't speak until I'd put the cleaning things away and was dusting the living room. Then he flicked off the TV and pointed the remote control at me.

"Sit down," he ordered, moving the remote between me and a chair, as if he'd finally found a way to get me to do what he wanted. The surge of rebellion I felt was maddeningly adolescent. I conquered it, sat, and tried to assume a pleasant expression.

"What did you do with the gun?"

My pleasant expression fled. "What gun?"

Dad thumped the remote on the chair arm. "You know what I'm talking about!" His voice rose. "I told that cop—"

"Shh!" I glanced toward the hall. "If you start shouting at me, I'll leave. Mom should get some sleep."

He harrumphed, but lowered his voice. "My gun."

I took a deep breath. "Why do you suppose I have it? I don't have the faintest idea where it was kept."

"Don't play dumb, girl." His face was suffused with red, the usual effect any opposition had on him.

"You say it's missing now?"

He looked at me hard. "I kept it in the same place for the last twenty-five years—a safe place. You didn't know where it was?"

"It was in a box or something, that's all I remember. You never used it that I recall, except to mark holidays once in a while."

"I nearly used it not long ago." He smiled in grim satisfaction. "On your husband."

"Mom said you threatened to shoot him. I could have told you that wasn't such a good idea."

He looked contemptuous. "Didn't have to shoot him, not with young Biff here aching to bounce him off the pavement. Just told him I would if I caught him bothering around here again." His swollen knuckles tightened around the remote control. "He was getting round your mother. Getting money out of her somehow." His laugh was not amused. "Fool pack of women I got around here."

"Did you tell the cop? O'Malley?"

Dad looked at me as if I were crazy. "Tell the cop? You think I'm a fool, too? He asked me about my gun—damn government knows everything nowadays. Told him it would take me awhile to get it out, and he didn't want to wait. Said he'd be back for it today."

"What will you tell him when you don't have it?"

"Danged if I know." Dad brooded. "It's not in its place. Thought you might have found it and shot that no-good weasel yourself." He scrutinized me carefully, like the deed would be written all over my face, and maybe it was. After a moment, during which I couldn't have spoken even if I'd thought of something to say, he leaned back. "Guess you didn't."

I couldn't tell whether he was relieved or disappointed. The hysterical laughter I'd been suppressing erupted.

"Nothing funny about this." My dad was offended. "If you didn't take my gun, who did?"

"Maybe the person who killed Tony. Maybe that person is trying to figure out a good way to use it to incriminate you or me right now. Wait—my bus!" I rushed to the front door. Babe sat there, serenely unlocked, with Barker's head hanging out the driver's side window. I had forgotten that he took his duties as car alarm seriously. It would be hard to plant a gun in my car while he was in it.

"Eh?" Dad was prying himself painfully out of his chair. "Is that cop back?"

"No, not yet." I dropped the curtain back over the window. "So what will you say?"

"Doesn't matter what I say." He lowered himself back in his chair, hands spread on his thighs, not looking at me. "He'll think you did it. Thinks so already, from what I could tell." He glanced over, and turned his gaze away again. "I thought so, too, then, but I guess you couldn't have. Not with my gun, anyway."

"Well, as long as we're being so frank, let me tell you that he told me you and Biff were also on his list of people who might have killed Tony."

Dad's jaw dropped open. It was, in a macabre way, the high point of my morning. I didn't want my dad or my nephew to be investigated by the police. But there was a certain irony in knowing that I wasn't the only Sullivan whose actions and motives were subject to scrutiny.

18

I wanted to talk to Kyle again, to see if he'd known anything about Tony's dealings with my mom and dad. Having them drawn into the murkiness surrounding his death was too scary. Scariest of all, I could see my dad shooting Tony. I just couldn't see him doing it the way it had happened, in that execution style that Drake had recognized immediately.

After dusting, I put off the vacuuming until Mom would be awake. There wasn't much besides eggs, lunch meat, and Molly's soup in the refrigerator. Dad was watching TV, and waved me away impatiently when I asked what he'd like for dinner. Hoping I'd remember the route to the market, I drove off to forage.

I stopped at the post office to mail the tape and transcript, and found my way to the King Sooper. Despite its name, the market wasn't too impressive next to the big, expansive food emporiums of California, where every kind of fresh produce gleams in beautifully stacked pyramids—or at least it can seem that way. The lettuce in Colorado wasn't bad, but the tomatoes were pale and firm, like some new species of apple. Between Dad's need to avoid saturated fat and Mom's invalid stomach, there wasn't much leeway. I got a chicken and some veggies, yogurt and oatmeal and more bread, some gelatin and fruit cocktail to complete the time-warp effect. There were batteries there, and I got the right size for Amy's tape recorder, but they didn't sell the tiny tapes.

Barker was holding his leash in his mouth when I put my groceries in the bus. I stopped at a park to let him run, so it was nearly noon when I got back to my parents' house. Amid the cars parked along the street, I almost missed the police cruiser halfway down the block.

Leaving Barker in the bus, I walked down the street. Officer Eva was sitting in the cruiser's front seat, her head bent over her notebook. When I stopped beside the window, she looked up.

"Hi, Liz." She gave me a brief smile, showing excellent white teeth. "I'm supposed to go talk to your dad. Want to come?"

"He told me about the gun."

She pursed her lips. "You're speaking? O'Malley thought you'd be the last to know."

"Dad doesn't have the gun anymore. He doesn't know when it disappeared. He last saw it a while ago."

"When he was brandishing it at a man whose description sounds a lot like your ex-husband's," Eva said, nodding. "We heard about that." She nodded toward Mrs. Beamish's house. "Your neighbor has good eyesight."

"Binoculars, probably."

"She said the man had stopped in several times in the preceding month." Eva flipped through the notebook. "Did you know that?"

"Mom told me when I got here." I shifted uneasily. "She had a kind of soft spot for Tony before we got divorced. He evidently was exploiting that."

Officer Eva looked skeptical. "Funny that you come home just when he's getting bumped off. It's no wonder O'Malley's looking so hard for the connection."

"Look, I can't help that. I came because Amy asked me to, said Mom was sinking and needed to see me. Turned out she wanted me to know that my louse of an ex-husband had been black—"

"Blackmailing her?" Eva spoke softly. "Thanks, Liz. I wasn't sure you'd tell me."

I cursed my nervousness, which had led me to babble. Normally I keep a tight rein on my loose lips, but I had let my guard down with this woman.

"He made up some stuff and said he'd smear it all over if she didn't pay." I shrugged nonchalantly. "She's old, credulous. Never thought to wonder who'd care about

Tony's lies. Just gave him what she could spare and hoped he didn't come back."

"So when your dad threatened him, he stopped coming?"

"Guess so." I could hear Barker whining from the bus; he doesn't like to see me standing around when he's locked up. "Talk to Dad if you want. He's gotten childish, you know. Surprised me how feeble he's become. He couldn't have killed Tony, much less heaved him onto the porch."

"But he wouldn't have had to, would he?" She smiled, revealing those strong white teeth. "Tony could have been shot by someone standing on the sidewalk in front of the porch, if he'd been coming out of the house. He would have fallen just like that, with his head on the mat." She studied me. "Your dad has an alibi, of course—he was at his lodge meeting. But the rest of you—your mother, you, your brother, your niece—could have conspired."

"That's a lot of people just to kill one lousy guy. And I thought the evidence showed he wasn't killed here." I didn't think she believed what she was saying, but I couldn't tell for sure. Police can be self-delusional when it comes to proving their own theories. "Wasn't there an exit wound? I'm sure your evidence people found no trace of a bullet anywhere. And if you think Mrs. Beamish would have missed a murder practically on her doorstep, you've seriously underestimated her snoopiness."

"Did you know your brother has a gun, too?" Officer Eva flipped through more pages of her notebook. "The firearms bureau's computer was down, or we would have known before."

"No, I didn't know, although it doesn't surprise me." I pushed the hair out of my eyes and realized my palm was sweaty. "Most people around here have guns, don't they?"

"We're going to need to test these weapons. I'd advise your family to get it together."

"I don't know anything about it. Ask Andy." A thought struck me. "There is one gun you haven't mentioned."

"Your own?" She looked resigned. "You packing heat, Liz?"

"No, Tony's." I could still remember its solid, reassuring

weight in my hand, in the instant before I'd fired ten years ago. "Did he get it back after my hearing?"

She frowned. "Haven't checked on that."

"If he was killed with the same gun as I used before— don't you have the tests you did then? Could you compare the bullets? Or did you guys spring-clean all that evidence away?"

"That would be embarrassing, wouldn't it?" She snapped her notebook shut. "Guess I'd better see if I can dig that up. Meanwhile, tell the menfolk to get ready to present arms." She gave me a narrow-eyed look. "It would go hard with anyone who lost their registered weapon and didn't report it."

"I'll pass that along."

"And you don't have a firearm yourself?"

"The pen is mightier than the gun, or so I've told myself." I put one hand on the car roof and bent to look in the door. "After the last time, I swore off firearms. If someone gets up against me, I just write them off."

Her chuckle sounded unforced. "Take care." She started the cruiser, and I watched her drive off.

Barker wanted to come with me when I collected my bags of groceries, but I made him stay. Growing up, I had never had a pet, though my brothers had coon dogs once, which were penned up in the backyard and not allowed many treats. My mother didn't like animals in the house— the mess, she always said, and it was true that Barker left a trail of fluffy white fur everywhere he went.

My dad was still sitting in front of the TV, watching a repeat of *The Dick Van Dyke Show* with intense concentration. I put away the food and used ice cubes to make the gelatin. The laundry had to be tended, too.

By the time I looked in on Mom, she was just waking up. She smiled sleepily at me, for the first time without that line of disapproval between her eyes. "I've had such a good rest," she said, yawning.

"I'll heat the soup for lunch, if you'd like."

"That sounds good. I believe I'm a little hungry."

She came into the kitchen while I dished up the soup, exclaiming how well I'd cleaned the bathroom, and for a few minutes we were in accord. Then Dad came in and took exception to the grilled cheese sandwich I'd made and the wheat bread it was made on, and Mom wondered how I could forget that he hated melted cheese and never would eat it. "We never have pizza," she reminded me, sounding wistful. "Your father simply can't stand it."

He's old, I told myself. Let it go. I made him a sandwich with pimento loaf and mustard on white bread, and ate the grilled cheese myself. It was good. I spooned up some of Molly's soup—also good—and watched the two old people at the table, and felt total isolation from them, as if we'd never been related. And yet everything they did, from my mother's periodic sniff to my dad's careful scrutiny of his sandwich before every bite, was familiar to me.

After lunch Dad went back to his recliner, and soon his snores mingled with the *Dallas* rerun. Mom wanted to do the dishes, but settled for snapping the beans I'd bought while exhaustively comparing the price of frozen beans to fresh, and concluding that I had been hopelessly extravagant to buy the fresh ones. I cleaned up the kitchen, feeling more and more closed-in. Though I had resented being called selfish, it seemed I actually was—I didn't want to give myself over to the maintenance of my old parents. If my services were gratefully or even graciously accepted it would be one thing, but the mother who condemned my extravagance didn't think of reimbursing me for the groceries I'd bought, and the dad who was so despising of my past actions saw nothing to commend in my present ones.

"I declare, I don't do anything but sleep," Mom said, after a mighty yawn.

"Go ahead, it's what you need."

"Maybe so." She allowed herself to be persuaded into bed, and I breathed a sigh of relief. Staggering up the steep basement stairs with a basket of clean laundry, I welcomed the sound of my dad's snores. They were the next best thing to peace and quiet.

I put the basket on the sofa and wondered if Dad would wake up if I turned *Dallas* off. A knock on the door distracted me.

When I lifted the curtain and looked out, Kyle Baldridge stood on the front porch. I glanced at Dad, still sleeping, and slipped out the door.

19

"LIZ!" Kyle grabbed my hands. "So I do have the right house. Tony pointed it out once when we were driving around, but I wasn't sure I remembered correctly. Are you staying here?"

"My mother's sick," I said, taking back my hands, "which is why I'm here in the first place. I came to help out."

He turned to survey Babe. A whining Barker hung out the window. "Is that your camper? Very adventurous." When he turned back, the smile was gone. "Where can we talk?"

"Let's go to my living room." He waited for me to open the door, but I led the way to the bus. "Both my folks are sleeping. We won't disturb them out here."

Barker bounded out to sniff Kyle thoroughly, putting his fur down almost immediately and accepting strokes with dignity. I gestured my guest to the rear bench seat and went forward to plug the immersion heater into the cigarette lighter. Uncovering the little sink, I filled two cups with water and started one of them heating. It had been a big day for Babe's hospitality, and it wasn't even two o'clock.

Kyle watched my preparations with bemusement. "I need a camper," he said. "It would make things easier on the dig."

"You still hanging out with the archaeologists?"

He nodded. "I should have gone into that field, instead of being a broker. But, of course, the pay is lousy. This way I can support myself and still get my excavating fix a couple of times a year." He frowned. "There's such a great need to get these sites identified and secured. Illegal pothunting is on the rise, and it really compromises our knowledge of the West's indigenous peoples."

He talked about the site he'd been working on for a few minutes, while I transferred the heater to the other cup and plopped a homemade tea bag into his cup. I set it in front of him and he broke off. "Sorry," he said, looking abashed. "Didn't mean to start my spiel. It always made Tony go to sleep."

"I enjoyed hearing about your work." I got another tea bag out for my cup. "This is my own herbal mixture. Very calming."

"Do you think I need calming?" He sniffed the cup and grinned at me. He wasn't conventionally handsome, but I thought him very engaging.

"Maybe you don't. I do."

He looked sympathetic. "What a mess for you. Come to visit your parents and all this happens." He leaned across the table and patted my hand. "Poor Liz."

A little cosseting was just what I needed. "What I can't figure out," I confided, "is why Tony's killer dumped his body on my parents' doorstep. How did that person know about his connection with them?"

A frown crossed his face. "That's a very good point. I mean, you'd been out of his life for what? The past ten years? It's pretty mystifying, though—" He set the cup back on the table. "I seem to remember Tony talking about your parents the time he pointed out this place. Something about how your mom still treated him like a son. Maybe he talked about them to other people, too—people he was working with."

"Actually, Tony had been bothering my mom lately." I explained about his threats, and how it had made my mother's illness worse. "My niece thought something to do with me was preying on her mind, which is why I came out."

"Just in time to take the rap." His gaze was serious. "You should know, Liz, that another detective came to question me this morning. He seemed to have the idea that you killed Tony because of me." He shrugged, spreading his hands. "I tried to explain I hadn't seen you or heard from you in years. Not that I forgot you," he hastened to add. "But I have to admit that long periods of time passed when no thought of you crossed my mind."

I matched his smile. "Ditto for me. In fact, mere survival has been the foremost thing on my mind for the past few years."

"Do you—are you involved with someone now?" He watched me closely as he said this.

"Not really." I gripped my cup with both hands. "I don't have much interest in relationships outside friendship. Actually, the very idea of getting close with a man scares me."

He nodded gently. "I understand."

"How about you? You were seeing someone when I—left."

He thought for a moment. "So long ago—I can't really remember. I've dated around. Been serious a couple of times, but it didn't last." He glanced up and away, as if such confiding was unusual for him. "There's a woman at the Four Corners dig—she really interested me, for the first time in a year or so. In fact, I was downright reluctant to leave when the police called me back. But then, when I saw you—"

I burst out laughing. "Now, Kyle. Don't say your heart stood still or anything like that."

He grinned ruefully. "No sappy romantic lines, huh? Well, I have to say it brought back my youth, for lack of a better word."

"You still have your youth," I pointed out. "What are you, thirty-five, thirty-six? That's not old."

"Not young, either," he insisted. "The days when we would stay out late and do wild things are gone. I feel positively middle-aged."

"You lead an exciting life, it sounds like." I enumerated on my fingers. "Frenzied stock trading in the pit, flinging money around with abandon. Indiana Jones–style vacations digging for the clues to ancient civilizations." I indicated the Harley parked behind my bus. "Is that your motorcycle?" He nodded. "And you roar around town on a Harley. That doesn't add up to middle age, if you ask me."

He laughed. "Thanks, Liz. You always could make me feel better."

We sat in silence for a while, sipping our tea. Under the table, Barker panted gently.

"Anyway, it's you I'm concerned about." He focused on me once more. "If the police are determined to pin this on you—"

"They can't." I spoke with more certainty than I felt. "I wasn't here when the murder was committed—I was getting my bus fixed in Idaho Springs, with the receipt to prove it."

Kyle cleared his throat. "The detective seemed to think you might have persuaded me to do the actual murder. Or that you hired someone."

"You? Kill Tony over me? He suggested that to me, too, and I told him what a dumb idea it was. I mean, if that was going to happen, it would have happened ten years ago." I laughed without amusement. "And his other idea is dumber. Like I know enough about the Denver underworld, if there is one, to hire a killer."

His smile seemed abstracted. "Well, thanks for defending me, although, of course, I was at the dig that night—or was that the night I stayed over in Cortez? I think it might have been. It was my turn to get supplies, and I had an infected cut I wanted seen by a doctor." His eyes clouded. "I keep thinking that I should have been around when Tony needed help. I always figured sometime he'd grow up, want to change. Be the kind of guy I would have been proud to have for a friend. Instead we grew apart, and now it's too late."

"It wasn't your responsibility to monitor Tony's behavior." I patted his hand this time, and he turned it over to hold mine. "How would you have done it, anyway? All your interference would have accomplished was driving Tony away from you."

"That's what I thought ten years ago," he admitted. "But I did feel guilty about standing by while he was treating you like that—I still do. I wish I could have made things easier for you."

"Don't worry about it." I spoke briskly, withdrawing my hand. "It's over and done with. The police will find the real killer soon and let me go back to California."

"Is that what you want?" He was intent again. "You could stay here, be near your family."

I repressed a shudder. "No, California is home now." I thought of my house, my garden—Drake. "I have roots there."

"I see." He took a deep breath. "Well, let's hope it blows over soon. Meanwhile, is there anything I can do to help you out? If you need legal representation—"

"I'll ask you for a recommendation," I promised. "But it won't come to that."

"I may need a lawyer, too, I guess." He pushed the shiny hair away from his forehead, looking worried. "I mean, I have an alibi, also—being a couple hundred miles away—but that doesn't seem to mean much to the police."

"Did Tony ever say anything to you lately about my folks? I can't figure out why he started hitting up my mom."

Kyle shook his head. "I didn't talk to him much the past year or so. He was drifting away from me, and I—just let him go. He scared me, if you want the truth. I really expected to hear that he was dead some way or other—reckless driving, getting into a brawl, something like that." He looked bewildered. "Not like this. This just doesn't add up for me."

"Me either." I opened the side door, and Barker took that as permission to jump out. Kyle smiled at me and touched my cheek with one finger.

"Thanks for talking, Liz. I know we didn't get anywhere, but it clarified some issues for me."

"Me, too." I was a bit at a loss for what to say. The subtext of male-female conversation is not an open book for me. Kyle had seemed to be asking if I was interested in starting something up. If so, I felt I had given a nonverbal negative. Of course, I could be reading more into it than existed, which is always a fear of mine. "It was nice to see you again."

"Hey, we'll meet before you leave." He grinned, putting on a helmet. "I'll be in touch."

I waved as he roared off. It did occur to me to wonder how he'd be in touch, but I figured it was one more example of taking conversational gambits too literally. What he meant, no doubt, was, so long, and thanks for the memories.

It was what I felt, anyway. Kyle was a nice guy. But talking about the past was painful for me in ways he couldn't possibly appreciate. I just desperately wanted my mother's health to mend, my dad to recognize that I was his daughter, no matter how wrongheaded, and myself to be tooling west on I-70. It didn't seem too much to ask.

Barker was sitting expectantly on the front porch. I called him back to the bus, and went in to finish the laundry.

20 _____

MOLLY came in a little later. Dad was still snoring in his chair. The sound of the front door opening brought me from the kitchen. It took me a moment to recognize my sister.

She was in her forties, I knew, but it was hard to tell. Her hair, which had been the same medium brown shade as my own, was now blond-streaked and carefully tousled. A sweater studded with glittery fake jewels came down to mid-thigh, topping stretch pants the same delicate shade of moss green, tucked into expensive-looking leather ankle boots.

When she saw me, she stopped short. "Liz?"

"Hi, Molly." I stayed in the archway, trying to gauge the hostility index. "Heard you wanted some help taking care of things here."

She looked from me to Dad, who straightened up the recliner, his eyes bleary with sleep. Her well-plucked eyebrows lowered. "Are you upsetting Mom and Dad?"

I shrugged. "Dad's more worried about the loss of his gun than he is about me."

"His—gun?" Her hand, with its fancy silk-wrapped nails, covered her slack mouth. The blusher stood out on her suddenly whitened cheeks.

Dad didn't notice—he was too busy railing at me. "Dang it, girl. What do you want to blab to everybody for? That gun's going to turn up. I didn't give you permission to talk about it."

I smiled at him. "The family might as well know it's gone. Maybe one of them borrowed it or something."

"What are you saying?" Molly whirled on me. "What are you insinuating? Biff would never—"

Dad emitted a harsh cackle. "That Biff. I wondered if he'd got his mitts on it a couple of weeks ago. Saw me putting it away after we tossed out Naylor, but he didn't say anything."

"See what you've done!" Molly had tears in her eyes, threatening her perfect makeup. She came over and shook me, hard. "You put him up to this. Not back two days before you're driving a wedge through this family again, just like you did the last time."

I could see she was hauling off to slap me, so I twisted away. "Hold on, Molly. I don't know anything about this Biff stuff. Dad told me I had stolen his gun a few hours ago."

"Probably you did." Her eyes widened. "You shot him, didn't you? You finally killed Tony."

Surprisingly, Dad came to my defense. "I've been over that with her." His voice was brusque. "She couldn't have done it, and I accept that. You'd better, too." He gave Molly the stern look I remembered from my childhood. "You're a good girl, but you go overboard," he said austerely.

I wouldn't have blamed Molly for hitting me at that point. Then a noise from the doorway drew our attention. A girl stood there, her eyes scared, her whole body tense. She was loaded down with a bucket filled with spray bottles, another full of rags, and a dust mop tucked under her arm.

We stared at her, and slowly she began to back out of the door.

"Conchita!" Molly went over and took her arm, speaking a steady stream of urgent Spanish. Conchita's reply was too subdued to hear, and in any case my Spanish is rudimentary. Molly drew her back into the room.

"This is my housekeeper, Conchita," she said brightly. "She's going to give things a good going-over and fix dinner. She's a very good cook."

Conchita shot her a look, much like one I'd seen on Amy's face, and I realized the two were probably the same age.

127

"Does she speak English yet?" Dad's face was wary. "I can't do that Mexican bibble-babble."

Molly raised her eyebrows at him. "She's learning fast. She understands better than she talks right now. Tell her what you want, and she'll probably know." She made a restless movement with her hands. "I have a lot of things to attend to—meetings at school and my aerobics class. You have my cell-phone number if you need me."

Rather pointedly, Molly had turned her back on me. She didn't see Mom coming down the hall.

"Molly, honey." Mom gave Molly a hug. "See, I'm on my feet today."

"You should stay in bed until you're better." Molly returned the hug, giving Mom a critical once-over. "You look wobbly."

"I've been up and down a couple of times today." She looked at me standing in the archway. "Gracious, are you still here, Lizzie? What have you been up to?"

"Pottering around." I retrieved my bag from the kitchen. "Looks like you won't need my help anymore today."

"That's right," Molly said, pulling Conchita forward. "I brought you Conchita, Mom. She'll help you out and make dinner."

Conchita set the buckets down and clutched at the cross she wore around her neck. Her gaze was fixed on the front porch, visible through the still-open door. She said something, her voice a little shaky. I made out the word *"espíritu."*

"That's ridiculous," Molly said impatiently, glancing at her watch. "There's no such thing." She added a Spanish phrase.

Conchita shrank back. She picked up the buckets and went into the kitchen.

"Lizzie already did the bathroom." Mom looked dubious. "I don't think we need to trouble Conchita, Molly."

"She's paid for her trouble." Molly shrugged, but a slight frown stayed between her eyebrows. "Look, I've gotta run." She hesitated, glancing at Dad. "About that other matter—I'll check into it."

"What other matter?" Mom was instantly curious.

"Nothing to do with you, Mary." Dad reached for the remote and turned up the volume on the TV. Helplessly, Mom shrugged.

"Go put your feet up, read a magazine," Molly urged, giving Mom's thin shoulders a squeeze. "Here, I brought you a *People*." She pushed it into Mom's hands. "I'll walk you out, Liz."

I went meekly after her toward the door.

"Wait. Lizzie, I didn't thank you for your help." Mom came after us, shutting the front door against the TV's noise. "Will you—are you going to come back?"

"Do you want me to?" I looked at her, straight, but she couldn't meet my gaze.

"If you want to come. It seems your Dad doesn't mind."

It made me smile, such a backhanded invitation, but my eyes felt hot from unshed tears.

"I'll come over tomorrow."

"Well, okay. Molly, thanks for the magazine." Mom went back inside, shutting the door on those three ill-assorted people.

Molly started in before we were down the front steps. "Just what do you think you're doing anyway?"

"Hanging around, waiting for the police to finish their investigation. I thought I could help out, free you from the burden, but it looks like you've freed yourself."

Her laugh was as brittle as the rest of her. "Right. I'm free all right, kid."

Kid. She was nine years older than me, and had always been a complete mystery. I used to watch her get ready for dates, putting on lipstick that made her lips so pale they practically disappeared. She wielded a variety of brushes as skillfully as Dad used power tools—a special hairbrush to make her hair turn smoothly under, a tiny brush to outline her eyes. Standing intently before the mirror, she stroked eyeliner on in a shiny, seamless river that flowed along her lid just above the lashes, ending in an upward slash at the outer corner. She crimped her lashes, already mascaraed into a thick, dark curtain. When she sashayed into the living room, her skirt decorously knee-length, my dad would grunt approval, though the eyelashes earned her a narrow look. As soon as her date arrived and the door shut behind them, I would run into my room. My window was right beside the front porch. I could see her as she followed her boyfriend down the sidewalk, rolling her skirt up around her waist under her sweater, to shorten it a good three inches.

I had always regarded her as possessing some innate wisdom about how to be female. Beside her grace and assurance, I'd always felt awkward and lacking in charm.

"Do you wear miniskirts, now that they're in again?"

"What?" The question put her off balance. "Of course not—never again." She studied me as I leaned against the car. "At least, I have some interest in clothes. You never did, as I recall—just wore those jeans and work shirts constantly. Almost like a prison—"

"Yeah, a lot like a prison uniform."

She looked at the ground for a moment. "I never felt so humiliated in my life," she said quietly, "as I did when my baby sister went to jail. I can never forgive you for that."

"Man, all you people really know how to hold grudges." I studied those downcast eyes. Her makeup was much more subtle now, but she still wore a lot of it, still looked fashionable and with-it, the kind of mom kids don't mind being seen with. "I've been working on overcoming mine."

"Don't you understand?" That well-manicured hand shot out and gripped my arm with amazing force. "They blamed me. Mom—Dad—even some of my own friends were asking how I could let that happen. Like I was supposed to be in charge of your life still, as if I hadn't had you around my neck constantly from the moment you were born—"

"Come off it, Molly." Her grip was harder to shake off this time. "You wrote me off just like the rest of them when I married Tony. The one time I came to you for help after he beat me, you told me to go back to him, that marriage was forever—"

"So it is," she said fiercely. "You're not the only one who didn't get what she bargained for in marriage. You're just the one who dragged her family's name in the mud trying to get out of it. I would never do that, never."

"You're a Fahey now, not a Sullivan. It wasn't even your name."

Her hand dropped from my arm, and she sighed. "Denver isn't really such a big place. There's always someone who knows where you came from. I was slated to be PTA president that year, but after people started whispering that I was your sister, it evaporated. Now that I'm up for school board and this close to being elected—" her fingers measured an infinitesimal distance "—you do it again."

I couldn't help it. I started to laugh.

"Damn it, Liz!" Molly reached out to shake me again. "It's funny to you that I had to work so hard to get accepted without a college degree or the advantages you threw away!"

I backed away from that angry hand and controlled myself.

"Sorry. It's not really funny. You're right. I blew my college education on a guy who regularly hammered on me. I went to jail, spent years hiding from him. And all the time you were being stigmatized by the PTA. Pardon me, Molly. I was so out of line."

She folded her arms and gave me a cold, level look. "It all came out of your own bad decision. Take some responsibility, Liz. Stop blaming us for your problems. Everybody's got problems, especially when it comes to marriage. At least when I married Bill, I knew there would be a comfortable future for us, for any kids we would have. You were just in a hormone haze. That's no way to make a decision about a lifelong commitment."

"What do you know about marital problems?" I gestured back at the house. "Live-in help, strapping boys—Mom showed me a picture of your house. Very fancy."

"Bill and I worked hard for our success."

"So if you made such good choices, so much better than mine, what's the problem now?"

For once she looked unsure of herself. "None of your business."

Silence settled between us. I waited for her to climb into the chrome-laden sport utility vehicle behind my bus, which I assumed was her upwardmobile.

131

"Well, this is all beside the point. What I wanted to say was, if you drag Byron into your problems, I'll see you put away again." She said it casually, but I didn't doubt the sincerity.

I wondered what had happened that morning to rile Biff, and if his mother knew. Somehow, I doubted that. Molly would have been a lot more pointed if she knew that Biff believed I'd told the police he was involved in Tony's murder.

"Look, I barely met your son. As far as Dad's gun goes, I know nothing except that the police want that gun and Dad doesn't have it anymore." I was getting tired of explaining myself. "Obviously I couldn't have taken it, since I was only in the house for half an hour, with Amy or Mom the whole time, before Tony was tossed on the porch."

She winced. "Poor Tony."

The words were muttered, but I caught them. "Poor Tony? So you had a soft spot for him, did you? Is that why you wouldn't help me out?"

She flushed. "Not a soft spot, but he wasn't the monster you made him out to be. There are two sides to everything, Liz, and your behavior frustrated him so much."

I had heard similar sentiments from Maud. I didn't care any more for them when they came from my sister.

"So, had you been seeing him all along?"

"Certainly not," she said, affronted. "I wasn't 'seeing' him to begin with. I simply ran into him every so often. We had lunch a couple of times."

I remembered that when Molly lied, her earlobes turned red. They were glowing rosily now.

"Had you seen him lately? Do you know what he was doing to make a living?"

"Really, Liz." She backed away. "I don't have to answer these questions."

I followed her, until she was pressed against the shiny flank of her vehicle. "You've already made it clear that you'd have no hesitation about getting me jailed. Why should I feel differently about you? Let me tell you, Molly, I feel threatened. And I think the police would be interested to know that you were buddies with Tony."

"We weren't buddies." The words burst out. "I did use him, and we had lunch once in a while. That's all."

"Use him? How?"

"I mean, used his placement service." She took a tissue out of her wallet-on-a-string and dabbed at her eyes. "You're really upsetting me, Liz. It's true that Tony worked under the table to avoid taxes. A lot of people do that. There was nothing wrong with it."

"Wrong with what? What did he do?"

"He helped people hire domestic workers and such." She gestured toward the house. "He found my last three house-keepers, including Conchita. It's a good deal for her as well as me." Her voice was defensive. "I treat her well, and make an effort to teach her English, give her time off for ESL classes and everything. I've gotten all the materials together for her so she can work toward being a permanent resident."

"So Tony was dealing in wetbacks."

"Shh, Liz. That's such a derogatory term." She actually glanced around to check if anyone could hear me. "They really hate to be called that. Besides, she has a green card. I insisted on that."

"How did Tony get hold of her?"

"I don't know. He found people on a corner somewhere, I guess." She shrugged her indifference, but her face was uneasy. "This has nothing whatever to do with his death. How could it?"

"I don't know." I didn't follow her when she scuttled around to climb into her vehicle. But I did know that Officer Eva would find it very interesting.

21

I didn't want to go looking for Eva at the police station. I'd already decided O'Malley wasn't on my side, and now that I knew who probably had Dad's missing gun, I wanted even less to encounter him. Despite what I'd said to Molly, I had no desire to get Sullivans or Faheys in unnecessary trouble. But certainly, given the family solidarity Molly showed, I wasn't taking the rap for any hulking young nephew who came along.

I drove slowly past the police station, but I couldn't recognize Eva's cruiser from anyone else's. I decided to go back to Andy's and call from there, hoping to escape O'Malley somehow.

The way led past Amy's high school. Judging by the crowds of bizarrely dressed young people milling around, school was just letting out. I remembered how much battling had gone on over the first slackenings in the dress code during my high school days—what a big deal it was when girls were allowed to wear shorts or jeans, just as boys were. Now there seemed to be no limits on dress, other than not being naked. The kids showed an incredible range of tribal costumes.

Amy was in a cluster of people of hair color, as I had started terming them during the summer. She saw me, gave a big wave, and hustled over, dragging Kimberly with her.

"Hi, Aunt Liz. Are you picking me up?"

"If you want a ride."

"Can we give Kimberly a ride, too?" Her companion looked up through a fringe of green-tipped black spikes—and those were just her eyelashes.

"Sure. Hop in."

They hopped in, with Amy making much of Barker and introducing him to her friend. "What a cool dog," Kimberly enthused. "I totally feel that you, like, belong together."

Amy giggled. "I could bleach my hair and put some black spots on, to match him."

Kimberly gave this serious consideration. "Not bleach, Amy. It, like, totally wrecks your follicles. You can strip it instead, but I don't know." She picked up a lock of Amy's persimmon-colored hair. "Some damage there already."

"Right." Amy blew upward through her bangs, causing them, for a moment, to stand along her hairline like gaudy sentinels. "I'm thinking maybe I'll let it all grow out. I've kinda forgotten what color it was to start with."

"Give it a chance to heal," Kimberly agreed. "And Ronnie Layton might like it better, too."

I could swear Amy blushed, from the peek I stole in the rearview mirror while I negotiated the streets. "So what?" She was defiant. "Like, who cares what that pimp thinks?"

"Pimp?" I was so astonished that I forgot the first rule of being an acceptable grown-up—always pretend you hear nothing. "Someone at your school is a pimp?"

"Well, yeah," Kimberly said, giving me a puzzled look. "I mean, some of them are pimping all the time, you know?"

Amy reached forward and gave me a condescending pat. "Aunt Liz. Whatever that meant in the olden days, it just means a guy who sleeps around a lot and gets as many women as he can, and stuff." She turned to Kimberly. "It used to have some obscene thing to do with sex, probably," she confided. "That's how they react to that."

"Yeah, that's right." Kimberly nodded wisely. "Like hoes. Whores," she enunciated carefully. "That used to mean getting paid for sex, you know. Now it just means girls who sleep around a lot or act like they do."

"Not even that," Amy contradicted. "Some guys will call you that if you won't sleep with them."

"Right." Kimberly twisted in her seat. "My house is down there," she said, pointing to a street of houses much like Andy's. "I'd, like, ask you in, Amy, but I'm grounded. Math bomb," she added dolefully.

I pulled up where she told me, and she hopped out, after a final pat for Barker and belated thanks shouted toward me.

"She seems nice," I remarked, surprised at how inane it sounded. Rule Number Two for being an acceptable grown-up—never comment on the friends of your teen, at least not out loud. Simply agree with any assessment the teen offers. I was really blowing it big-time.

"Kimberly? She's always grounded." Amy coaxed Barker to the seat beside her—not a difficult task. "At least I get my homework turned in."

"The math bomb—is that heavy-duty homework?" I broke Rule Number Three—never ask questions.

Amy was in a tolerant mood. "It means you've gotten a warning notice and you're cruising for an F," she said. "They never give you an F unless you're a total screw-up, though."

I hoped I hadn't used up my quota of answers, because I had more questions. "Amy, about your cousin Biff. Do you see much of him?"

"Biff is scum," Amy said vehemently.

"You don't like him."

Amy appeared to get a grip. "Let's just say he sends the needle off the vomit meter." Her face was screwed into an expression of distaste. "He went to another school last year, but they kicked him out. So now he goes to my school. And he's even in my grade now, because of being held back a year."

"Is he stupid?"

She considered this. "Well, not really. He just acts like an asshole all the time. Aunt Molly wants to be on the school board, partly because she's always fighting with the teachers over Biff."

"What's the worst thing about him?" This question is much better at eliciting answers than the blander, what-kind-of-person-is-he type.

"He backed me into a corner at Aunt Molly's Labor Day cookout." Amy sniffed. "Not the first time, either. He's always trying to feel me up, going like this—" she made smacking noises with her lips "—and telling me we're kissing cousins. He stuck his hand right down my T-shirt!"

I love Amy dearly, but she brings out the reactionary in me. I had to bite my lip to keep from telling her that girls who wear low-cut, skimpy T-shirts are asking for negative attention from creeps like Biff. My brain says women should be free to wear whatever they want without suffering masculine harassment. But my gut wants to stand up and shout, "Beware, young ladies! The world is not a fair place, and it's run by men!"

I didn't do that. "So what happened? Did you tell your parents or Molly?"

"My mom says if I don't want him to do that, I shouldn't dress like I do." Amy's curled lip showed what she thought of that advice. "And Aunt Molly yelled at me because she's always afraid Biff will knock up some girl and have to pay her off." She sniffed. "As if I'd let his dick anywhere near me!"

"So what did you do?"

"I kneed him," she said calmly. "You know, Aunt Liz. You're the one who showed me how."

"Well . . . good. Guess that took care of it."

"He was in a lot of pain." Amy looked undecided. "I mean, it served him right, but I almost apologized. Then he said he would make me sorry, and I told him if he bothered me again I would spread it around that he tried to have sex but couldn't get it up, and that his weenie was really the size of a Vienna sausage."

I pulled up in front of Andy's house, fighting the impulse to burst into hysterical laughter.

"Besides, he stole Grampa's gun," Amy added, and the laughter congealed.

"Are you sure?"

"He stole Grampa's gun. I told Daddy, but he just brushed me off—don't think he even heard me." Amy's lower lip stuck out. "They never listen to me. Anyway, Biff's had the gun at school a couple of times. Once he was showing it around his group of moronic friends, and my friend Shayla told the principal, but he cut school that afternoon so they didn't find it when they searched his locker."

"Does he still have it?"

"Maybe." Her eyes grew round. "Aunt Liz—do you suppose—nah, even Biff wouldn't kill someone just because he thought his mom was banging him."

I sorted through that confused sentence. "Biff thought Molly was having an affair with Tony?"

Amy looked undecided. "He saw Aunt Molly with some guy in a bar one afternoon. In the assembly next day he was sitting behind me, and I heard him tell one of his so-called friends that if some dickhead was moving in on his mom, he'd make dog meat out of him. Maybe it was Tony—I don't know."

"Did anyone else hear him say that?"

"Yeah, about half the school is all. He's really loud." Amy looked at me. "Are you going to turn him in?"

"No." I hadn't known what I thought about it until the word was spoken. "After all, he's my nephew. And he's probably no more likely to have murdered Tony than I am."

"You didn't." Amy sounded positive. "I've planned your defense for you. We all have alibis—except Daddy, and he was just hanging around waiting for Grampa to get out of the VFW meeting." She breezed on past this little nugget before I could quite take it in. "Mom was cooking dinner, and I had so much homework I hardly lifted my nose from the computer until just before dinnertime. Gramma was sick in bed, and Grampa didn't have his gun anymore, anyway." She faltered a bit. "I don't know about Aunt Molly and Uncle Bill, but Uncle Dan's been in Montana with the oil rig crew for the past three weeks, and Aunt Dot went up there with their boys last week to spend a few days. So you see, we're all okay, except probably for Biff."

"What about his brothers—Brewster and—who's the other one?"

"Brendan." Amy dismissed him with a wave of the hand. "Brewster's at the Air Force Academy—that's in Colorado Springs, you know."

"I know." I blinked. "He must be pretty smart. I thought it was hard to get into that."

"Aunt Molly put pressure on some government guy Uncle Bill was working with, and got Brewster a recommendation." Amy shrugged. "He's not dumb—none of those guys are. And he'll grind some. He wants to be a Top Gun."

"I see."

"And Brendan's at UK in Lawrence, Kansas." Amy waved in a vaguely eastern direction. "Biff's the only one who says he doesn't want to go to college. He works construction with Daddy in the summers." Her lower lip stuck out. "Daddy thinks he's so cool because of that. As if any jerk couldn't form concrete."

So Amy was jealous of Biff. I would have to take her confidences with a grain of salt.

"We'd better go in," she said, opening the side door and jumping down, with Barker all around her legs. Then he began growling, and I saw Eva's cruiser pull up.

22

"WE'VE found a rental van. We think Tony Naylor was in it after his death," Eva said. She'd waited for Amy to go inside, which Amy reluctantly did. The kitchen curtain was pulled aside, and Amy's face joined Renee's in the window.

"How could you do that?" It sounded like searching for a needle in a haystack to me.

"It's a piece of luck for us. This big rental place lost their maintenance guy, the one who usually vacuumed and washed the cars. When we looked at all the places that rent white vans, there it was, on the back of the lot, still not cleaned." Her voice held great satisfaction. "Found traces of blood and hair in one of the movers' blankets, and the initial tissue typing makes a match with Naylor pretty certain. He was rolled in a blanket after he was killed, then driven to your place. Whoever dumped him is pretty strong."

I thought immediately of Biff, toting that concrete. "Well, guess that lets me out."

"You look strong." She eyed me consideringly. "And you would have had an accomplice, of course. Right now, all I want is for you to come and look at the vehicle, see if you can identify it."

I shrugged. "It was dark, and I just got a glimpse of it. But sure, I'll come with you. Let me tell my sister-in-law I'll be back." I raised my eyebrows. "If I will, that is."

Eva allowed herself a brief grin. "I'm not arresting you," she said. "You'll be back, unless something comes up."

Renee sniffed when I said I wouldn't be there for dinner.

I was trying to be an unobtrusive guest, but she didn't seem to appreciate my efforts.

"Are you taking that damned dog with you?" She pointed to the floor she'd been sweeping when I interrupted her. "He's leaving his hair everywhere."

"I can't take him, but Amy would probably sweep up for him if you asked her."

Renee sniffed again. "You're out of your mind. Amy never does anything I ask her."

I held my tongue, a difficult task, and went on out to Eva's cruiser. Silently, we drove to the police station. In the back parking lot, a white van was getting a real going-over by technicians armed with weird-looking little vacuum cleaners and other arcane equipment.

I stood behind the van. "Does it look familiar?" Officer Eva stood beside me, looking at me instead of the van.

"Sort of." I tried to remember the brief flash I'd seen when the van turned the corner, its taillights flickering. "The license number actually does look familiar. Those last three digits—I vaguely remember they had some relationship to each other in the glimpse I got."

"Seven-two-eight?" She raised her eyebrows.

"Twenty-eight is a multiple of seven."

"Oh, yeah." She didn't look convinced. "It's pretty vague."

"Sorry. If I'd been sure about anything, I would have told you at the time."

"Right." She didn't sound convinced, either.

One of the technicians shut off the vacuum cleaner and spotted Eva. "Hey, O'Malley was looking for you a little while ago. He's gone now—tore out in a big hurry."

Eva looked speculative. "Did he? Maybe he left a message."

I hung back when she headed for the building. Even if O'Malley was gone, I didn't like gratuitous sitting around in police stations.

"I can wait in your car."

"You come with me." She didn't grab my arm, but her gaze commanded me. "I might need you again."

Resigned, I trailed after her. No one paid any attention;

nobody came at me with handcuffs. I perched on a chair in front of Eva's desk and watched her go through her messages.

"Nothing here from O'Malley. I'll call and see if Phil's in—maybe he knows what it's about."

I wasn't paying much attention, but after a cheerful greeting, Eva stiffened, her eyes fixed on me. She lowered her voice, and I couldn't hear what she said, but I could see something big was happening. After a moment she slammed down the phone.

"Come on."

"Where are we going?" This time she dragged me out of the chair. I found I didn't want to leave it.

"Up in the mountains a little. Want you to see something."

We rushed out. I found myself in the front seat of the cruiser again.

"Is this a time for sightseeing?"

"We're not sightseeing." Officer Eva's face was grim. She turned on the flashing lights, and we sped through the streets, swerving around slower traffic. At a red light she touched her siren and we blasted through. "Not the kind you mean, anyway."

I sighed. "You're not going to tell me what's going on, are you?"

"Nope." She drove with cool competence, her face intent on the traffic, a swift shark cleaving schools of lesser fish. "But I want you to talk. Tell me everything you did today."

My boring day made a monotonous recital, since I left out anything to do with Amy, Molly, or Biff. She didn't slacken her pace while I talked; I held onto my seat and hoped we didn't get crosswise with any ambulances.

Eva turned onto Coal Creek Canyon Road and headed straight west to the mountains. She still hadn't spoken, and I wouldn't ask, but I was glad I'd told Renee not to expect me for dinner. Having run out of incidents, I'd been quiet for several minutes.

"Tell me something else," Eva said, keeping her eyes on the unfolding highway. "When did your ex-husband show up in California? Your pal Drake says he's your neighbor, and he hadn't seen any sign of Naylor. But you told Bald-ridge you'd touched base with him."

I cleared my throat. "It was before Drake and I became neighbors. And I just saw Tony once. Then he left."

"Without hurting you?" Her question was casual.

"What does that matter?" I wondered if Tony beating me up so recently could be used to make me look stronger as a suspect.

Eva shook her head. "So he did hurt you. And you didn't report it."

"He agreed to leave," I said feebly. "I wanted him gone, not detained for questioning. And chances are, he would have talked his way out of it and then come back to show me a thing or two. Besides, I knew he wouldn't bother me again."

"Sure," Eva said, her voice without inflection. She thought I'd been protecting Tony by not calling the cops on him. Really, I'd been protecting myself. But I had learned years ago that people don't admire you for adapting your-self to circumstances, trying to slide through the tough places as easily as you can. You are admired when you stand up and make a lot of noise, even if that makes you a better target.

We rode in silence for a while longer. The sun was in my eyes on its journey toward the peaks. The road plunged into valleys and climbed flanks of hills. I reached for the visor, and Eva glanced sharply at me as I pulled it down. All I could think about was that Drake knew, now, that my shameful past as a battered woman was not as far past as he'd thought. Would he, too, feel a kind of disgust for a woman who could let that happen to her again without call-ing the authorities—one of whom was him?

When the silence got too heavy—or maybe it was my thoughts—I spoke.

"So are we going to Boulder?" We were heading some-what south of Boulder, but there wasn't nearly enough traf-fic for a commute destination.

"No." She turned her attention back to the highway. Without the flashing lights, our progress was much more sedate, although she drove fast—too fast for that road, I thought.

"Are we meeting O'Malley somewhere?"

"Probably." She slipped the cruiser around a lumbering semi, leaving it in her wake.

"Are you going to tell me anything about it?"

"No." She thought for a minute. "Why did you think we're going to Boulder?"

"Where else does this road go?" I spoke patiently, and she answered with the same exaggerated diction.

"There are other places."

Vague memories stirred in my head, and I pressed my fingertips against my temples, as if that would cause my thoughts to coalesce sooner. "Tony used to visit someone in one of the little towns around here."

"Who?" Her voice sharpened.

"He didn't tell me, and I was too grateful to have him gone to ask." I didn't want to remember it—certainly not to tell Eva about it. But my memory was in a constantly churning state these days, and a lot of unpleasant stuff was boiling up.

On this particular occasion, a few months before our lives together ended, Tony had not wanted me to enjoy myself while he was off on his weekend of fun. I remembered sipping the glass of wine he had, with unaccustomed gallantry, poured for me. Next thing I knew, I was waking up on the bathroom floor, with a jar of peanut butter and a box of crackers beside me. The door was securely locked, from the outside. I tried to get the window open, but it was nailed shut. I yelled a bit. When no one in the other apartments responded, I threw the jar of peanut butter through the window.

Some kids playing outside had helped me down from the window. I had been hungover from whatever drug Tony had given me to knock me out. And, of course, the front door of the apartment was locked, too. Luckily, the landlord believed the story that my purse had been stolen, and brought over a spare key. I'd reglazed the window myself, and then on my landlord's advice, changed the door locks. I really wanted just to leave the apartment, but Tony always kept our checking account low, and the rent was paid through the end of the month. I'd had nowhere to go, thanks to my family's hostility, and no means when I got there.

The odd thing was, Tony had appeared to forget how he'd left me when he came back three days later. He showed up at dinnertime that Monday evening, wearing his work clothes, as if he'd left that morning as usual. He'd brought me flowers—his usual make-up offering, augmented by a box of candy for this special occasion. When I asked him where he'd been, he just laughed and sat down at the table, ready for dinner. I wouldn't have had any clue if I hadn't found the filling station receipt on the bedroom floor the next time I swept.

For the past few years, I'd blocked my life in Denver from my conscious mind so successfully that it had come to seem a hazy dream, a formless mental cloud that was never examined. Now I needed to bring it into focus, and sometimes it sprang into my mind with a dreadful, painful clarity. Despite what Eva might think, I was a different woman now, incapable of enduring such treatment. And Tony's appearance in Palo Alto had proven that. I had known he wouldn't come back, and he hadn't. Others could believe what they liked.

Eva was waiting for my reply. "It'll come to me, probably. The town had a funny name, the place he bought gas once. He never told me about it or why he went."

"Hygiene?"

For a moment I was offended. "I had a shower—"

"The town's name." Eva appeared to be struggling with a smile. "Hygiene is north of Denver, you know."

"Yeah, I know." I felt sheepish. "No, it was something else—Nederland." Pleased with my memory for leaping into the breach, I smiled. "You know, I saw something recently that reminded me of that. Let's see . . ."

"Something since you came back?" There was tension in Eva's voice again.

"Yes, just in the last day or two." I frowned, chasing the elusive thought. "In someone's house."

"Your friend Kyle's, perhaps? He's got a lot of nice stuff,

I noticed." There was resentful admiration in Eva's voice. "I wonder if he came by those artifacts legally."

"He works with archaeologists. Maybe they give him stuff." I felt another synaptic connection. "No, it was Maud's place. She had a watercolor of a quaint-looking little Main Street. I thought it might be Central City, but now I remember the name underneath was all one word. I couldn't read the word, but I'm pretty sure it started with an *N*. She must have been up there with him."

Officer Eva's shoulders relaxed a little. "So Maud knew about this place of Tony's."

"It wasn't Tony's place, I'm pretty sure." I shook my head. "Well, I'm not sure, actually. He could have acquired a vacation house or something in the past ten years. But if he had a house, why was he mooching off Kyle and Maud?"

"Not much work in Nederland, maybe." Eva made the suggestion. "He couldn't make a living there, and he could in Denver."

"It would surprise me, somehow, if Tony owned anything." I fell silent, and so did Eva.

The road went on. The sun dropped behind the mountains, in that abrupt way I'd forgotten, and dusk closed in. We passed a signpost that said Nederland was twelve miles away. The road got steeper, the darkening landscape more forbidding.

Eva reached for her radio receiver and spoke into it. I couldn't decipher the squawking that came out, but I saw her glance at her odometer and she said, "Within a couple of miles, then," More squawking. She glanced at me. "I'm bringing her."

The squawking got louder, and I thought I recognized O'Malley's voice. Eva said, "I thought she might help us out." She sounded defensive. "Be there soon."

I sat forward, knowing now that we were near something that would affect me—probably in a negative way. We drove for another couple of minutes, and then we rounded a curve and I could see the flashing lights in the distance. As we drew closer, Eva slowed. She parked behind another patrol car on the narrow shoulder. Just ahead in the deepening gloom, the road took a sharp bend. The guardrail there had obviously failed in its duty. It was twisted and broken away in one place. A knot of dark forms was gathered there, bathed in the eerie glow of the flashing lights. More lights flickered below the road.

"Come on," Eva said, springing out of the cruiser and wrenching the door open on my side. "Let's see what we've got here."

She marched me down the road toward the cluster of other people. Dread grew inside me. I knew I wouldn't want to see this; whatever it was, it would somehow be laid on my plate, which was already unpleasantly overfull.

One source of the flashing lights was an ambulance. Each vehicle we passed seemed to have a muttering radio inside it. One car looked like O'Malley's. My steps hesitated, but Eva dragged me along.

Three men stood at the break in the guardrail. The wind was cold and dank off the mountains; I shivered in my thin cotton sweater. The men were looking down the mountainside; Eva and I came closer to the edge and looked, too.

A car was poised amid the scree and boulders that cloaked the sides of the ravine, its nose pointed downward as if eager to finish its journey. After a moment, letting my eyes get used to the shifting patterns of gray shadows, I saw that it was held back from a free fall by a granite outcropping that dwindled away further down. White-jacketed figures toiled up the slope, back to the road. They carried a burden in a sling between them.

One of the men at the guardrail turned. It was O'Malley. He frowned impartially at Eva and me.

"I don't know what you think this will prove," he grumbled.

"Neither do I, but she was there when I heard about it, and she's already shed some light." Eva didn't look at me as she spoke; all her attention was focused on those laboring figures. "Says Naylor used to visit someone up here occasionally."

"Who?" O'Malley barked at me.

"I don't know. Maud Riegert, maybe." I was watching as the emergency medical technicians rose from the ravine, like Orpheus ascending. "He didn't tell me, and I didn't ask."

O'Malley shook his head, but his attention was also distracted. The EMTs handed up their burden to those waiting at the guardrail, then scrambled the rest of the way on their own. The phalanx of police and technicians gathered around the stretcher.

"Come on," Eva said, pulling me over. As we breached the circle, one of the EMTs pulled the body bag open.

Maud Riegert's face stared up sightlessly. Half of her face, anyway. The other half had been blown off.

23 _____

EVA stopped the cruiser in front of Andy's house and looked at me soberly. "You were lucky," she said.

I was unlucky, really, in seeing poor Maud Riegert with the left side of her head blown away. Unlucky, not just because of that, but because it wasn't the first violent death I'd seen. But lucky because O'Malley had come very, very close to arresting me. After we'd gotten back to the station, I had spent a long time alone in an interrogation room while he and Phil and Eva had huddled to discuss what to do.

In the end, Eva was allowed to bring me back to Andy's, as long as I knew I was on a short leash. The past twenty-four hours of my life, from last seeing Maud at her condo, to Eva's picking me up to check out the van, were scrutinized minutely. Evidently they could tell that Maud had probably been killed the previous evening. My message was still on her answering machine, and helped verify my story that I was just asking her questions to establish my own innocence, not to scare her.

At one point Eva had left, returning about forty minutes later with a statement from Amy verifying that I'd been with her that evening until long after dark. And a check of my odometer showed totals that made it impossible for me to have driven so far since the police had written down my mileage just after Tony's death. They would be checking the rental places, but people who rented vehicles in the evening and brought them back before morning would be pretty conspicuous, and when that didn't pan out I felt secure in proving yet another alibi.

"I know." I looked at Eva's sober face and didn't feel secure anymore. "Things don't look good, do they?"

"You've got motive," she said, and added over my protest, "or something that can be made to look just like it. Your ex-husband, the woman he was cheating on you with—both dead. You might have had opportunity. You even had access to weapons—your dad's gun, your brother's. We need to see those guns ASAP."

"Well, my dad's hasn't turned up."

Eva gave me a look. "Why hasn't he reported it?"

"Take it that he's reporting it now."

I didn't mention Biff. Judging from his temper tantrum that morning, the police were already talking to him. Let them connect him to my dad's gun on their own. Besides, Molly would have my liver and lights if she thought I'd finked on her son. Unless it was him or me, I wasn't going to throw my nephew to the mercy of the cops.

Eva sat for a moment. "So why didn't he just tell us it was gone, not that he couldn't find it?" She glanced at me. "He thought you took it, right? And used it."

Either me or Biff. "I'm not even sure where he kept it—he never told anyone, as far as I know. I guess if I'd known, I could have gone for it after talking to my mom, before I joined Amy in the kitchen. That assumes I knew Tony was going to drop by, of course."

"And if we assume Amy was in on it with you—"

"We assume nothing of the sort! The whole thing is ridiculous." I could see the pale shine of Eva's eyeballs turned my way. "If you think that, I don't know why you're letting me roam around in the world."

"I'm not." Her voice was hard. "Understand, Liz. I'm going to do my job. You may believe the two of us have gotten to be buddies because we're both women, but that won't stop me from arresting you if the evidence points your way. That won't stop me from using force against you if I decide you're a danger."

"I never thought differently." She was definitely preaching to the choir.

"So remember." She reached over and opened the passenger door. "O'Malley's giving you rope. Don't hang yourself."

I stood on the sidewalk, watching her lights disappear. Then a motorcycle rumbled to a stop and Kyle jumped off.

"Liz. Your dad told me you'd probably be over here."

I didn't respond to his outstretched hand. Knowing that the police are as close to you as fleas are to a dog is enough to make you hold back from everyone, for fear those fleas will start jumping.

"Hi, Kyle." A light came on in the kitchen; I could see it from the corner of my eye. The curtain would twitch any moment. I hated the fishbowl I was living in.

Kyle looked concerned. "Was that the police? Are they still bothering you?"

"Until they solve this, yes." I rubbed my hand over my eyes. "What's up with you?"

"I was worried about you." He pointed to a second helmet on the motorcycle's seat. "Wanna take a ride? I'll buy you an ice cream."

The thought of it brought goose bumps to my already chilled arms. "No, thanks." I was too tired to go anywhere or talk to anyone who might want to be entertained. "But thanks for asking."

He took one of my hands. "I'm sorry this whole scene is so miserable for you," he said earnestly. "But I'm glad to be in touch with you again." A shadow crossed his face. "I've been making arrangements for Tony's funeral, as soon as they release his body. Do you—would you consider being there?"

"I might be back in California by then." I hoped so, desperately. "No, I don't want to go, Kyle." I thought of Molly's coziness with my ex-husband. "But I'll pass it along if I see anyone who's interested."

"Like Maud." He frowned. "I left a message for her. Her answering machine says she's not available until Monday. I know she'd want to be there."

I shivered, thinking about Maud's missing face, but I didn't say anything to Kyle. Those fleas—those police officers—probably had their own ideas about letting people know of Maud's demise. "I'm freezing," I said instead.

"And my sister-in-law is waiting up for me." The truth of that was obvious to anyone who glanced at the kitchen window.

Kyle fumbled for a card. "Listen, in case you don't have my number." He pressed the card into my hand. "You need a friend, Liz. I'm worried about you."

"Thanks." I was touched by that and by the expression in his eyes behind the horn-rims. But his niceness was like a barrier between us. I saw the echo of Eva's disapproval in him, whether he judged me for it or not. His knowledge of how I'd let myself be abused in the past made it impossible for me to get close to him. I had learned the hard way to respect myself; how could anyone else who'd been there then respect me?

"Well," Kyle said with reluctance. "I'll be off then. Call me if you need me, okay? Promise?"

"Okay." I watched him drive away, with a mixture of regret and relief warring within me. It's convenient to have good reasons to avoid involvement with men. It prevents you from having to work at a relationship, risk the emotional, sometimes physical, damage that men and women cause each other.

Renee was waiting to pounce in the hall. "Who was that?" Subtlety wasn't her strong point.

"An old friend—Kyle Baldridge. He stopped by to tell me about Tony's funeral."

Renee wrinkled her nose. "Why would you care about that? The man was a creep."

I felt marginally warmed by this. Everyone else in my family seemed to be on Tony's side.

"You and I know that, but that's not how he seemed to others."

Renee moved into the kitchen for her omnipresent cup of coffee. I don't know how she slept. She pointed to a cup on the counter. "I made you some herb tea—that's what Amy said you like."

The offer was grudging, but I accepted it anyway. The peppermint smell was clean and sharp, and seemed to cut through the muddle in my head.

"Thanks." I took a sip and followed her lead, sitting at

the high counter between the kitchen and dining room. The house was quiet, the lights low. "Where is everyone?"

"Andy's at the union meeting, and Amy's got homework." The familiar hostile expression took up residence on Renee's face again. "She's having a very hard time settling, with you getting her all stirred up."

"I'm sorry." I had another calming sip of the tea. "I know it's a drag—for both of us. It'll be cleared up soon, and I'll be out of here."

Renee appeared to accept that. We were both silent for a moment.

"Will you tell Molly? About the funeral?" She spoke abruptly, her voice harsher than usual.

"Will she want to know?" I put my cup down.

"She might." Renee gave her usual contemptuous snort, this time, however, not directed at me. "She let him get around her—hiring those wetbacks of his!" I had no trouble deciphering the envy in her voice. If Renee had been able to afford an illegal immigrant to do her scut-work, she would no doubt have had one. But since she couldn't afford it, she was taking the high ground here. "I told her no good would come of it. I reminded her about why you'd tried to kill that bastard, but she has such a good opinion of herself. Too busy to do her own housework!" Once more, the snort. "What's she want to be going to college for at her age? And this school board stuff. Everyone knows she just wants to get elected so Biff can graduate, finally."

"He's not going to graduate?"

She shrugged. "Well, he's always in trouble. My friend who works in the school office said there was a rumor he had a gun at school, but nothing was proven. If he brings it again, they'll suspend him."

There was a rush and a scrabbling from the hallway, and Barker bounded into the kitchen, followed closely by Amy. "Aunt Liz! You're back. What did they want, anyway?"

Renee looked expectant, too, although she took time to admonish Amy for the chocolate she was eating. "Do you want to break out in pimples?"

"I'll wash my face." Amy offered the last bite of the

153

candy to the room at large, and finished it herself when there were no takers. "So, were they grilling you?"

"Not exactly. They think they found the van I saw the night Tony was killed. Wanted me to try and identify it."

"Could you?"

I shrugged. "I only got a glimpse of it."

"Well, what took so long?"

"Paperwork. Bureaucracy is slow."

Renee looked skeptical, but didn't press the issue. "Did you get any dinner?" She was certainly fixated on feeding people, even those she didn't particularly care for.

"We had enchiladas," Amy chimed in. "They were great—Mom makes wonderful enchiladas."

Renee, pleased, offered to heat one up for me, but I couldn't face it. "No, thanks. I'll just wash up and get out to my bus for the night."

Amy looked disappointed. "I wanted to show you something on my computer, Aunt Liz. It'll just take a few minutes."

"You need to get to bed," Renee said, putting her cup and mine into the dishwasher.

"I will, right after I show Aunt Liz."

I followed her down the hall, Barker prancing at my heels, and wondered if Renee's mellower mood would last.

"It's e-mail from Mr. Drake," Amy whispered when we got in her room. "I printed it for you." She handed me a sheet of paper and watched eagerly while I read it.

Drake had written,

Received more inquiries from local PD. Can't you stay out of trouble? Want me to come out and give you a hand? Please cooperate to fullest extent with local force or you'll put yourself at risk. What's this about Naylor visiting last Halloween? I didn't notice any extra vampires around. Seedlings look good. See that you're back soon to plant them. Love, Drake.

"See," Amy said, pointing. "He signed it, 'Love.' "

"Everyone does that." I felt an unfamiliar ache behind my eyes. Ordinarily, I'm not much of a crier.

"Aren't you going to answer?"

"Maybe later." I glanced over at her computer. "How do you send e-mail, anyway?"

She gave me a brief rundown of the procedure for going on-line, and showed me what Drake's message looked like on the screen. Then Renee stuck her head in the doorway, and I escaped to the bathroom for a quick washup, and then to my traveling bedroom with Barker. At first my gulping sobs disturbed him, but finally he settled down. Even after I let the backlog of tears out, I couldn't sleep. The night was too full of questions, and when I closed my eyes, my brain was too full of horrible pictures.

24 _____

I dreamed of stroking through the warm, embracing waters of Rinconada Pool. Weightless, I moved; effortless, I floated. In the dazzle of sun on water I saw a figure, waiting at the end of the lane. At first I thought it was Drake. Then, as I neared the end, it looked more like Andy or my father. I watched the aqua tiles that edged the pool come steadily closer, and I felt more and more agitated. Before I touched the tiles, I looked up, but the sun behind the figure's head made it impossible for me to see the features clearly. I knew, though, that it was Tony, my dead ex-husband. And I felt menaced—by him, by the water, by the very sunlight that glinted painfully into my sleeping brain.

I woke feeling heavy with dread, the sun shining into my eyes through a chink in my curtains, and Barker's insistent nose nudging my arm.

"Yeah, yeah." Groggily, I put on my shoes and took him out for his morning run. The sunshine should have been a welcome change from the gloom of the past few mornings, but it couldn't lighten my spirits. I felt disaster in the offing, and wondered if I'd be back in jail by nightfall.

Amy was waiting by the bus when I got back. "Don't you want to send an e-mail to Drake?" She, at least, was unoppressed by the formless worries that beset me. "And then would you give me a ride to school?" She gamboled ahead of me down the sidewalk, Barker leaping around her. "Daddy's already gone to work, and Mom says I can catch a bus."

"Can't you?" I paused in the door, hit by the wonderful smell of bacon. I rarely indulge in it, but that doesn't make its perfume any easier to pass up. "If that's what your mom wants, you should do it."

Renee, standing in the kitchen doorway, gave me a look of grudging approval. "I've got some more eggs and bacon, if you want them," she told me. "Get your stuff ready, Amy. If you have that room picked up by the time your aunt is through eating, and she wants the trouble, she can take you to school."

I felt honored by this great favor. The breakfast was outstanding; despite her sour moods, Renee was a great cook. I complimented her sincerely, and she unbent a little farther.

"I talked to Molly this morning." She shook her head as she refilled her coffee cup. I politely declined more hot water on my grocery-store tea bag—those aren't strong enough to take a second dunking and still provide any flavor, let alone the caffeine I need in the morning. It ill befits my poverty-stricken lifestyle to crave good tea, but there it is.

"Is she upset? She was pretty stirred up yesterday."

"She said to tell you that Conchita is going back to Mom and Dad's today, and that your Mom is better and won't need your help."

I smiled a little. "I'll stop in, nevertheless. That's why I'm here, after all."

Renee looked at me curiously. "That's really why you came—because your mom was sick?"

"Is there a better reason?" I savored the last bit of scrambled egg, fluffy but not dry, with little cubes of garlic jack cheese melting into it. How Andy kept out of the coronary care unit was a mystery to me. "It sounded like Mom was on her last legs, and I thought it was time we made up our differences."

"Well, I'm surprised." Renee added cream to her cup with a liberal hand, and left a lipstick smudge on the rim after she sipped. "Nobody in your family ever really gets over their grudges. Dan and Andy still barely speak after some investment they made went sour." She looked at her coffee for a moment, then looked at me, her expression rueful. "As for Molly and me, I guess it's partly my fault, but she really rubs me the wrong way. Always acting so above us—as if she was one bit better! Her with that fancy house, shopping at Lord and Taylor's instead of K mart—well, it sticks in my craw, let me tell you."

"I can imagine." And I could. My sister had always had a restless need for approval from her peers, to run with the popular crowd. "So she hung around with Tony, even though I was in jail?"

"No, not then." Renee didn't seem to find this question strange. "Three or four years ago she met him somewhere and told me he was really charming, not the monster you said he was. They met once in a while when she needed new household help. He got her those maids, you know."

"That's what she said." I still wondered why Tony had ended up importing illegal laborers, and whether this had been his sideline or his major income. I wanted to tell Eva about it, but that might lead her right to my sister, which wouldn't do much for my future relationship with my family.

"I told Andy about them." It took me a while to realize Renee was still dwelling on Molly's live-in help. "He said I didn't need help, since I didn't have a job or do anything. And we can't really afford it. Besides, he said, they're illegal, and after all that publicity about it, I had to admit he had a point." She glanced at me sideways. "I certainly don't want to get in trouble with the police."

"How does Molly avoid trouble? She's running for school board and all."

Renee shrugged. "I don't know, but Bill makes a lot of money, and she knows people on the city council."

I couldn't picture Molly paying anyone off so she could have a live-in maid. Illegal immigration is a given throughout California and the Southwest. It had been no secret when I was growing up that officials would turn a blind eye to undocumented workers for a consideration.

Amy came in. "I have to leave in ten minutes," she announced. "Didn't you want to do something on the computer, Aunt Liz?"

I rinsed my plate and put it in the dishwasher, along with my juice glass and cup. Renee looked almost approving, until her eye happened to fall on Barker, who was licking up a fallen morsel of egg. I smiled. "He's good at cleaning the floor, huh?"

Amy hustled me away before I could put my foot any farther into my mouth, and Barker followed us, innocent of guilt. The computer screen in Amy's room was crowded with a multitude of symbols. My elderly computer does only one thing, or at least I know how to do one thing on it, which is to print what I write on the loud daisy wheel printer that Bridget had donated when she and Emery got a laser printer.

Flicking the mouse around expertly, Amy sat back. "Now we're going on-line," she announced. "Then you can send Drake an answer. Do you know what you're going to say?"

I didn't. But when Amy finally yielded the chair to me, and I looked at the little message screen I was supposed to fill, I found some words.

Drake, thanks for your concern. Things will be fine, and at least I don't have to worry about Tony anymore. He wasn't very scary last Halloween. Don't bother coming out here; I'll be heading home soon. Make sure you don't let the seedlings dry out, or I won't give you any tomatoes next summer. Liz.

"How do I send it?"

"I'll show you." Amy pushed me aside, then coolly read my message before clicking on a couple of boxes on the screen which I believe the computer set call buttons, for some reason. "It's not very romantic."

"There's a reason for that." I watched her while she dispatched my e-mail and opened a different file, or folder, or whatever they're called. This one asked for the names of various stocks. She typed a series of incomprehensible letters and studied the graphs displayed on the screen.

"What's the reason?" Her printer started chugging away, and she gave it a dissatisfied glance. "Wish I had a laser printer like Biff's," she muttered. "No way does he deserve it."

"Drake and I aren't romantic." I watched her rip the paper from the printer. "Biff has a fancy computer?"

"Everything's fancy about him." She looked smug. "But he's flunking out just the same. Come on, Aunt Liz. I'll be late!"

She rushed down the hall, and Barker rushed after her, getting all worked up at the prospect of frenetic action. Renee stood in the kitchen doorway, uttering encouraging cries like, "Don't forget your homework!" and "Do you have lunch money?" This last caused Amy's hand to extend automatically toward her mother, who just as automatically dug into her pocket and slapped a five-dollar bill into the beseeching palm.

Urged on by Amy, I made my best speed through the streets, which luckily weren't too clogged with traffic. She sat in the front passenger seat, sorting through a bulging backpack.

"What you need is a laptop computer."

"Oh, yes!" She closed her eyes for a brief moment of ecstatic yearning. "I'd love one—and a cell phone. That way I could keep up with the markets no matter where I was."

"Maybe one of your stocks will pay off big-time."

"Maybe." For a moment she was the mature, fiscally responsible teen I'd lived with the past summer, instead of the giddy, often sullen girl who inhabited her parents' house. "I lost some bread in mutual funds, and the bottom fell out of the futures market. But I did get a couple of hot tips on technology stocks last summer, and those are starting to take off." She sighed. "I'm supposed to put my earnings into my college fund, though. Laptops cost too much."

"That sounds sensible." She shot me a look, but I kept my attention on the road. I knew from the eight weeks she'd stayed with me that editorial comments were unwelcome and possibly detrimental to future confidences.

We pulled up in front of the school, and Amy got her stuff together. Students were standing around outside in attitudes of extreme leisure. "We're early," Amy said, glancing at her watch. "I thought we were late."

"Your clock must be fast."

Amy shrugged and slid down from the passenger seat to

the sidewalk. "Thanks, Aunt Liz." Barker stuck his head out the window, whining eagerly, and she rubbed his ears. "Sorry, guy. They don't let dogs in school."

"They let you in, didn't they?" Biff stood beside the bus, his face wearing the same sneer I'd seen before. He stared rudely at the cleavage Amy's deeply-scooped T-shirt revealed. "Of course, you have your points."

"Not funny," Amy said coldly. She started to move away, but Biff crowded her against the bus. He looked from her to me, and his eyes were cold and angry.

"So the police bugged me twice yesterday. Twice!" He leaned over Amy. "You been tattling, Amy? You know what that gets you."

Barker didn't like his tone of voice. He started growling, his hackles rising, and Amy, who had been looking around cautiously, smiled a little.

"Watch out, big guy," she said to Biff, her sneer matching his. "Fang here will tear your balls off if I tell him to. And I didn't tattle on you. I don't know what you're talking about."

I hadn't noticed Eva pulling up behind me, so fixed was I on the scene Biff was creating, but she strolled up in full uniform, her hand gripping her nightstick. "Is there a problem here, Ms. Sullivan?"

Biff gave her the once-over, still insolent. "Yeah. Too many nosy bitches in my life."

Eva's smile curled her mouth, and it occurred to me that she was attractive, with her strong body and well-constructed face. She didn't appear intimidated by Biff.

"This is my charming nephew, Officer Gutierrez. Byron Fahey."

Eva looked him up and down, to the accompaniment of Barker's growling. A little crowd of students collected, their faces watchful. I wondered whose side they were on. Biff's side? He had the look of a popular guy, with his muscle shirt showing off a fine build, and the gold earring glinting in his ear. Amy's side, and by extension, mine? Or maybe just against the police, whichever side that was.

"So you're the one we've been hearing about." Eva settled herself firmly, hands on her hips, near her weapon and nightstick. "Several folks have let us know you've been bringing a gun to school. Do you have a license for a gun, Mr. Fahey?"

Biff didn't back down. The expression in his flat blue eyes gave me a cold chill. He seemed so big, exuded such a sense of menace. "I don't know what you're talking about."

"That's your story, is it?" Eva pulled out a little notebook and flipped it open. "You want to come to the station and give me a full report?"

"I got nothing to say to you." Deliberately he turned back to Amy.

"You want to charge him, Miss Sullivan? Liz?" Eva looked at us, and back at Biff. "He's bothering you?"

"This is private," Biff said, swinging back around. Red flooded his tanned face and neck. His fists clenched, and a couple of young men stepped a little closer. They, too, looked well built and pumped up.

Unmoved, Eva surveyed them. "You boys are spoiling for a fight, is that it? Come on. Take me on. I'm just a woman, right?" Biff seemed to be considering it, but the other boys looked at each other uncertainly.

"Of course," Eva went on, her voice conversational, "after I whip your butts, I'll arrest you. Book you for assaulting an officer. Down at the station, they don't like punks who try to beat up officers. You'll get the full treatment—strip and body cavity search. They're not always too gentle. Probably won't call your parents for a while, so you can get the full benefit of the holding cell. Probably set your bail high, too. So, you want to give it a shot? Or do you want to get on to class?"

The other boys melted back into the crowd, and the crowd began to melt away. Biff, sullen, turned also, but Eva's arm barred his way.

"I'm not through with you, Mr. Fahey." She smiled easily at him, her white teeth gleaming. "Think you'd better come with me."

"Why?" He flung himself back against the bus, crossing his arms over his chest to make his biceps bulge. "Because

I had a gun? Why don't you ask Miss Priss there about her gun?"

There was a moment of startled stillness. Amy was the first to break it. "My gun?" Her voice was a notch higher. "I don't have a gun!"

"You did last May." Satisfied with the sensation he'd created, Biff straightened. "Saw you myself, when they—" he jerked his head toward Eva "—were trading concert tickets for guns."

"Oh, yeah." Amy looked a little self-conscious. "Yeah, that's right." She grinned suddenly. "So it's obvious where the gun is, moron. I gave it to the cops."

Biff was slightly cast down from his failure to think that one through. "Well," he demanded, sticking his face toward her, "where did you get it? And how many more have you gotten since?"

"Where did you get yours, if it comes to that?" She stuck her face out, too. They looked like nothing so much as second graders having a playground confrontation. It would have been funny if they hadn't been arguing about who had the most firearms. And if Biff hadn't had such an ugly edge.

"Children." Eva's voice was calm. "Simmer down. Amy, where did you get the gun you traded?"

"It was Daddy's," Amy said, her eyes on the ground. "He still doesn't know I took it. I hated having it around the house, and he left it unlocked. Mom hated it, too. So when they said they were trading tickets for guns, no questions asked, I just took it and got the tickets."

"I see." Eva's mouth twitched, but she maintained her sober expression when she turned to Biff. "And where did you get yours?"

"I—uh—borrowed it."

Eva waited, and finally Biff added, reluctantly, "From my granddad. He—doesn't exactly know I did. And now it's gone from my room," he added with resentment. "Guess my mom or dad found it."

"So neither of you has a gun at this moment?"

The bell rang before they answered. Amy looked toward the building, where a few students were running toward the doors. "I don't, of course. I didn't have one before, really." She caught my eye. "I know it was bad, Aunt Liz, and I'll tell Daddy tonight, and I'll pay for a new one if that's what he wants, although I'm totally against guns, but I really have to get to class now."

Eva nodded. "Go ahead, but have your aunt bring you by the station this afternoon to sign a statement."

Amy scurried off, and Eva turned to Biff.

"I already signed a statement yesterday," he said sullenly.

"But you lied in that one. Said you had no access to firearms."

"Yeah, well, I'll change it. At lunchtime." He gave her a look of intense dislike. "So get off my back."

A man came hurrying up.

"I'm sorry you've been bothered, Officer," he said. "This young man is working on straightening out his problems. Why were the police called?" He gave Biff a severe look.

"I was just passing by, Mr. Hedges." Eva smiled brilliantly. "Just shooting the breeze. There's no problem. Right, Mr. Fahey?"

Biff stared at the ground, not answering. Mr. Hedges made an impatient noise. "You know, Byron, you are at risk of expulsion if you don't start cooperating. And you can tell your mother I said so!"

"It'll be fine, Mr. Hedges." Eva spoke soothingly to the man, turning him aside for a moment. Biff melted toward the buildings, and by the time Mr. Hedges looked around, he was vanishing inside the door.

The administrator sighed. "I appreciate your coming around sometimes, Eva. It's good for these kids to see police presence."

"Fun to check out my alma mater sometimes, too." Eva waved and climbed into her cruiser. I started up Babe, and Mr. Hedges trotted back to his school.

I wouldn't have had his job for anything. Facing down muscle-bound young men with the kind of chip on their shoulder that Biff carried seemed downright dangerous. And how did the students feel about it? High school was a place of seething hormones and raging disappointments in my day, but I never felt physically frightened of anyone.

And I had been frightened of Biff, for a moment. Looking at him brought to mind every news story about disaffected, amoral youth I'd read in the past few years.

Barker hopped into the passenger seat, and I was glad he was the only adolescent I was responsible for.

25 _____

I wondered if I was being followed. How else had Eva known where I was?

I stopped at the King Sooper to pick up some groceries. Walking from the parking lot, I tried to get a good look at the cars that might have followed me. Inside the market, I moved slowly past the fruits and vegetables, gathering nectarines and grapes. I got a pound of the coffee Renee used, and some decent tea bags. All the turmoil was making me forget that I should be a good guest and contribute to the household. Renee and Andy didn't have to worry about their food bill like I did, but if I'd thought it was rude of Renee to visit me and my sparse refrigerator without helping out, then I should practice what I preached. Cruising up and down the aisle in a leisurely way, I kept tabs on anyone who paused nearby while I read the labels on everything.

By the time I went to the check stand, I had some little cans of tuna and some dried soups in cups—ready to take to the road the minute I could. Naturally, the same people who'd been shopping in the store were also in the checkout line. It turns out that in grocery stores, someone generally is following you.

The checker was a lean, hollow-eyed fellow with darkly nicotine-stained fingers and a chesty cough. The way his hair receded reminded me of Leonard Tobin. I wondered if Leonard had heard about Maud's death yet. On an impulse, after I'd put my groceries away, I drove south along Broadway, taking a roundabout route to Leonard's house. I had a fancy to see how he would react to Maud's death.

Nobody screeched through yellow lights to stay near me.

Nobody showed any interest in me at all. It was almost insulting.

Leonard's house looked just the same. It had occurred to me that Eva might be there, or even O'Malley, motivated by the same questions that bothered me. But the driveway was empty, although I could see a car in the garage when I stood on tiptoe to look through the windows.

I rang the bell and heard the same hollow echo. After the second ring, footsteps dragged down the hall. "Who's there?" Leonard sounded cautious.

"Liz Sullivan." I smiled my best when he opened the door a slit. "I wanted to talk to you for a second, Mr. Tobin."

"Yes?" His eyes were bleary; the only sign that he'd done anything but drink since two days before was the clean shirt and tie he had on. Evidently he dressed for success even in the midst of failure.

"Uh—has Eva been here? Officer Gutierrez?"

He squinted at me. "Yeah. She came along day before yesterday, not long after you. She was a little steamed when I told her you were bugging me."

"She hasn't been here today?"

"No one has. Except you, and I don't particularly want you here." He started to close the door. I had a hasty debate with myself.

Just before the door closed, I said, "So you didn't know Maud was dead?"

He froze for an instant. "Maud?" His face was expressionless—so much for making a discovery there. "You mean—my Maud? We spoke of her yesterday."

"Yes." The door swung a little farther open, and then I saw the shock in his eyes, the increased slackness in his jaw. "I thought you might have heard already. I'm sorry."

"Maud." His eyes focused again, on me. "She wouldn't even speak to me afterwards, you know. Pretended it had never happened. If I hadn't had pictures, I would have doubted my own memory."

"Pictures?" I followed him into the house, shutting the door behind me. He didn't seem to notice, just moved unsteadily down the hall to that bare living room. A fresh bottle of Jack Daniels adorned the table.

"Of her—enjoying herself, so to speak." His face turned a little pinker while he filled his glass. "Photography's my hobby, you know." He nodded toward the framed landscapes on the wall. "I offered once as a gag to take some boudoir shots of her, and she took me up on it." He gulped some whiskey. "It led to—it was—very exciting. I couldn't stop thinking about her." He squeezed his eyes shut. "She acted like it never happened. Said—"

Head bent over his glass, he lapsed into silence. After a moment I cleared my throat.

"So she's dead?" His head came back up, his hand tightened on the glass. "She deserved it, that bitch." His voice was rough, but tears glistened on his face. "What happened?"

"Her car ran off the road."

"Accident?" He gazed into space, not looking at me or anything. "She drove that Beamer like the devil was after her."

"In this case, he was." I stood directly in front of him, trying to look into his eyes. "She was shot first."

His immediate response was fear. "She—you—did you—"

"It wasn't me." He scrambled away from me so fast his chair almost tipped over. "I'm still trying to find out who could be doing these things, especially since that person wants me to take the blame."

"I don't have anything," Leonard said in a high gabble. "It's all gone. You can see for yourself. Don't bother me anymore. Don't hurt me."

"I'm not going to." Sweat glistened on his face, and his eyes darted around the room. I began to worry that he'd find a weapon and kill me in needless self-defense. "Look, calm down." I sat in the other chair, moving it farther from him. "I just want to know if you knew about Tony bringing in illegal aliens."

That got his attention. "How did you find that out? Did she tell you?"

"No. I just heard some stuff." I leaned forward. "Evidently you knew. And Maud knew?"

Leonard didn't speak for a while. He sipped his whiskey, his fingers tight around the glass, as if he was afraid I would try to take it away.

"He called me," he said suddenly. "Just after I got the ax—after he got me fired! Had the gall to say he was sorry, and offer me a new job—temporary, he said. Help out some people he knew. He didn't say what it was, and I was too depressed to care. Once I got down there—"

"Down where?"

"In New Mexico, somewhere." He gestured south. "I've forgotten where."

I doubted that, but let it pass. "So you were a coyote, too."

He looked stung. "No. When I knew—when I understood—I said I wouldn't, and I left—rented myself a car and drove back. He—Tony said they'd be around to get their deposit back. I didn't know what that meant, but then a few days later my truck was stolen, and someone called to say I'd better not report it." He licked his lips. "I was scared," he admitted. "But nothing else happened, so I forgot about it. Tried to, anyway."

He fell silent again, and I thought he might have reached the end of his communicative mood. I wished I'd had Amy's tape recorder this time. I prompted, "Was that the end of your association with him?"

He darted a glance at me. "Damned if I know why I'm telling you this," he mumbled. "But what does it matter, anyway? What does anything matter?" He tossed off the rest of his whiskey and poured another generous shot into the glass. "Want some?" Unsteadily, he offered the bottle to me.

"No, thanks." I took it from him and set it on the floor beside my chair. "It matters to me, Mr. Tobin. I didn't know about this stuff or have anything to do with Tony's death, but the police have put me at the top of their suspect list. I just want to find out the truth."

"So you say." He swirled the liquid moodily in his glass. "Can't trust you. Can't trust anybody."

169

"Tony was untrustworthy." I kept my voice steady, not insistent. "Did he call again recently, try to blackmail you again?"

"How did you know?" Leonard took another sip, and answered himself in a mincing falsetto. " 'You have just told me, Mr. Tobin.' " He giggled a little. "I watch *Sherlock Holmes*, you know."

"What did Tony say?"

Sighing, Leonard set down the glass and appeared momentarily more sober. "He said he would tell the authorities I was involved in a smuggling ring if I didn't give him money. And you know what I told that bastard?" He leaned toward me, smiling, "I told him, go ahead. Do your worst, Tony old boy. Nothing left. Nothing left for you to get your fangs into. I told him, 'Damn you to hell, Tony Naylor. Even if I have to send you there myself.' "

He raised his glass triumphantly and drained it. His eyes were glazed, and I wasn't surprised to see him slump over in his chair. His pulse was strong when I felt it. I wiped my fingerprints off the liquor bottle, just in case, and set it beside him on the floor. Then I left.

Driving back to Mom and Dad's, I found myself deeply sorry for Leonard Tobin, though he was a repulsive little guy in many ways. Tony had really ruined his life. In fact, I felt lucky myself—I had had nothing Tony wanted in the end. I hadn't even had fear, and that was what he'd really wanted from me.

At my folks' house, I knocked briefly and let myself in. Dad was sitting in his chair, pulled up close to the TV, which he watched intently. Some kind of sport was on the screen, with an announcer braying excitedly. He barely responded to my hello.

I looked in the kitchen, which gleamed spotlessly. The oven door was open, half-swallowing a slender form. For a moment I worried that Mom had felt impelled to rise from her sickbed and scrub; then the woman emerged from the oven, and I saw she was Conchita, Molly's live-in help.

She gave me a scared look. With a murmur in Spanish, she turned back to her work, sweeping the blackened bits out of the oven and giving it a final polish. Industriously, she tidied the area around the stove, then rose and tried to slip past me.

I put out one hand to stop her. *"Dónde está mi madre?"* That was about the extent of my Spanish, learned on the side during high school and rusty with disuse.

She murmured something I didn't understand, and I shrugged and said, *"No entiendo."*

That made her giggle. "You speak well," she said softly, ducking her head.

"So do you. Is Molly teaching you?"

A guarded look came over her face. *"La señora es muy amable.* She me speaks."

I let that pass. "Sit down here, Conchita." I pointed to the chairs at the table, and after a moment she sat on the edge of one, pulling it out from the table so it didn't look like she was getting too comfortable.

I let the silence stretch out for a moment, then asked abruptly, "Do you remember the man who brought you here?"

Immediately all the shutters came down over her face. Now she murmured, *"No entiendo."*

"Was he dark, with springy hair?" I gestured with my hands, trying to sketch the way Tony's hair grew, and a sudden recollection pierced me. The man who drove a white van on Highway 70, as I approached Denver. I had thought myself paranoid because he looked like Tony. Now I wondered if that had been Tony, if he'd even then been plying his trade. "How long ago did you come here?"

Still she said nothing, her eyes cast down, hands clenched together in her lap.

"Look, Conchita," I said, leaning forward. "I'm not from Immigration. *No soy La Migra."*

"No?" She looked at me assessingly, and then said in painstaking English, "Why you ask so?"

"That man—" I re-sketched the springy hair, and this time she nodded, "was once my husband. He was—very cruel." I searched my memory for the right Spanish to describe this, and couldn't. "Now he's dead."

She nodded vigorously. *"Sí. El espíritu*—still it lingers. Not resting." She glanced through the archway toward the front door.

"He wasn't killed here." I tried to reassure her. "Just dumped off after someone killed him."

"No fué aqui?" She looked relieved and broke into voluble speech, none of which I understood. When I shrugged, pantomiming bewilderment, she smiled, and I remembered again that she was the same age as those thronging students who appeared to put no value on school at all. I wondered if they'd rather scrub ovens than go to government class.

Speaking more slowly, she began again. *"Señor Jefe—*he tell us to call him so. He come to drive at end. We are so tired." She laid her cheek on her hands, closing her eyes to indicate how tired they were. "But he drive fast and slow, laughing loud, *muy loco.* Once he take Maria out, and she come back crying." Conchita looked fierce at this. "When we get here, we hate him much, but what we do? *La Migra* take us away if we complain." She twisted her hands together. *"Mi familia*—I send money."

"How long ago?" She wrinkled her forehead over this. "How many days—*cuántos días*—since you arrived?"

"Días?" She thought. *"Ocho? Nueve?"* She shrugged.

So if it were Tony I'd seen on the highway, he had been making another trip. I didn't know what the frequency of his haulings was, or whether he was his own boss or worked for someone else. And when I tried to ask Conchita, I got quickly out of my depth. She heard my dad stirring in the living room and jumped to her feet.

"I work now. Bye-bye."

Dad came in and went to the refrigerator. "Guess nobody in this house is going to eat lunch anymore," he grumbled, looking at me out of the corner of his eye.

"I'll fix you something, Dad. What do you want?"

"Anything," he said expansively. "But none of that sloppy cheese."

I heated soup out of a can, and made a thick and meaty sandwich, with plenty of Miracle Whip—no effete mayo for him. I found some sandwich cookies and cut carrot sticks for him to complain about, but eat anyway. It was pretty much what he'd taken in his lunch box for thirty years, and he wasn't a man who liked changes.

I added some fruit to his little stack of carrot sticks. He

came to the table, sat down, grunted at the grapes, and tucked in. I went looking for my mother, passing Conchita, who was polishing the window sills in the living room. At least, the house would be clean after she'd spent a couple of days there.

Mom was in her room, sitting up in bed with a book open on her lap, her head down on her chest while she dozed. She woke up when I touched her shoulder.

"Mercy. Sleeping all day—don't know what I'm coming to."

"There's some lunch in the kitchen, Mom. Or should I bring yours in here?"

"Oh, no. I can get up. I should be doing something, not letting that girl of Molly's take care of everything." I gave her my arm, and we shuffled down the hall. "She scrubbed the kitchen floor on her hands and knees today," Mom said as we passed through the living room, her tone reverent. "*Buenos días,* Conchita."

The girl looked around with a smile. "*Buenas tardes, señora.*"

"She means I'm tardy, I suppose." Mom shook her head. "Can't seem to get around anymore, and that's a fact."

"Takes awhile to get over these illnesses." I made her comfortable in the kitchen, where my dad acknowledged her presence with a pat on her hand between slurps of his soup. I got her a bowl, too, and half a sandwich, and some grapes, and sat down with them at the table. Every time I did this, it felt strange. An awkward silence fell over the room, broken only by Dad's insistent slurping.

"Really, Fergus," Mom began.

"Just cooling my soup," Dad said. This exchange, well-worn by much use, brought me close to tears for some reason.

"So, Molly brought my gun back this morning. Said young Biff 'borrowed' it," Dad said into the silence.

Mom gasped, her hand going to her heart. "Biff—took your gun?"

"I couldn't find it the other day—told Lizzie about it. Anyway, seems young Biff wanted to look like a big shot

173

or something, so he snuck off with it." Dad fell silent, coping with a big bite of sandwich.

"Whatever would he want to do that for?" Mom looked worried. "Poor boy. It must have been a shock for Molly."

Dad laughed. "Biff needs a good thrashing," he said, pushing his plate away. "Boy's spoiled rotten. Gets anything he wants out of Molly—she's got no notion how to manage a young fellow like that."

Mom stared at him. "And I suppose you know so much about it? I seem to recall you having awful fights with your sons."

Dad actually winked at me. "I learned something from that, woman. Shoulda made them boys go to work sooner. You notice a paycheck settled them right down."

"If you can call it settled." She sniffed. "Seems to me they were out drinking and fighting five nights out of six."

Dad shrugged. "So? That's not what hurts a boy. What hurts a boy is idleness."

I could tell they were settled in for a nice long bicker. The afternoon was wearing on; I was supposed to take Amy over to the police station, and I hoped I could do that without Renee ever finding out, or my life wouldn't be worth a plugged nickel.

"Well, is there anything I can get you—any errands to run?"

That gave Mom's thoughts a different direction. After a little thought, she produced a couple of items she wanted at the drugstore—a new hot water bottle and some eyewash. Dad disdained my offer, but she recalled that he was out of denture cream. I promised to bring them the items before bedtime, and left them comfortably arguing while Conchita attacked the dusty shelves of the linen closet.

26

I did my errands at the drugstore, and was waiting for Amy when she got out of school. She didn't talk much on the way to the police station. I hated having to take her there, hated having her involved in this. Not nearly as much as Renee would, though. I asked Amy what she'd tell her mom about this excursion.

"I won't." She shot me a look, half-defiant, half-pleading. "It's for her own good. She'd just get all bent and start raving. The less she knows, the happier she'll be."

It had the ring of a philosophy. I wondered if Renee had applied it to Amy—I think most parents do. And probably most kids turn around and use it against their parents.

We sat in the holding area of the station for a while, waiting for Eva to see us. Then we sat in front of a desk while she churned out forms and statements about our various activities. I didn't like having to sign statements about Biff, but he looked like the kind of guy who can take care of himself. It made me twitchy to sit there with cops all around. I thought I'd gotten used to being around the police—after all, one of them lives right in front of me. But it was different when they were sizing you up for a possible jail cell.

"That's about it," Eva said finally. "I just have to get some information from O'Malley. You two wait here for a minute."

She bustled off down the hall. Amy, sighing, got a big tome on U.S. history out of her backpack and applied herself to it. I shifted around in my chair for a few minutes, trying to sort out my chaotic thoughts.

"Oh," I said, jumping up. Amy blinked at me. "I just remembered that I never asked Eva who rented that van they found."

"She said to stay here."

"I know where O'Malley's office is." I patted Amy's shoulder. "You work on your homework. I'll be right back."

I strode down the hallway, looking purposeful so no one would stop me—and no one did. It had occurred to me a couple of times that the police must know who rented the van, and I had a good chance of finding out if I could take them off base. I wanted to ask before I forgot again.

O'Malley's door was ajar, and Eva's voice came through it, passionate and loud. I didn't mean to eavesdrop, but I heard my own name—who can resist that?

"You told me to be on Liz, and I've been on her. I don't think she had anything to do with the killings. She didn't really have time, for one thing, and if she's got the money to rent that van, I'm Ross Perot."

Laughter from Phil's side of the room. O'Malley's voice came through, cool and clear.

"I'm telling you, Gutierrez, lay off. You're out of this investigation, as of now."

"Why?" There was frustration in Eva's voice. "I know we're close to cracking it. I know we're going to nail the perp. Why do I have to quit? So you can get the glory?"

O'Malley's voice sounded tired. "These orders don't come from me—they come from higher up. And that's all I have to tell you. But I will say that you keep on the way you're going and you'll get a rep as not being a team player. You gotta learn, honey. Poke your nose too far into some internal affairs around here, and your nose ends up shorter."

There was silence for a moment. In that silence, I tiptoed away from the door. It sure sounded like O'Malley didn't want me cleared. Feeling sick, I crept back the way I'd come, wondering how long before he arrested me.

I sat back down; Amy was deep in her book and didn't even notice me. I murmured, "Just went for a drink of water. I couldn't find the office after all."

"She'll be back soon," Amy said absently. "She'd better.

If I don't get home, Mom will be tearing up the roads looking for me."

Eva stomped in a moment later, her eyebrows etched in a frown. "Sorry to keep you," she said gruffly. "O'Malley doesn't seem to know the answers to my questions."

"Aunt Liz wants to know who rented that van," Amy piped up helpfully.

Eva looked at me, her hands gripping the file she held. "I can't say," she said finally. "I have to go make copies of your statements." She put the file on the desk with a certain emphasis, took the papers she needed, and went off again.

I sat on the edge of the desk, trying to look casual, then started leafing through the file. Amy regarded me with a troubled frown, but I paid no attention. A bewildering variety of paper was contained between those stiff leaves. I went through it, looking for the information on Tony that had interested O'Malley that first night after his death. I didn't find that, but I did run across the van rental agreement. It had been booked by phone, paid for with a credit card. A copy of a driver's license was stapled to the form. Though the name—Carlos Amador—was strange to me, Tony's picture was on the license.

So he had rented the van that had carried his dead body. And he had an alias to use in his coyote business.

Amy hissed at me, and I clapped the leaves of the file folder together and slid off the desktop just as Eva came into the area. She gave me a glance of mingled suspicion and complicity. I thought she might have been offering me information to keep me going on the case, since her hands were tied. I only hoped that if I did manage somehow to stumble on the truth, I would be believed by the higher-ups. O'Malley had already written me down in his scenario as the sacrificial goat.

Eva dismissed us brusquely, and Amy, her face troubled, raced for the bus, looking over her shoulder.

I had to walk fast to keep up with her. "Do you think they're going to come after us?"

"Aunt Liz, you read her confidential file!" Amy jumped into the bus, not even greeting Barker. "She'll probably figure it out—after all, she is a detective. Then she'll arrest you for meddling or whatever it is they do."

"Relax, Amy." I took my own advice and loosened my death-grip on the steering wheel. "She meant me to look at it. She wanted to give me answers but it's against the rules or something."

"Really?" Amy considered this. "She wanted you to look at the file, and that's why she left?"

"Well, she really did have to make those copies, probably. Seems like they spend a good part of every day in any office making copies. But yeah, I think she wanted me to know."

I wished now that I'd told Eva how Carlos Amador probably linked up with Tony's self-employment as a coyote. It opened up another whole area of inquiry, one she might not find out about anytime soon.

We pulled up in front of Renee's house. Molly's shiny sport utility vehicle glittered at the curb; I parked behind it with a sinking heart. She was there to give me hell about Biff, I knew.

Renee and Molly were sitting at the kitchen table. Renee wore her defensive look, but I was coming to realize that her prickly behavior stemmed more from feelings of inadequacy than from outright hostility. And Molly would be capable of making anyone feel inadequate. Today she was Mrs. Fast-Track, in a linen jacket and pants, with a scarlet silk top making the most of her coloring. The heavy chain around her neck and the big hoops in her ears would have to be gold.

She greeted Amy effusively, and Amy was charming back to her—and for once nice to her mom, as well. I could see that Amy admired Molly's elegance, but she had a clear-eyed way of assessing those around her, and though her parents didn't seem to rate with her, she knew their value.

"I have to finish my homework," she announced, when Renee asked who would like something to drink. "I'll just take a Coke in my room, if you don't mind, Mom."

Renee handed it over, forgetting for once to warn Amy against all the dangers of soft drinks in the bedroom—ants, spills on clothing, ruined upholstery and computer keyboards—that I had heard her mention several times in the past few days. Amy thanked her for that with a hug, and withdrew.

Molly turned to me as soon as her niece was out of earshot. "I'm surprised at you, having the gall to drive the child around after the scene you staged this morning."

"Were you there?" I raised my eyebrows. "I didn't see you. If you had been there, you would have known who staged the scene."

"I know what my son told me." Molly's cheeks warmed to match her shirt. "You as much as accused him of killing Tony! You brought that policewoman into it. You got him in even more trouble."

"He did that without my help." I took the cup of tea Renee handed me, noticing with appreciation that she'd used the new tea bags I'd given her. "Thanks, Renee. I'm sorry to have to break it to you, Molly, but your boy Biff must act differently around you than he does around the rest of the world. I found him rude, arrogant, self-centered, and threatening."

Renee looked at me with something close to approval, but prudently didn't say anything. It would have been hard, anyway, with Molly sputtering. Renee and I looked at her, and after a few minutes she stopped hollering and burst into tears.

Renee handed her a box of tissues. "Sorry, honey," she said, not sounding sorry at all. "But it is true. Amy's mentioned to me several times that Biff tries to corner her at family parties, and it's not for any cousinly stuff either."

"Well," Molly flashed, "if Amy will wear those tight shirts with her endowments, she has to expect that kind of attention from men."

"Not from her cousin, she doesn't." Renee dug in her heels, glaring right back at Molly. "It's sexual harassment at the very least, that's what it is. I haven't said anything to Andy, but if it goes on, I will. And he might just make sure that boy of yours doesn't have the equipment to hassle pretty girls again."

How long they would have faced off I don't know. I cleared my throat, and both of them rounded on me.

"Actually," I said, trying to be mild, but consumed with a wild desire to laugh, "Biff did have Dad's gun at the time of Tony's murder. And he had mixed it up with Tony at Dad's house that day. I also heard he was making other threats against Tony."

I directed a questioning gaze at Molly, and her eyes dropped. "He had some silly idea—at one time, he thought—"

"He thought you and Tony were carrying on. Other people thought that, too."

"You told that policewoman? You—"

I held up one hand. "I haven't so much as mentioned your name or that of anyone in my family. The police aren't stupid—they're checking things out, talking to everyone who knew Tony." At least I hoped they were. "It was only a matter of time before they came across you."

Molly looked unconvinced. "I advise you to tell Officer Gutierrez all about it," I added. "The more information she has, the more likely they are to find the person who killed Tony. Unless you don't want that to happen?"

"Don't be ridiculous," she snapped. "I have nothing to be afraid of. I'm confident my son couldn't possibly kill anyone."

"That's good," Renee announced, again at her favorite post, the kitchen window. "Because she's here. Your policewoman, Liz."

Sure enough, there was the patrol car outside. Eva was still sitting in the driver's seat. I went out and stood in the street, next to her door.

She didn't give me her usual smile. I cleared my throat. "Somehow, I got the idea you were washing your hands of me."

"Not exactly." She stared straight ahead, through the windshield. Car doors slammed as people came home from work and went inside. "I'm watching you. That way if anything happens, I'll know if you were the one doing it or not."

"Well, while you're watching me, come inside. I think my sister has something to tell you."

"Your sister?" Surprised, she got out of the patrol car. "The mom of that kid this morning—what was his name?"

"His name is Byron. That's why he's called Biff by everyone. My sister, Molly, knew Tony. In kind of a different capacity than I did." I pushed open the front door. "But I'll let her tell you about it herself."

I wasn't sure Molly would talk, but Eva knew how to get people to confide in her. Soon she was sitting at the table with Renee and Molly, commiserating about raising teenagers—although I couldn't believe she was old enough to have one herself. By gentle degrees, Molly was led to unburden herself of her connection with Tony's illicit employment agency.

Eva extracted everything she could, including information about Conchita, whom she wanted to interview that evening. Molly, glancing around, realized how late it was.

"Heavens," she said, collecting her smart handbag. "Bill will be home by now, and no dinner on the table, since Conchita is cooking for Mom and Dad. I'll have to get takeout. You're welcome to join us," she told Eva.

"No, thanks." Eva nodded politely. "I'll stop by your parents' to interview her. And it would be better if you didn't let her know beforehand. Some of the illegals get pretty antsy when it comes to the police. I value her testimony, and I don't see any reason why the INS needs to know anything about it."

Molly left, and Renee, also looking at the clock, wondered aloud where Andy was, and if her roast was done. Thus hinted, Eva and I took ourselves out.

I stood on the front porch with Eva, who was frowning down at her notebook. "Does that help you any? It shouldn't be too hard to find out more about what Tony was doing, now that you know he was a coyote." I remembered the copied driver's license. "That explains why he had another identity established."

Eva glanced at me. "So you took advantage of your moment, did you?" She was almost smiling, but a moment later her somber mood returned. "I don't like this, Liz. It smells dangerous for you."

"For me?" I stared at her. "I thought it would let me out entirely. A whole different line of questioning, one I couldn't be involved in. I wasn't here—didn't know anything about what Tony was up to."

"Nevertheless," she insisted. "Traffic in illegals is connected with pretty unsavory stuff around here. I'm going to go on investigating, although," she added under her breath, "it could get me in trouble." She pointed a finger at me. "But you need to keep a very low profile. Don't go anywhere or do anything for a couple of days. Especially don't go around checking up on people like Leonard Tobin."

I looked guilty, I suppose. She almost smiled again. "He was awake when I got there," she added. "But he didn't remember too much, although he did remember you told him Maud was dead. I don't like that, Liz. I want you to keep clear."

"I will, if you guys aren't going to just settle for me instead of finding out who really killed Tony."

Her brows drew together. "I don't 'settle' for anything. I'll find out the truth, whatever that is. Meantime, you stay put."

"I was going to go to my parents' place tonight for a while, make sure everything's okay with them."

She considered. "Well, okay. But go straight there and come straight back. Will your brother go with you?"

"No way. He spends evenings snoring in front of the tube." I felt disloyal the moment I said that. "I mean, he's tired, you know. He works construction."

"I know." She gave me a look. "There isn't a whole lot I don't know by now about your family, and I'm finding out more every day. So keep your nose clean, Liz. And watch your back."

She strode to her cruiser and drove away. I went slowly back inside to help Renee finish up dinner. Somehow I couldn't dismiss Eva's warnings, much as I wanted to. A cloud of foreboding settled over me, and I saw everything through it, stained by its darkness.

27

MOM let me in when I knocked. She still looked a little tottery, but just being up after dinner was a good sign. Dad, as usual, was intent on the TV, which he'd turned up to suit his age-deafened ears.

"Your sister is very angry with you," Mom said, shaking her head. She sat back down on the couch and picked up her crocheting, fumbling with the wool.

"I know. But we've talked, and she's pretty much over it."

Mom sighed. "I don't know what I did wrong with all of you. Most people's grown children don't fight and squabble like you all do."

"I don't—at least, not until recently." I sat in a chair next to the sofa, trying to talk under the roar of the TV. Dad turned and gave me a nod. I realized that I tended to treat them as they treated me—children who needed things smoothed over and made simple. Neither of us liked that. My parents had been through trouble and adversity. It was instinctive to try and spare them, which was what Molly tried to do, but that didn't take into account their own resilience.

Dad turned the TV down a little. "That woman cop's been here again. Took my gun. Don't know when I'll see it again."

"I don't care if you never do," Mom sniffed.

"You don't know anything about it." Dad got that defensive note in his voice. "There's times when you need a firearm—like when Naylor came around bothering you."

"Well, all that accomplished was to worry me to death for fear you'd actually shoot someone and then have to go to jail yourself." Mom looked indignant. "Better just to be shot, if you ask me."

"Nobody did ask you, so shut up." My dad, after this gracious utterance, turned back to the TV.

Mom wasn't done with the subject. "You should have asked me in the first place, before you wasted your money on it. People in this family never talk to each other about anything." She sounded mournful.

"We're fine." Dad banged the remote control on his chair arm. "Nobody needs to come around trying to make us feel bad." He directed a look at me.

I managed to avoid the loud, defensive Sullivan Arguing Voice that usually took over any quarrel in our family. "It's not so bad to admit you made a mistake. We've all made mistakes. You guys wouldn't even talk to me for fifteen years because I made a couple of big ones. At least, I learned from that. What I learned was—don't make the mistake bigger by pretending it didn't happen."

Mom turned to me, her eyes wet. "We were wrong, too, honey." She put her hand on mine, a rare demonstration. "We shouldn't have been so rigid with you. Like you say, it just made the first mistake worse. I didn't mean to send you back to him, that time you told me he was beating you. I just wanted you to—well, be really repentant or something. Instead you left and never came back."

"I never thought I'd be welcome." I squeezed her hand and looked at Dad. "Would I have been?"

He looked down at the remote control in his gnarled hand. "Of course," he muttered. "You're our child. We have a duty to you. But dammit," he burst out. "Why do you have to stir up so much trouble? Every time you come around—"

"I didn't make the trouble this time," I pointed out, striving for that reasonable tone of voice. "I didn't kill Tony—didn't even try to this time."

"Shoulda been shot a long time ago," my dad grunted, apparently without irony. "That's what guns are good for." He glanced sideways at Mom.

"I never want to see that thing again." My mother spoke with surprising strength, considering a lifetime spent deferring to this man. "It's just a source of trouble. Anyone might get hold of it—that Conchita, for instance." She turned to me. "Thought she was such a nice little thing, but she just up and left this afternoon."

"Before Eva came over? Oh, dear." Here was something else that might be my fault. I hoped I hadn't driven off yet another witness—or been the means of endangering her.

"Yes, she was here until nearly four, stirring around. Then the phone rang and she answered it—told me it was a bad number or some such thing. I dozed off for a while, and when I woke up she was gone."

"Didn't take nothing, though." My dad added this, determined to be fair. "I checked."

"Maybe someone called to tell her the INS was after her." I hoped that was all it was. I hoped she wasn't meeting the same fate as Maud.

"Now, I thought Molly told me she was an exchange student."

I had to smile. "Nope. Molly probably suspected she was illegal. She got Conchita and whoever came before her through Tony. He was a coyote—bringing in undocumented workers from Mexico. Usually they pay the coyote to bring them, and he collects a fee for delivering them."

Dad shook his head. "He was a bad one, that fellow. Never liked him. What was Molly about, to pick up with him?"

"Maybe she was rebelling, too, after being so good for so long." I was worried about Conchita. "Did the girl go back to Molly's?"

"No. Molly called here right after dinner to say she'd be over to pick her up soon, and we had to say she'd already gone." Mom clasped her hands together. "What does all this mean, Lizzie? Why is this happening?"

"I don't know," I admitted. "It does sound like someone has it in for the Sullivans, though, doesn't it?"

The phone rang, and I leaped up to answer it, having the youngest knees in the room. It was Amy.

"Aunt Liz, there's another e-mail from Drake. Shall I read it to you?" She was eager to do so—hoping for some tender phrases, I supposed.

"No, don't bother. I'm about ready to leave here."

"Who was that on the phone?" Mom put down her crocheting, looking at me over her glasses when I came back into the living room. It took me back so far I almost lied from habit, as I'd done in my teenage years.

"Amy. She had a homework question."

Mom nodded, satisfied. "Now little Amy isn't mixed up in all this, is she?"

"Not if Biff lets her alone. He's given to annoying her, I gather."

Mom tsked, but Dad shook his head. "The girl should put more clothes on," he growled. "Not that that's any excuse for Byron. That boy needs a good whipping."

Mom disagreed. "He can be a very sweet boy," she insisted. "But Molly lets him get away with that bad behavior, so of course he keeps misbehaving. She should be stricter with him."

It was none of my business. I was just glad Amy knew a couple of ways to discourage unwanted masculine attention. She was unlikely to change her style of dress, and although I found it tacky in the extreme myself, I didn't see why she shouldn't wear what she wanted. When men wear tight pants and muscle shirts, do women molest them under the philosophy that they just can't help themselves? A man who can't control his hormonal behavior is going to find provocation everywhere, even in women who wear muumuus. Such a man may need help reining in his impulses; an occasional knee to the groin does wonders.

I didn't say this to my parents—protecting them from reality, but I thought they needed it. They looked a little shaken, and I felt bad about spreading so much truth around. When you're used to ducking unpleasantness, to find it in your face is scary.

"I'm sorry all this is happening," I said, giving my mom a tentative hug. "But I'm not sorry I came back. Maybe we can stay in touch after I leave this time."

"You'll be leaving." Mom looked like she didn't know whether to be glad or sorry. "I was sort of thinking you might stay here, since you've come back."

"My home is in California now. But you two could come

visit me. The train runs between Denver and the Bay Area, if you don't want to fly."

"It's so expensive," Mom said vaguely. "But we'll certainly think about it, honey."

"It's nice in the winter out there," I told them. "Sunny until Thanksgiving, and warm. And spring comes early—February instead of May."

"Sounds lovely." Mom was a little more enthusiastic, but Dad just grunted. Sun or snow, he never paid much attention to the weather. He wore his heavy parka and fur-lined hat from October to April, along with long underwear and wool socks, and wondered why other people complained.

I left them in the living room, the TV turned back up, reminding my mother to lock the door after I left. She shook her head, but I heard the lock click.

Barker bounced back and forth through the bus when I climbed into the driver's seat. I felt sorry for his boredom that day. I'd dragged him around without giving him a good walk, but he didn't complain.

I felt like complaining, though. I wanted my swim. I wanted a long walk through the streets of Palo Alto, admiring the nice yards and well-kept cottages while managing to ignore the monster houses mushrooming up on small lots. I wanted to plant my seedlings and pick my green beans and tomatoes and smell my roses. I wanted to sit in front of my elderly computer, sending queries out and hoping they came back with positive answers.

Instead I pulled up outside my brother's house at nine o'clock on a chilly Denver evening, hoping to escape a lecture from Andy on how I was sinking the family into the mire with every moment I stayed around.

I left Barker in the bus, despite his whining protest, and slipped in the front door quietly. Renee was at her usual post in the kitchen. She nodded, and I smiled back.

"Amy wants to show me something, so I'll get that done so she can get to bed," I said. "I left Barker in the bus."

"I can hear." She sighed heavily. "You might as well let him in. He'll bother the neighbors."

"He's fine there for a little while. I'll be going to bed soon myself."

"You don't have to sleep out there," Renee said after a moment. "You could use the other bed in Amy's room, you know."

"I know. But I like it out there. All my stuff—" I waved vaguely, but Renee understood stuff.

Loud honking and roaring sounds came from outside. I flinched, and Renee ran to her curtain. "That Biff!"

"Is that him?" I joined her at the curtain, just in time to see a white pickup disappear.

"He's done that a couple of times this evening—driven by revving and honking." Renee tightened her lips. "I'm going to give Molly an earful, I can tell you." She stalked over to the phone, and I went on down the hall to Amy's room.

She was cross-legged on one bed, bent over a big text, but with one eye fixed wistfully on the phone. "Aunt Liz!" She bounced up when I appeared. "Here's your e-mail."

She had printed it; the piece of paper trembled a little when I took it.

Got your message. Naylor under investigation by FBI as member of a ring bringing in undocumented aliens. Ring is still active. Naylor may have been killed because he was a danger to other members. The FBI won't shake loose of any other names—had to work like hell just to get this out of them. Be very careful. These people are obviously prepared to kill.

"I read it," Amy confessed. "And I'm worried." She turned frightened eyes to me.

"Don't worry, Amy. That's just Drake's way of trying to scare me into my burrow like a good little rabbit."

She was silent for a moment. "Will it work?"

I laughed. "You bet."

"Good." She slammed her book shut. "Did you want to answer it?"

"Sure, if it's no trouble." I watched her bustle around the computer. "Renee was just on the phone, if that matters."

Amy lifted the receiver and listened. "She's off now. I need my own phone line." The computer made little dialing noises. After a moment, Amy said, "There. You're all set. Tell it to send when you're finished writing, then exit, like I showed you."

I sat for a few moments, trying to compose something that would express everything I felt in a few non-revealing words. In the end, I just thanked him for his message and repeated that I hoped to be home soon.

As soon as I was finished, Amy confronted me. "Are you really in danger, Aunt Liz?"

"No. I don't know anything. I'm as mystified as everyone else is."

"You know about—Tony," she said, pronouncing his name hesitantly. "You read that file."

"Yeah, but the police know that, too. It's no secret."

"Right." She seemed relieved.

I stretched. "Well, Barker's already in the bus, so I'm headed that way, too."

"This once, will you sleep in here?" The pinched look was back around Amy's eyes.

"I'm just as safe in the bus." I didn't believe that anyone would be after me—what would harming me accomplish? But if anyone was so deranged as to wish to harm me, better that they didn't go through Amy first.

It was cold outside and seemed darker than usual. Barker had stopped whining. His head was still out the window, his ears pitched forward to something down the street that claimed his attention. He barely looked at me as I walked toward Babe.

I opened the side door to climb in, and he was out of it like a shot, dashing down the street toward whatever he'd been watching—probably a cat, maybe even a raccoon. I grabbed the leash out of the bus and set off in pursuit, whistling to him. I didn't want to yell, for fear that Renee would deprecate any commotion I made.

The streetlight at the corner was out, and Barker was close to invisible, like a dog in camouflage streaking through the darker shadows where trees overhung the sidewalk.

Halfway down the block I figured I was far enough from Andy's house to yell. "Barker!"

He checked momentarily, turning back toward me. I saw his eyes shine, and his happy doggy smile. When I came closer he pranced away. I dangled his leash temptingly, but a dog who'd been without exercise as long as Barker wasn't going to give up a run for a tame walk on a leash. He circled coyly toward me, then his head came up again, alert. Once more he dashed toward the corner.

A big catalpa tree threw darkness over the corner. I thought I could see a figure standing in the black heart of the shadow. Barker disappeared into that blackness, but my steps slowed.

"Barker! Come!" I heard a whine from the shadows, and I could dimly see a few white spots that I assumed were my dog. Then he cried out sharply, as if someone had kicked him.

I hurried forward, unable to leave him to whatever threatened him, even though I knew it was foolish. The only weapon I had was my Swiss army knife in my pocket. I wrapped the leash around my hand a couple of times, its heavy hook swinging free.

My eyes were growing used to the darkness. I could see the moving shadow of a person, standing under the trees, stooping actually. I heard the clink of Barker's chain collar and his soft, puzzled whine.

Just as I got under the tree, Barker jumped up, bounding at me, uttering sharp barks of distress. His approach took me off balance, and in that instant someone slipped behind me and wrapped an arm around my throat. I felt cold metal on my temple.

"I blew poor Maud's head off," a voice whispered in my ear. It was familiar somehow, but not recognizable. I remembered Leonard Tobin, talking about poor Maud. "I'll blow yours off, too, if you don't do just as I say."

I turned my head a little, and the arm around my neck tightened. "Don't try to see me or you're dead," it warned.

I tried to nod. Barker seethed around my feet, and I was torn between the hope that he would trip the person holding me, and the fear that it would cause my death.

Then something roared around the corner, and bright lights pierced the shadow. Brakes squealed, and a white pickup truck swerved across the sidewalk. I felt the arm around my throat slacken. Impelled by some atavistic impulse for survival, I threw myself forward, lashing out behind me with my improvised leash-whip. A sharp crack and a smothered cry answered my movement. With a clatter, something fell to the ground. And Byron Fahey jumped out of his pickup truck, his face contorted in a scowl.

28 _____

SO it wasn't Biff who'd been threatening to kill me—who had killed Tony and Maud. Even so, Barker wasn't glad to see him.

"What's going down here? You partying, Auntie?" Biff's sneer was in excellent shape. It distorted his features, colored his voice.

I didn't have time to waste answering. Whirling, I saw Kyle groping on the ground behind me. His glasses dangled from one ear; the lenses were cracked from the heavy hook of Barker's leash.

He'd dropped the gun when I'd lashed out at him. I located it a second before he did, half-under some dead leaves at the edge of the sidewalk. I kicked it away from Kyle's groping hand, and it skidded toward Biff.

"What's this?" He bent and picked it up, glancing from Kyle to me. "You playing rough, Auntie?"

"I'm not playing at all, Biff. This guy killed a couple of people already, and now he wants to kill me. Give me the gun, please."

He was still being Mr. Tough Guy. "You kidding? Give you the gun—that's a good one. You're the man-killer, right, Auntie? Gonna shoot this guy, too, like you did your rat of a husband?"

Kyle stood up slowly, adjusting his broken glasses on his face. "That's right," he said, holding Biff's eyes with his. "She's trying to kill me. Broke my glasses, too."

I could see Biff's thought processes as clearly as if they were written on his face. Kyle wore glasses. That made him a wimp. Wimps didn't carry guns. Therefore, I was the bad person here. Barker made up his mind by growling at him. Biff took a firmer grip on the gun.

I fastened the leash on Barker and made another effort to communicate, trying to stabilize my shaking voice. "Biff, if you don't believe me, I suggest you call the police. Renee will let you use her phone."

"Right, call the cops." Biff was inclined to sneer again, but Kyle spoke, using a quiet forcefulness that looked good next to my shaking voice and nervous hands.

"I think you should call the cops. Let them sort this out."

Biff stood undecided, scratching his head.

"Give me the gun. I'll keep her here until you get back," Kyle added.

"No!" I yelled when Biff started to hand it meekly over. By then it was too late. Kyle yanked the gun from Biff's slack fingers.

"Okay, over by Liz." Kyle gestured with the gun barrel, and when Biff didn't move, he adopted a commando stance. "Move it now, buddy."

Slowly Biff shuffled over to stand by me, his eyebrows pulled down in great displeasure. I thought of several names I could call him, but didn't waste my breath.

"This is your nephew?" Kyle glanced from Biff to me, maybe looking for some resemblance.

"Yes." I remembered reading somewhere that shallow breaths were better than deep ones if your head was whirling. I wasn't the only one there who was confused. Barker, interspersing growls with whines, had his fur up, but he began sniffing Biff's leg with great interest. The dog's presence hampered me—he seemed so vulnerable. But then, in a funny way, so did Biff. I wondered how I could get us out of this. I sent mental telepathy to Renee, only half a block away, to call the police. If we stayed here on the corner long enough, someone would surely get suspicious and do just that. Wasn't Eva cruising around keeping an eye on me? We should be easy to see, with the headlights from Biff's truck trained on us.

Kyle didn't plan for us to stay there. "You have a nice truck," he said to Biff conversationally. "We're all going to get in it. You'll drive."

Biff didn't take orders well.

"The hell I will," he said angrily, as if the gun in Kyle's hand meant nothing. "What's going on here? All I did was stop when I saw my aunt playing bondage games with some weirdo. This has got nothing to do with me." His voice cracked on the last word, reminding me that this huge, stubbled-bearded male was only a few years away from playing with GI Joe dolls.

I shrugged when Biff directed his scowl at me. I still didn't understand what was happening. Somehow, given the two guys in front of me, I would have expected their team affiliations to be reversed.

"Your aunt was right," Kyle said gently into the silence. He was getting himself in hand, smoothing back that shiny hair. Noticing his leather jacket, I wondered where the motorcycle was. "I was threatening her. Now that you've given me back my gun, I can keep tabs on both of you. So, you can either drive or I'll shoot you."

Biff backed reluctantly toward his truck. Kyle pointed the gun at me. "You get in the middle, Liz. Behave, now, or I'll have to hurt something you're fond of."

"She don't give two hoots about me, Mister," Biff said. He didn't look too good—his beefy face was glazed with sweat, and his eyes flicked back and forth like a cornered animal's.

"I meant the dog." Kyle glided a step forward and snatched the leash out of my nerveless hands. He jerked the leash, and the choke collar tightened. Barker yelped.

"I just don't understand." I wasn't faking the fright in my voice. I was very frightened. But I thought the strain of trying to keep both of us in line would tell on Kyle, and work to our advantage. And I had some lame idea of making him relax his vigilance. "You were the one to kill Tony? And Maud? Why, Kyle? I never thought you were capable of something like that."

He held the gun with one hand while he tried to keep Barker from winding around his legs, but he was still dividing close attention between Biff's dragging footsteps and my frozen body. My question made him hunch up one shoulder, as if shrugging it away. After a moment, he said,

"Tony was just—too dangerous. I didn't want to kill him, God knows. But the way he was going, we'd both be taken out." He stopped short, as if he'd said too much.

"Tony? Your ex, right?" Biff slanted a hostile glance at me. "The one my mom—"

Kyle laughed. "Tony heard somewhere that you thought he was fucking your mom. He thought that was pretty funny. In fact, he thought it would be even funnier if it was true." He smiled gently. "You should be glad I killed him. He might have succeeded."

"But why? Were you a coyote, too?"

Kyle darted a narrow glance at me. "If I tell you about it, you'll be dead. You know that?"

"And otherwise you won't hurt us? Biff will just drive us to the Dairy Queen and home again? Right. What's the real agenda here, Kyle?"

Biff stopped, his hand on the truck's door. "Yeah. Why don't you just go ahead and shoot us, punk? You're going to anyway." His bravado came out sounding a little thin, and it wasn't a great way to keep Kyle occupied and talking until Eva made her next swing through the neighborhood.

"I want to know what's behind all this before I check out." I tried to be genteelly insistent. Barker was straining at the leash, wanting to come and sit on my feet, like he used to when he was smaller and worried or upset.

Kyle jerked him back, and for an instant the gun slipped in its vigilance. I darted a glance at Biff and caught his eye. He moved away from the truck, back toward Kyle. The moment had passed, but there might be another one. Maybe we'd be ready for it.

"Damned dog," Kyle muttered. "I should have thought of some other way to get you down here on your own, Liz."

"You—called Barker somehow?"

"Dog whistle." He jerked the leash again, and Barker cowered. He had no idea he'd been my Judas.

"But why did you want me? I don't know anything."

He almost looked uncomfortable—he wouldn't meet my eyes. "You know the police have suspected you from the beginning. If you'd only run away, kept their attention on you—everything would have worked out. As soon as they arrested you, I was going to tell them how you'd told me you were still in love with Tony, still jealous of Maud. You would have looked good," he assured me earnestly. "That cop who questioned me—he thought he could get a conviction with you, even without hard evidence. The only problem was, you wouldn't run. I was—just going to get you out of town, make you look guiltier."

"So you were going to kill me." I don't know why that seemed like such a letdown. The likelihood was that he would still kill me.

Kyle looked uncomfortable. "Just a little accident," he insisted. "You might have lived. I was going to drive you in your bus out to the Interstate. You would be fleeing, you see."

I still couldn't make sense of it all. "But—why? Why are you doing all this?"

He sighed; I could hear it over the rumble of Biff's truck engine and the sound of the wind in the stiff catalpa leaves. "For the Anasazi, of course. I thought you'd understand, Liz. You've always understood about them. I found this cache of pots on government land. I couldn't get any funding for a full-scale dig without revealing the location, and as soon as one other person knows, the integrity of the site is compromised. You know. We've talked about this."

True. But I hadn't realized that Kyle's fervor was homicidally strong. I said, "So that's why you worked with Tony, bringing in illegal aliens."

"I needed money to finance my dig. It was good money, and didn't interfere with my other job." He nodded, pleased that I'd understood, but the gun still moved steadily, pointing now at Biff, now at me. "I didn't mind those long night drives down to New Mexico with Tony. That's when I heard about him finding you in California. He didn't say just what happened, but he did talk often about what you deserved." Kyle shook his head. "It kind of made me sick, when he'd talk like that. And he was trouble in other ways, too—skimming profits, making both of us look bad to the—"

He hesitated. I filled in the gap. "The people in charge, whoever they are."

"They're very results-oriented," Kyle assured me. "Tony was dodging them, but I wasn't so lucky. They brought me to a—meeting, and told me Tony would have to go if he couldn't make up the money."

"He wanted you to make it up?"

"I had just managed to get together enough for an excavation permit and three months of supplies." Kyle sounded outraged. "I told him he had one month to find the cash. That's when he started hitting up your mom—thought that was funny, too, to make her pay. Maud, Leonard—he tried everyone he could think of. Then he stole my pots."

"What?" That woke Biff up. "Pot? Drugs?"

"No." Kyle shook his head. "The Chaco pottery from the site I'd discovered. Like a fool, I'd told him once how valuable it had become on the black market. When I found the site had been vandalized—" His lips tightened. "I knew it was Tony. Hell, he left some of his dumb imported cigarette butts there. He'd followed me, rifled my find, disturbed the layers."

He took a deep breath. "I was supposed to be in Cortez that night. Instead I drove to Denver, to the rendezvous point where Tony was bringing a shipment. I waited until he was alone. I knew he always carried a gun when he was working. I ran up, said someone was after me, grabbed the gun, and—shot him. Just like that. Then I wrapped him up in a movers' blanket from the rental van so his brains wouldn't get all over everything. I put my bike in the van and drove away." His monotone ceased.

"And Maud?"

"She knew about our business sideline. Tony blabbed it all to her." He shook his head. "He had such a big mouth. He told me about your old man waving a gun at him— that's why I ended up dumping his body on your folks' doorstep. Seemed like a good diversion. I called Maud the next day, to make sure she'd keep her mouth shut. She told me you were in town." He shook his head in wonderment. "It was like the gods were smiling on me, you know? I'd put the body on the doorstep, and you turned up to take the rap." He smiled at me, and I could still see that nice guy. "Maud said the police did suspect you, but she was nervous. I knew she'd spill her guts. After you and the cop left my place, I got on my Harley and went over to Maud's. She was just leaving. I followed her. The gods were smiling again—she picked a route with practically no traffic. On the bike, it was easy to pull up beside her." He glanced at his gun.

I held myself very still, hoping he would go on. Biff had been listening, his mouth slightly open as if it were all an action movie. When Kyle stopped talking, he shuffled his feet, and instantly the gun was trained on his chest.

Down the block, a car door slammed. Barker leaped up, facing the sound, and barked frantically.

The leash's jerk threw Kyle off balance an instant. Biff tackled him, and the gun went off with a deafening roar. Barker tore free, galloping back toward Andy's house. Kyle was submerged under Biff's big body, but I couldn't tell who was hurt and who wasn't. I overcame my first urge, which was to curl up whimpering on the ground in a fetal position, and edged closer to the seething tangle on the sidewalk.

Although he was on top, Biff wasn't moving. Kyle still had the gun—the headlights of Biff's truck caught the gleam from its barrel. Kyle flailed, trying to get out from under Biff's inert body.

I did the only thing I could think of. I stood on Kyle's wrist, trapping the gun.

"Kid—weighs—a ton," Kyle gasped. His wrist turned under my feet, and I lost my balance, staggering to avoid ending up in the clump. The gun came up, leveled unsteadily at me.

"Look, Kyle. Give it up." I sidestepped, and the gun followed me. Kyle was still working at getting out from under Biff. I couldn't tell if the boy was dead or not, but I noticed a dark rivulet of blood making its way along the sidewalk. "You're doomed. Someone's calling the cops right now. Kill me, and you make it worse for yourself."

"It can't be any worse." For a moment Kyle stopped

struggling, then he heaved Biff off—toward me. The boy's head struck the pavement with a resounding crack.

"Well, if he wasn't dead yet—" I knelt beside Biff, ignoring the gun for a moment. His shoulder was wet with blood from a jagged hole. I pulled his T-shirt up and bunched it over the hole, pressing as hard on the wad of fabric as I could. When I looked up, Kyle was holding the gun on me.

"I just wanted you to leave town, Liz. Even if it had come to a trial, you would have gotten off light—abused wives do these days. I didn't want to kill you. I like you." Kyle's expression was rueful.

"That's nice." I looked beyond him, where headlights beamed from a car pulled up in front of Andy's house. I hoped all the civilians had the sense to stay away. Then another car rounded the corner and pulled up, boxing us in next to Biff's truck. Kyle blinked uncertainly when the harsh spotlight found him. A man's voice barked, "Drop the gun!" Kyle laid it slowly on the ground, and held his hands up.

"Liz." It was Eva's voice. "I'm covering you. Stand up slowly."

"I can't! Biff is bleeding too much. Get an ambulance."

The next few minutes passed in a blur. Two uniformed officers took Kyle away. I could hear him as they led him off, and my heart sank. He was already spinning a story to account for holding a gun on me. Maybe he would be able to turn me into his fall gal.

Eva brought an emergency kit over and nudged me gently out of the way, and then the ambulance was there. I had felt Biff's pulse still fluttering weakly in his neck before the EMTs took over. All the same, I looked anxiously after the ambulance. Obnoxious or not, Biff had courageously tackled an armed man, and maybe saved my life.

"So, I thought you were going to lay low tonight." Eva turned to me after the ambulance left.

Andy came up, reaching into Biff's truck to turn off the engine. When its rumbling ceased, I realized for the first time how much noise it had made. We must have been talking quite loudly to hear each other.

"Are you okay?" Andy was awkward asking this question of me in front of an audience.

I looked down at my bloodstained hands. There was blood everywhere. I hoped I wouldn't faint.

"Yeah, I guess so. Hope Byron makes it all right."

"So why did you shoot him?" For once, Andy just looked puzzled, not angry. "I mean—he could be rude, sure, but—"

"I didn't shoot him." I turned to Eva. "Is that what Kyle was saying? Why would I try to stop the bleeding if I shot him?"

"I didn't hear it all, but his theory had something to do with a flashback to when you shot Tony."

"Oh, brother." I turned back to Andy. "That guy killed Tony and this other woman. I guess I was next on the list. Biff saw him and stopped, and got shot when he interfered."

Andy just stared at me numbly. "None of this makes any sense," he said. "All I know is, Molly's going to go ballistic if that boy doesn't get well."

"Even if he does, probably." We exchanged wan smiles.

Andy turned to Eva, showing more deference than before. "Can I move my nephew's truck, ma'am? It's going to get hit if it stays there."

"In a little while." Eva was watching the various crime scene people bustle around. "We need some pictures and stuff. Someone will let you know."

"I'll take the keys, then." He pocketed them, gave me a funny half nod, half bow, and walked back down the block. A few feet away he turned and yelled, "Amy's keeping your dog."

I signaled my appreciation. Beside me, Eva cleared her throat. "Think you'd better tell me what happened," she said, flipping open a notebook. "We can compare it to Baldridge's statement."

I shook my head in wonderment. "I don't know why he's bothering. If Biff makes it—"

"He had a nasty lump on his head," Eva said. "Might not remember what happened. Baldridge is probably counting on it being your word against his. Tell me."

I told her, trying to remember everything Kyle had said, wishing I'd had Amy's little tape recorder on me. Eva whistled when I was done.

"So now I guess we just see who's telling a better story, you or Baldridge." She looked at me sympathetically. "Do you want to clean up first?"

The blood had dried on my hands. "Yeah, I guess so."

"I'll have to stay with you. Or you can have a matron, if you want."

"You'll do." I walked next to her back to my bus. The door was still open, just as it had been when Barker had jumped out—hours ago? Minutes? I couldn't tell anymore.

I didn't go in the house. Let Renee and Andy and Amy remain undisturbed. I stood beside my little sink and washed my hands and arms and then, not caring who was watching, substituted a clean sweatshirt for the bloodstained one. Eva picked up the discarded shirt and stuck it in an evidence bag. I shut up the bus and locked it, hoping I'd be back before long, and followed Eva to her cruiser.

29

I spent some time making an official statement, then some more time in a small, featureless room by myself. I kept wondering how Biff was. Surely he was too tough to die. As the numbness of shock receded, I began to feel terribly guilty, as if I'd caused his death or, at least, done nothing to avert it.

Finally Eva came to escort me to O'Malley's office. Phil was there, too, sitting at his desk flailing away at his computer, smoking a very smelly cigar right underneath a NO SMOKING sign on the wall. Eva sat down at another computer. At a long table covered with piles of paper, Kyle was sitting, sipping a steaming cup of something, and looking so normal that I could hardly believe what had happened.

The apprehension with which he noticed me was a good bolster for his story of my being some kind of weirdo executrix of men. I had a sinking feeling that such a story would be very attractive to men of a certain age, playing right into the Black Widow archetype.

O'Malley greeted me with some reserve, and seated me across the table from Kyle. "Now," he said, glancing at each of us in turn. "There appears to be a large discrepancy here. You—" he pointed at me—"tell us what happened tonight."

I tried to be succinct, but the fright I'd felt made my narrative shaky.

"So you claim this guy lured you down the block, threatened you, then when your nephew stopped to see what was happening, tried to kidnap both of you and ended up shooting the boy. Is that it?"

It didn't sound too likely. "That's what happened." I

wished I had something to drink. "What does he say happened?"

O'Malley put on a pair of bifocals and looked over some notes. "He says you had the boy at gunpoint when he stopped to see what was happening. You had evidently gotten your nephew to kill Tony and Maud for you, then you were going to kill him. Something like that."

I looked at Kyle. "You'll be in trouble when Biff wakes up."

Kyle leaned toward me. "Why, Liz? Why did you do it?"

O'Malley looked at me over the bifocals. "You care to answer that?"

"No, I don't." I felt anger warming me, stiffening my spine. "This man has killed a couple of people, and you're letting him snow you! He told us all about it before he tried to kill Biff." I looked at Eva. "You should search his place. And don't bother to treat the artifacts carefully. He won't care if you smash them all."

Eva raised her eyebrows, but Kyle jumped up. "Don't touch my antiquities!"

"Tony stole some from him—that's what tipped the balance. That, and him skimming the profits from their coyote business."

O'Malley shuffled his papers again. "That's right. Bringing undocumented workers into the state. According to Ms. Sullivan's statement, you're involved in that." He fixed Kyle with the bifocal glare.

"It's ridiculous," Kyle sputtered. He was either a great actor or a man with selective amnesia. "I make a good living as a stockbroker. I don't gamble or do expensive drugs. Why would I want to do anything so unsavory?"

"Who is it that grants permits to conduct archaeological explorations on government land?" I tried to make eye contact with Kyle, but he stopped talking and stared at the table. "There's a paper trail somewhere that ends up with Kyle shelling out big money to excavate a site he has his eye on."

"That's really stupid." Kyle finally looked at me. "I already get to excavate, and my experience is valued at the dig. I get all my archaeology strokes there."

"You get a few at home, Officer Gutierrez says." O'Malley nodded toward Eva, who turned away from the computer.

"I knew if those pots you had in your apartment were authentic, they were worth a lot of money. At first I thought it was just your expensive vice—collecting them. But asking around, I found that some folks thought you were a bit of a pothunter."

Kyle turned white. "That's not true! They would never say that. Everyone knows about my expertise—they ask for me—"

Eva shook her head, her face stolid. "Not everyone says that. The dig you were on last year didn't want you back. They think you ripped off a couple of pieces."

"I didn't steal them." Kyle was vehement. "I'm keeping them safe! You don't understand. The best things always get stolen. Those would have been stolen, too, if I hadn't protected them!"

O'Malley was watching Kyle with a kind of fatherly detachment. "You see, the problem is, Mr. Baldridge, that we've been paying a lot of attention to Ms. Sullivan's movements. She's been traced all the way back to California, from the campgrounds she stayed in to the place her car was repaired, and then to her brother's house—right before the time Naylor was shot, the pathologist says. No way could she have killed him. So unless the two of you are working together, she didn't do him. And it would be pretty hard for her to have done Ms. Riegert, either. And it sure doesn't look to Phil and me like the two of you are working together."

"It doesn't have to be me, if it's not her!" Kyle's control had been shaken. "Her nephew—the one that got shot. He threatened to kill Tony—Tony himself told me about it!"

"When was this, Mr. Baldridge? According to the statement you gave Officer Gutierrez Thursday, you hadn't seen Mr. Naylor for some time." O'Malley glanced at Phil, serene in his noxious cloud. "For God's sake, Phil, put that thing out. We're all dying here."

"Sorry, O'Malley." Phil got up and carried his cigar out of the room.

Kyle watched him go. He took off his cracked glasses, looked at them as if he'd never seen them before, and then cleaned them. "I—might have just seen him in passing recently. A week or so ago. And he told me this hulking kid had declared a vendetta against him. It actually worried him."

"You told us tonight he thought it was funny." I put in my two cents' worth.

Kyle shot me a glance of entreaty. "Liz, don't make it worse."

"It is worse."

"I'm sorry I said it was you trying to kill your nephew. Maybe you were just trying to defend yourself from him. He could have been threatening you, saying if you didn't back off trying to find out who killed Tony, he'd get you. Right?"

"No, Kyle. That's not the way it was. Try telling the truth."

A uniformed officer came in. "There's a woman here demanding to see whoever's in charge of the Naylor investigation," he said nervously. "Don't know what you want me to do with her."

He didn't have to do anything. Molly barged into the room, pushing him out of the way.

"Where is he?" Her hair was wild, as if she'd driven fast with the window down. "Where's the scum that tried to kill my baby?"

Eva was on her feet. "Mrs. Fahey! How's Bryon doing?"

"He's alive." Molly gulped convulsively. Her makeup was smeared around her eyes, making her look like a wild Celt ready for battle. She turned that bleary, molten gaze on O'Malley, who visibly quailed. "Is that the slimebag? He deserves to have his balls ripped slowly off and roasted over an open fire!"

"Molly—" It was the bravest thing I've ever done, to get in the path of her slow, mesmerizing stalk toward O'Malley. "Molly. Doesn't Biff need you? Shouldn't you be by his side?"

"They threw me out." She switched the basilisk glare to me. "Told me I was upsetting him, so I left the hospital.

Renee said there was some kind of fight on the corner, that they had arrested everyone involved. Were you involved, Liz?"

"Byron saved my life," I said.

Her eyes narrowed further. "Why did you make that necessary, damn you? If you hadn't come back, none of this would have happened!"

Eva cleared her throat—she also seemed to feel brave. "Actually, Liz saved your son's life, too, probably. He lost a lot of blood. If she hadn't acted quickly, he would have lost more—maybe too much."

Some of the red faded from Molly's face. She'd always had a talent for a good rage, but I had never seen her like this before. "Did you?" She faltered a little. "His blood—"

I pushed her into my chair just before her legs turned to rubber. Eva bustled around, finding a glass of water. O'Malley wiped his balding head with a handkerchief.

"You've had a shock tonight," Eva said, handing Molly the water. "Is your husband at the hospital? Do you want me to call and let them know you're here?"

"That—that would be kind." Molly gulped the water and seemed to revive. "I wasn't doing poor Byron much good. He was just covered in blood—his own blood!"

"He'll be cleaned up when you go back," Eva said soothingly. She was dialing from O'Malley's phone, and turned her back to talk softly into the receiver.

Molly drew herself up, and I hastened to introduce O'Malley. "This is the detective in charge of Tony's murder."

She looked him over and didn't seem impressed. "And you did arrest someone for shooting my son?" She noticed Kyle, who had been very quiet, as if hoping to be forgotten. "Why, Mr. Amador."

"I beg your pardon." Kyle looked blank. Too blank. He held himself as still as the rabbit that scents danger.

"Mr. Amador," Molly insisted. "Don't you remember me?" She sounded a little hurt, and indeed I thought most men would remember her face, although not in its current state. "We met at lunch one day. With Tony—" Her eyes widened.

O'Malley moved swiftly, pushing Kyle back down when he rose to his feet. "Just sit still, Mr. Baldridge," he said jovially. "We'll get to the bottom of this." He turned to Molly. "Now, Missus—"

"Mrs. Fahey." Molly frowned. "Did this man shoot my son? Why does he pretend he's never met me?"

"Did you know your sister's friends, when she was still living in Denver?" Eva hung up the phone and slipped a quiet question in.

Molly stiffened. "I don't see what business that is of yours."

"Answer the question, please." O'Malley sat on the edge of the table, his expression satisfied. Phil came back in, accompanied by the young uniformed officer, who moved to stand behind Kyle. The very air in the room seemed to change.

"Well—no." Molly turned to O'Malley, impatient. "I barely saw her—we were estranged. I actually thought she didn't really have any friends."

"So you didn't recognize Mr. Baldridge when you were having lunch with Naylor?" O'Malley had taken over the questioning.

"Mr. Amador? Isn't that his name? It's what Tony called him." Molly's eyebrows drew together. "I'd never seen him before then. He wasn't very polite, actually. Tony called him over and looked delighted to see him, but Mr. Amador—whoever—" she turned a laserlike stare on Kyle. "He sort of mumbled for a minute and went away. Of course I remembered him because he didn't look particularly Hispanic, in spite of his name." She flushed, glancing at Eva.

"And it was Naylor who called him Amador?"

"Yes." She stared at Kyle again.

"How long ago was this?"

"Just a few weeks ago. I was arranging with Tony for—" she caught herself.

"For a little immigrant help?"

Molly bridled. "Well, it's always worked out in the past. The last young woman I got wanted to go to school and work toward residency. I arranged for her to take ESL classes and to enroll at the junior college." She looked at Eva while she spoke. "I understood I was doing her a favor. And she did end up enrolling in school, and in fact left me to go full-time." She was triumphant at this vindication of her patronage. "So I needed another one."

"How much does it cost you up front?" O'Malley barked the question. "How much did you pay?"

"Really, am I under arrest here? I thought—"

"Just answer the question, and maybe we can all go home."

Molly pressed her lips together, but then answered. "I gave him five thousand," she said defiantly. "That was for the paperwork, you see, and prepaying her first four months. And she did have a green card—I saw it."

O'Malley glanced at Phil. "Forged," he said.

Eva flipped through the papers she'd been given. "There was a portable offset press and a supply of rose-colored cardstock similar to what the INS uses, as well as a laminating machine, in Baldridge's storage locker at his apartment house."

Kyle let out a cry of outrage. "You—searched my place? My artifacts—"

"Relax. We didn't break anything. Not that it will matter to you in the long run." Phil spoke, his voice a deep, bearlike rumble.

"But you can't—"

"We've had a search warrant since earlier today," O'Malley said briskly. "One for you, too," he nodded toward me, "but it looks like we won't be needing it. Thanks, Missus." He clapped Molly on the shoulder, ignoring her wince. "All we wanted was something linking him to Naylor's sideline. Can you pin that date down better, when you saw him?"

"I suppose." Molly looked bewildered again. "It'll be on my calendar. You mean—this is the man who shot Byron?"

"Kyle Baldridge, we're charging you in the assault on Byron Fahey." O'Malley wasn't paying attention to Molly anymore. He bent toward Kyle, as if he found him fascinating. "If the boy doesn't recover, that's a capital charge. In addition, we're charging you with the murder of Tony

Naylor, and probably with Maud Riegert's as well. Do you want to press charges?" He looked at me.

"Not unless everything else evaporates. Sounds like you've got plenty."

Molly's hands curved into claws. "If he gets off—"

I pulled on her arm. "Don't make any rash remarks here, Molly. Byron will be well enough to testify, I'm sure."

Her expression changed. "Oh, my God. My son, on the witness stand? How humiliating! I'll never be elected to the school board!"

Kyle was led away, with O'Malley and Phil in attendance. Eva paused beside us. "Don't worry," she said, smiling. "These things can take awhile to come to trial. And I'll vote for you in November!"

"So, we can leave?"

Eva nodded. "I told the hospital someone would drive Mrs. Fahey over there. Do you want to?"

"Sure. It's as easy as that? Everything's settled?"

"Lots of work ahead, but not for you." She patted my shoulder. "Thanks for your help, Liz. You shouldn't have gotten mixed up in it, of course."

"I felt I had to. I heard O'Malley tell you to back off, and I figured someone wanted me to take the fall."

"I know. I thought that, too." Her gaze fell. "An internal investigation was going on, but only a few cops knew about it—and O'Malley was one. When he got orders to slack off, he had to appear to slack off. The investigation was completed late this afternoon. I can't tell you about the results—although they might end up in the paper—but some people rather high up have been found guilty of impropriety at the least, in both the INS and police services. Evidently Naylor hadn't been making the proper payoffs, and had threatened to do some whistle-blowing if he was pressed for the money." She shrugged, glancing at Molly, who had clearly checked out of our conversation and was gnawing nervously at her knuckle. "Anyway, we moved as soon as we could to get the search warrants and things. But by the time we were ready to pick up Baldridge, he'd slipped away. I was coming to tell you to be careful, but it was too late."

"So, can I go back to California?"

"Probably." Eva nodded. "Come in Monday to wrap up the paperwork. If they need you to testify, whenever that is—" she glanced at the school board candidate—"they can fly you back."

"Cool." I took Molly's arm. "Come on. Let me behind the wheel of that monster you drive."

My sister's face was wan. "What if Byron—"

"He's too ornery to die," I predicted, pulling her out the door.

30 _____

    BIFF was asleep on the cranked-up hospital bed; he was pale, and his breathing sounded labored. A patchwork of bandages covered his shoulder and torso. Among them was a very nasty-looking plastic tube which the nurse last night had told me was a drain. In the pale daylight that came through the vertical blinds, he looked surprisingly attenuated.

    Amy stood beside me. She'd been complaining all the way up in the elevator about visiting a jerk like Biff, but once in the room, seeing the evidence of his danger, she turned thoughtful.

    "Maybe we should just leave the book," I said, low-voiced. "Looks like he's racked."

    "I'm surprised Aunt Molly isn't here." Amy laid down the book we'd brought on the bedside table. "He looks, like, below the absolute lowest." She clutched my arm. "I mean—it's not like I like him or anything, but he is going to get well, isn't he? Not be, like, on screen-saver forever or anything?"

    "Molly said the doctor said complete recovery after the wound heals. Maybe some limited motion for a while—"

    "Oh, shit." Biff opened his eyes. "You mean I can't lift? Damn—"

    Amy actually patted his arm. "Probably just for a while, Biff-boy. You'll be whirling the dumbbells in no time."

    He looked up at her, and a touch of his old arrogance surfaced. "Had to come to my sickbed, did you, Amy? Gonna figure out a way to take my mind off my pain?"

    I expected her to turn around making gagging noises, but

she surprised me by smiling tolerantly. "You're in no condition to chase anyone around the room, sonny."

"Yeah. Right." He closed his eyes again. I hadn't noticed before, with his eyebrows lowered so far over his eyes, that they were a nice shade of blue-green.

"We brought you a book," Amy said, thumping it on the bed beside him. Biff flinched. "Sorry." She patted his arm again, and shot me a look. "Aunt Liz picked it out." Amy had wanted to give him *Backlash*, which she was currently reading for a social studies class, and which she thought he really needed.

"Sort of for younger kids, but I thought it would be easy to read." Now I was sorry I'd selected *Redwall*, by Brian Jacques. I'd read it out loud to Bridget's kids one night, and gone on reading when they'd gone to bed. Admittedly, Bridget's oldest is nine, but I figured a recuperating Biff would regress from his current emotional age of about fourteen to right around Corky's age.

Biff examined it. "Looks good." He sent me a shy glance. "Mom was wishing she had something to read aloud to me. I always liked that when I was sick."

"Well, great." I had something to say, but didn't really want to say it in front of Amy. "Can we—do anything for you? Get you anything?"

"My water pitcher is empty," Biff said hesitantly.

"Would you?" I handed the pitcher to Amy.

"Sure." She started for the bathroom.

"Why don't you find some ice for it somewhere?" She started to protest, glanced at me, and then shrugged.

"Sure thing, Aunt Liz."

Biff lay back on his bed, eyes still closed. I took a step closer. "Listen, Biff, I'm glad you're awake, because I wanted to thank you for tackling Kyle last night. I'm sure you kept him from shooting me. I'm just sorry he shot you."

"He didn't really mean to, I think." Biff surprised me, wrinkling up his forehead in thought. "I went over it this morning with Officer Gutierrez. She's actually pretty cool." He licked his lips and glanced at me. "Actually, I pretty much acted like a jerk. I was just looking for something all the time to keep myself amped." He sounded wondering. "I mean, like, I almost died! I mean, people were always telling me I was looking for trouble, and then—bam! I found it." He glanced at me again. "Mom said you kept me from bleeding to death. Thanks. I—I owe you."

"No you don't. We canceled each other out." I smiled at him, and he smiled back.

Molly bustled in, followed by Amy, who carried a brimming pitcher of ice chips. "Now, my boy needs his rest," Molly said, edging me aside and lovingly smoothing the sheet that covered Biff's stomach.

"Look, Mom. They brought us a book to read." Biff turned to his mother.

Molly looked at the book, then at me. "This looks—interesting, Liz."

"I liked it." I watched Amy set the pitcher down. "We should go. Don't want to tire the patient. I might not see you again, Biff, so I hope you get well quickly."

Molly turned quickly. "You're leaving that soon?"

"In a day or two. I'm going to talk to Mom and Dad this afternoon, and then tomorrow or the next day I'll be pulling out."

Molly started to speak, glanced at Amy, and bit her lip. "Maybe I'll stop by Mom and Dad's later, too."

"Okay. See you." I waved at Biff, and he waved *Redwall* back.

Mom answered the door. Her color was better than I'd seen it, and she looked pretty steady on her legs. "Lizzie." She smiled at me. "Molly just got here. She said Biff is doing so much better this afternoon. He might get out of the hospital by Wednesday." She stepped aside for me to enter. "And at least, the police finally got the man who killed your husband. And Conchita came back this morning, she said—just visiting her sister." She guided me into the kitchen. "Come have a cup of coffee. Molly brought a tea cake."

Dad sat at the kitchen table, a big slice of tea cake in front of him. He nodded at me, but didn't look pleased. "That policeman was by," he said, setting his coffee cup down with a solid clunk. "Said I can't get my gun back because I didn't report it stolen, and my permit's expired."

"I'm glad," Mom said, sitting across from Dad and sipping from her cup. Molly sat between them, and I sat across from her. For a little while we were a microcosm of a happy family, even if we all knew it wouldn't last. "I don't want that nasty thing around here. If someone wants to break in, let them. We don't have anything worth stealing anyway."

"You need a good dog," Molly said, with a sly smile at me. "To bark and scare the burglars away."

Mom seemed divided as to which was worse, a dog or a gun. Dad paid more attention to his tea cake than to the conversation.

I was feeling liberated. One more stop at the police station on Monday, and then I was free to leave.

So I made a cup of tea with the flow-through tea bags which had probably been in the cupboard since before I left, and took some cake myself. I looked at Mom and Dad, arguing now over whether it was going to rain next week, and felt ashamed of my eagerness to be gone. I had lived a loner's life too long, and family closeness felt too smothering. Besides, the internecine squabbling in my family would drive me mad before long.

"So," Molly said, guessing some of what was in my mind. "You're leaving soon?"

Mom and Dad stopped arguing and looked at me. I looked down at the murky surface of my tea.

"Yeah. I gather it may be a while before Kyle even comes to trial, and if they need me then, they'll fly me out." I glanced quickly at Mom, and then away. "The writers' workshop I teach starts a week from Tuesday, and I have other responsibilities, too."

We were silent for a moment. Mom reached over and squeezed my hand. "So it's all over now," she said softly.

"I guess so."

Dad shook his head. "It'll never be over." He eyed me narrowly. "Her husband may be dead, but he's not forgotten."

That was perceptive of him—I was surprised.

"You should marry again," Mom announced. "You're not too old to have children."

Molly choked on her sip of coffee. "For heaven's sake, Mom. Let her breathe for a while before you start throwing men at her head."

"I'd duck, anyway." I smiled at Mom. "I'm not the marrying kind."

She looked troubled. Dad thundered, "You'd better attend Mass, girl, and get yourself straightened out. You're asking for damnation, the way you're going."

"Actually, I'm going West." I cleared my throat. "But I wondered—Mom, you want to go look at the leaves tomorrow afternoon? I noticed on my way into town, the quakies are turning."

"What a nice idea!" Mom was delighted. "Why, it must have been two or three years since we've been out to look at the quakies, isn't it, Fergus?"

Dad just stared at me, amazed. "A big game is on TV tomorrow!"

Molly laughed. "I think it sounds great. I'd go if I didn't need to be at the hospital with Biff. But Amy and Renee might want to go. You could take my car."

"And we'll stop for pizza."

Molly looked puzzled, but Mom clapped her hands. "Yes," she cried. "I love pizza."

We settled on a time, and I got up to leave. Molly followed me to the door.

"We've been planning to go to Hawaii this winter," she said casually, walking me out to the bus. "Maybe we'll stop over in San Francisco and visit."

"Sure." I tried to sound welcoming, but I felt dismay. Molly, the family princess, visiting my humble little cottage? I couldn't see her sleeping on the lumpy sofa bed that Amy had used.

"We'll stay at a hotel—I know you're hard up for space." I could forgive her the condescending voice in which she said this, since it relieved my mind. "But maybe you can show us around a little."

"That would be fun." We smiled at each other, and her eyes filled with tears.

215

"My little sister." She hugged me once, fiercely. "I've missed you all these years."

I hugged her back. We stood there, silent, not knowing what to say.

"Well," Molly said finally, brightly, "I'll come by tomorrow, and you can drive me to the hospital. And go on for your aspens and pizza!"

"A truly cheesy excursion." I got in the bus and drove away.

31 _____

I crossed the Bay Bridge at dusk, with the lights of San Francisco tempting my gaze away from the traffic that whizzed past me. When you drive a bus, you sit up high; I could see the Transamerica Pyramid and the fantastic top of the Mariott, which is nicknamed the Jukebox for its extravagance. My whole body hummed with road vibrations; I'd been driving since early that morning, stopping at Donner Summit to fix some lunch and let Barker run. He'd been sitting in the passenger seat for the last twenty miles, scenting the ocean in the breeze.

We cruised down 101, mingling with commuters. After the airport, the traffic lightened considerably. I was low on gas, but figured I could make it home. And that's all I wanted—to be home.

By the time we reached the Willow Road exit, I wasn't really safe to drive any more. But Babe knew the last few miles like the back of her tires. I turned off Middlefield, wound around Palo Alto Avenue, turned onto my street. Babe slipped down the driveway and stopped, panting, in front of the garage.

Drake's lights were on. When I opened my door, Barker bounded past me and tore wildly around the yard, revisiting all his favorite smelling posts. I shut the driver's door and had a big stretch, breathing in the fragrance of freshly cut grass and the roses next to the driveway.

Before I could start hauling my stuff out, Drake came hurrying out of his back door. His frizzy hair stood on end, a sign of emotion for him, and his wire-rimmed glasses made him look like a young, fit Einstein.

"Liz!" He grabbed me in a bear hug, and it felt good.

Real good. I hugged back. When he kissed me, I kissed him back. That felt good, too, but remembering how attractive I'd found Kyle, I doubted my ability to know what was what with men.

"It's good to be home," I said, and Drake seemed satisfied with that.

"I've missed you a lot. And yes, your seedlings are fine, but I think they need to be planted soon."

"I'll get on it tomorrow."

"And I got you some milk and eggs and bread and stuff."

My stomach growled. Barker stood on the front porch, gazing commandingly at me—he was ready to remember his way around the house.

"Come on in, then," I told Drake. "I'll fix you some tea."

VALERIE WOLZIEN PRESENTS

THE DARKER SIDE OF SUBURBAN LIFE.

You just never know where a body will turn up—the bathtub, the PTA meeting, the Christmas party... who knew suburban life could be so dangerous?

Meet Susan Henshaw—wife, mother, chauffeur, chef, friend—and amateur sleuth.